WOLFE ASYLUM

The Complete Series

ABIGAIL GRANT

FANTASY & PARANORMAL ROMANCE

DEDICATION

Thank you to my incredibly supportive husband for believing in me and taking our three little hooligans away long enough for me to write to my heart's content!

Thank you to my family and friends that always ask how the writing is going or tell me you miss me when I've been stuck to a computer for far too long.

And an extra big thanks to those readers that tell me when I drop the ball or when I blow you away. I never imagined making it this far, and I wouldn't be here without you!

CONTENTS

PART

1

CHAPTER 1

Don't break Jackson's perfect nose, I tell myself. *It's not worth it. Yes, he deserves a few punches. Yes, it will feel so damn good to mar that pretty face of his. But, just another month, just one, and we're out of this place. We can make it to graduation and become something in this life while Jackson grows fat and sweaty as the manager of the 5th street drug store. Do. Not. Break. His. Nose.*

"Come on, Loner Girl. Just a little kiss. I won't tell a soul." Jackson's voice is dark and his words are slurred.

It's not the first time our star lacrosse player has come to school with a few drinks in him, but it's certainly the first time he has cornered me in the stairwell while he breathes liquor-breath down my neck. I don't believe the stereotype that all jocks are jerks, but this one gives them a bad name.

Of course, Jackson won't get in trouble, but me on the other hand. I'll be punished if I choose to defend myself. I've been in too many fights in my life for this to be taken as self-defense. My anger is something I have little control over, and the shoplifting didn't help things.

"Get away from me, Jackson. I have a class." I speak through clenched teeth, trying my best to suppress the anger building in my gut.

Don't get angry, Ivy. Keep it together.

I shove his chest just a little. Enough to make sure he knows I'm not caving. Jackson doesn't budge as he leans in too close, his lips nearly touching my ear. "Everyone knows your life is tragic, Loner Girl. Let me give you something to smile about." His hands grab at my waist, squeezing me hard, and that last thread of control snaps. *Screw it.*

I shove him, hard enough to make him stumble backwards, and I swing my fist against his face with a sickening crack. Jackson doubles over as blood drips from his too-good-looking face. He lets out a whimper before he looks up at me with a dark glare. I can't deny the flutter of joy that rises inside of me at causing him pain.

I smile cockily back at him. "Thanks, Jackson. That really *did* make me smile."

"Ivy Hart! Principal's office, now!"

I turn toward Mrs. Cramer's squeaky voice and my smile drops. *Of course someone would see.* When have I ever gotten away with lashing out? Oh, right. *Never.*

"Seriously, Ivy? Will you ever grow up?" My sister, Lorelei, crosses her long arms and looks at me like a dog who just tore up her favorite shoes.

I sigh and slide down in the plastic chair where I sit in Principal Foster's office. Moments ago, Mr. Foster walked out to make a phone call to my probation officer, which means I'm in for Hell in about five minutes.

"I'm sorry, Lor. I had no choice! What would you have done if a guy cornered you? It was sexual assault!"

She rolls her blue eyes and shakes her head. "I get it, Ivy, okay? I understand *why* you broke the guy's nose, but *you* don't get to do stuff like that! You're on probation for all of the other crap you've pulled in the last three years. That means *no* fights, and *no* principal's office!"

Three years? Has it really been that long already since Mom and Dad died? I feel like I've wasted my teenage life since the day they went down in that little plane. I still can't even look up at planes in the sky. I truly haven't grown up.

I groan and drop my head into my hands, letting my long black hair fall around me in a curtain of protection. "I've messed up a lot, haven't I? I've been an awful sister to you, and an even worse daughter."

Lorelei's hand lands on my back and she sighs loudly. "Maybe I've been a sucky guardian. I didn't get a lot of training for this stuff, you know? Suddenly having to care for a fourteen-year-old when you're not even twenty yourself is a lot of work."

"I'm sorry," I whisper again. She shoves my arm hard and I jerk up in my chair. "Ow!"

Lorelei rolls her eyes again and she flips her blonde hair over one shoulder. "You're not going to get off easy, Ivy. I'll help you in any way I can, but I just want you to know that life could potentially suck a lot more after today."

I nod. "I know. I'm just glad Mom isn't here to see the failure I've become."

"Oh, stop." She scoffs. "If Mom were here, you'd have your ass kicked into behaving years ago."

I laugh. "Very true." I imagine my mom's dark eyes being enough to put me in my place with just a stern stare.

The office door opens and Mr. Foster saunters into the room to plop his heavy body into his swivel chair. "Well, it doesn't sound good, Ivy. Officer Knight says it's the end of the road."

"What does that mean," Lorelei and I ask in unison.

Mr. Foster frowns. "It's juvenile detention, Ivy."

Lorelei gasps and throws a hand to her chest. I shake my head, holding my tears back. "No, it was one punch. I'm not a bad person, Mr. Foster!"

He leans forward, his eyebrows creased at the center. "Nobody thinks you're a bad person, Ivy. You broke Jackson's nose with that punch, and I commend you for sticking up for yourself, no matter what people may say. You have had it tough in this life, and no offense to you, Lorelei." He looks sympathetically at Lor. "You are twenty-two years old, halfway through college, and supporting the both of you on a part-time income. Officer Knight said he could send Ivy to a girl's home for behavioral help, but it's expensive. There's no other choice."

"I'll drop out," Lorelei says, tears running free. "I can take on full-time hours and make payments to the girl's home. Ivy won't go to juvie!"

My heart breaks for my big sister. She has never done a thing in her life to deserve this. She is perfect, or as close as you can get to it. All she wants is to be a nurse, to help people, and dropping out of college will end that dream.

I stand up, pushing my chair back. "No!" I look between Mr. Foster and Lorelei. "I'll go to juvie. I'll do whatever they want me to do and then I'll move on."

"Ivy," Lorelei starts, but I hold up a hand to stop her.

"Stop. You are going to finish college and get an incredible nursing job at the best hospital in Chicago. No more sacrifices for me, okay? I can't live with it."

She blinks rapidly as she stares up at me. Her blue eyes are like pools, filled with water as she cries for me, and maybe for herself too. "What kind of parent sends their child off to jail for standing up for herself?"

I shrug. "That's the thing, Lor. You're not my parent. You're my sister, and what kind of sister lets her amazing *big* sister give up everything she ever wanted?"

Lorelei stands and wraps me into a tight hug. "I'll miss you, little bear," she says, using a pet name that I normally despise. I don't hate it right now, though.

"I'll miss you too, big bear."

CHAPTER 2

I already miss home. It has been sixteen hours since Lorelei dropped me off at this place, and I want to run away. My roommate snored all night long, but she otherwise hasn't said a word to me. I don't mind that.

Dinner last night was spaghetti, served in a cafeteria setting, not too different from high school, except that all of us were wearing the same blue pants and white t-shirt. I'm not huge on fashion, but I normally get to wear clothes my size. My new uniform was made for a girl two sizes bigger than myself.

My phone was taken when I got here, supposedly sent back to my sister, and any of my personal items were also seized, except for the few books I packed away. Reading is welcome, and that's probably the only upside to this whole situation. As long as I get to fall in love with made-up, angsty vampires in the safety of my twelve-by-twelve room, I'm doing alright.

"Find a seat. Don't cause trouble," the female guard says beside me after walking me to the big cafeteria and helping me find breakfast.

I nod, trying my hardest not to salute sarcastically as I make my way through the crowd of eating girls. They're all mostly teamed up in groups of two to five. All I need to do is settle in with a couple of them and make friends. At least, that's what the counselor here wants me to do.

I'm not big on friendships, though. Never been good at it. I move to the empty end of a long table, having to hike my baggy pants up before sitting down with my tray. Eggs, a sausage patty, and orange juice. Not bad for prison food.

Before I get a chance to dig in, someone clears their throat behind me. I turn toward the sound, coming face-to-face with a thick girl, maybe my age or slightly older. She has two more girls standing at her back, all of them carrying the same dark expression.

"Yes?" I ask, looking from one glaring girl to the next.

The big girl scoffs and points to the table in front of me. "You're sitting in my seat, new girl."

I look around me for a name tag, not finding any. I shrug. "I don't see your name on it. I wasn't aware that the benches were assigned."

Her lips twist in a sneer. "When you've been here for some time, you get used to sitting in certain places. This," she gestures to the table again. "Is *our* place. *You* have not earned the right to sit with *us*."

I try not to smile at her dramatic attitude, but I'm sure it shows through. "Okay. I get that you're all used to sitting here, but I'm here right now. Let me finish my food and I'll

18

be happy to move." I gesture to the rest of the cafeteria. "There are plenty of open seats. Take your pick."

Big girl practically snarls as she drops her tray onto the table, directly on top of my food. I jump up from my seat, narrowly avoiding getting a glass full of orange juice down the front of me.

The three girls all laugh as I back away, but their laughter just makes me mad. *No, no, no, Ivy. Not here!*

I can feel the heat of anger rising in my body, but I keep it in check. Big girl snickers and flips her ponytail over her shoulder. "Awww. Looks like the new girl might throw up."

"I'm not going to throw up," I growl back at her. My fists clench at my sides, and I take an extra step back.

Big girl moves closer. "You're like a scared little bunny rabbit. Go ahead and find some carrots, little bunny."

I close my eyes to calm myself, but it's a mistake, because my new bully and her posse circle me. There's nowhere to go now, and I can't start a fight on day one. I only have four months in this place and then I'm free.

"Just leave me alone. I'll find another seat." *Good, calm.*

The bully leader jabs her finger against my chest, pushing me against the girl at my back. I'm shoved from behind, into the big girl, and then it's a game of Pinball as each of them shoves me back and forth to the others. My anger rises until I'm ready to scream, but a dark growl leaves me instead.

I throw my arms out toward the girls at my sides, and kick out in front of me at the same time. All three of them go flying, hitting the linoleum floor on their backs. I spin in a circle, panting like a wild animal as all eyes fall on me. *Well, crap.*

None of the bully girl's make a move, staring back with wide eyes. It takes me a moment to wonder why they look so shocked, and I realize that I somehow threw them a good few yards away with just one blow. I look down at my hands, wondering when I became so strong, and a woman clears her throat from behind me.

"Dammit," I mutter under my breath, turning slowly toward the tall woman.

"Come with me, Ivy," she says. I don't know this woman, but she seems to know who I am. She's at least six-foot tall with dark brown eyes and dark hair down to her thin waist. Her skin is smooth and tan, gorgeous in a white blazer and black pencil skirt.

I follow after her, my shoulders slumped in defeat. It's time for my first punishment in juvie. *Great.* "Am I in trouble?" I ask, keeping pace with the woman's long legs as she leads me down a dimly lit hallway.

She shakes her head but doesn't turn around. "No, you aren't in trouble, Ivy. I saw what happened in there, and it was clearly self-defense."

My jaw drops and I don't know what to do with myself. I've never been let off the hook for fighting, ever. Maybe the rules in here are more slack than out in the real world. The woman stops inside the doorway of a clean office and gestures for me to take a seat.

"Uh…Ma'am, if I'm not going to be punished, why am I here?" I lace my fingers on my lap, shifting uncomfortably under her intense gaze.

She doesn't take a seat in a chair, but she leans against the large black desk in front of me. "You can call me Stella,

Ivy. I'm not exactly part of the faculty, or the security in this building. I am a...counselor of sorts." She smiles like she made a joke. "I go around to different foster homes, detention centers, and correctional homes. Young people like yourself are important to me."

I draw my chin back. "You mean orphans? I'm not an orphan. I have a capable guardian."

Stella shakes her head with a sigh. "No, Ivy. Not orphans. These are exceptional students with bright minds who often get caught up in trouble for reasons they can't explain. People tell them they are bad kids, or have behavior problems, or even anger issues, but I don't see it that way at all."

It's a pretty solid description of me and what I've gone through, but I don't see why she even cares. "So, you're going to be my counselor? Like, help me with my problems and teach me how to calm my anger?"

Stella scoffs, as if I'm hilarious for suggesting such a thing. "Oh, not at all. I think your tenacity and anger are incredible tools that shouldn't be pushed aside. The reason I'm here is to offer you a different life."

"What do you mean?" I'm feeling impatient now.

She leans forward, and I realize how young she is. She can't be more than thirty-five. "I am the headmistress of a place called Wolfe Asylum, and I want you to join our student body."

I stand from my seat, needing to step away from Stella's piercing eyes. "You want to take me to an asylum, like, for crazy people?"

She leans back, helping me feel like I can breathe better. "Why does everyone say that?" She chuckles softly. "It's an asylum, as in 'a safe place'. There is a difference."

I shake my head, feeling like I've lost my marbles finally. "Why? Why would you want a girl like me to be under your care?"

She grins widely. "Because you are one of a kind, Ivy. Like I said, you have strength in you, and incredible tenacity. Wolfe Asylum is the perfect place for you to become something better than a prisoner."

I shrug, but I don't know why. What can I say to her? I'd love to get out of juvie, but none of this makes any sense. I watch Stella stand up and open the office door again.

She stands to the side and waits for me to leave. "Think about it, okay? You don't deserve to be here, Ivy."

I make my way back into the hallway, but as I pass Stella, a calmness envelopes me and I know what my answer is. "I'll do it." I look up at her soft expression. "I'll go to your asylum."

CHAPTER 3

LOR: "Did you land safely?
LOR: "What part of California is it?"
LOR: "Will I be able to visit?"

I groan, exhausted from my flight, and unable to answer my sister's incessant questioning. To be honest, I don't know all of the answers. Deciding to fly across the country to Wolfe Asylum was sort of spontaneous. Did I ask Stella for details when I said yes? No. I'm probably about to get murdered in some Sacramento alleyway and have my body parts sold on the black market.

ME: "I'm safe, Lor. Stop worrying. Just landed in Sacramento."

She doesn't need to know about the random taxi driver that dropped me off at the airport back in Colorado with a plane ticket, my cell phone, and a suitcase full of clothes. Or about the fact that I went along with it, no questions asked. It's fine.

I grab my checked bag from the conveyor belt and make my way out to the passenger pickup stalls outside the huge airport. The city towers high above everything, and the setting sun is gorgeous behind the buildings. I've never been this far west, and I am in awe.

Even if I do get murdered, at least I go out in a new outfit, a full belly, and in the *City of Trees*. There are worse ways, right? I check my phone for the information about the car that should be picking me up. Stella programmed her number into my phone under "Miss Wolfe" and then messaged me the important details. Do I know where this car will be taking me? No, but I know it's a royal blue Jeep. *Good enough.*

I find the Jeep easily, and I run up to the parked vehicle with sweaty palms, and my nerves running wild. A boy climbs out of the passenger's seat and reaches for my bag with a big smile. He has to be only fifteen years old.

"Hey, you must be Ivy. I'm Silis." He looks me up and down. "You're pretty." He grins and tosses my suitcase into the trunk.

My cheeks flush red as I nod to the boy, about my height with a lean body and fluffy red hair. "Uh…thanks." *What do I say to that?*

"Silis, boundaries!" A deep voice makes me jump, and I spin around toward the driver of the Jeep.

Something lodges in my throat as I take in the stranger. He's older than Silis, and gorgeous. He could easily be

24

twenty years old, and everything about him makes my body heat up. I've never had this kind of reaction to a stranger, or anyone really.

His hair hangs down to his eyebrows, a sandy-brown color. I can't see his eyes clearly from this distance, but they're dark as he glares at the younger boy. He's taller than the Jeep, which means he has to be at least six-four, with wide shoulders and a five-o'clock shadow dusting his square jaw.

He rolls his eyes before turning his attention to me. Our eyes meet, and the dark confusion that crosses his face makes him look younger. He licks his lips, and my entire body shudders against my will. *What the hell?*

I blink, breaking the brief contact as Silis closes the trunk of the Jeep. It feels like I have been standing here, staring at the man for several minutes, but it was just a moment in time. An incredibly intense moment.

"Here, you can take shot-gun." Silis gently nudges me toward the vehicle.

I eye the front seat, realizing how close it is to Mr. Tall, Dark and Sexy. "Uh, no thanks. I'm fine taking the backseat. I'd like to stretch out a bit."

Silis smiles at me, opening the back door to the Jeep and waving me forward. "As the lady wishes."

I can't help my smile. He's a charmer, that's for sure. I climb into the lifted vehicle, settling into the most intoxicating scent, like pine trees and spearmint. *Yum.* The two guys buckle up in the front, and Mr. TDS starts the rumbling engine.

"It smells incredible in here. Do you have one of those plug-in car scents?" I look around the car for the source of the smell. Whatever it is, I want a dozen of them.

Silis twists around to lock those sparkling green eyes on me. He really is adorable. "So, you like the smell of sweaty teenage boys? I can make that work."

I blush again. "That's not exactly the smell I was referring to." We drive around the outskirts of the city, heading east, as far as I can tell. "So, where are we going? I'm not sure where this place is actually located."

"Alta," the driver says. His eyes flick to the rearview mirror, meeting mine for half a second before looking back at the road ahead. *Blue*, they are definitely blue.

"Alta?" I ask, having no idea where that is. "Will it be a long drive?"

Silis looks back again. "Just about an hour. Wolfe Asylum is tucked away in the middle of nowhere, but you will love it. As long as you're a fan of never-ending forest."

I actually love the sound of that. "Do you both live at the asylum?" I try not to look over at Mr. TDS, but a part of me is desperate to know more about him.

"Yeah. Alden and I grew up there," Silis says, nudging the driver's arm. *Alden.* "Well, except for when Alden lived with his—"

"Silis!" Alden glares over at the boy, a warning in his tone as he cuts him off.

"What? I'm just getting to know the new girl." He smiles back at me. "How old are you, Ivy? It *is* Ivy, right?"

I nod. "Yeah. I'm seventeen. I'll be eighteen in a few months."

"Aw, man. You don't happen to have a thing for younger men, do ya? Particularly fifteen-year-olds with wild red hair?" Silis's green eyes plead to me as he waggles his eyebrows.

I chuckle, unable to help it. He has a way of making people feel happy, peaceful. I don't get that feeling often. "Sorry, Silis. I don't date anyone."

It's the truth. I've never been one for chasing after boys. Alden's eyes find me again in the mirror, and he studies my face for a moment but doesn't say anything. His hands clench on the steering wheel, and he licks those lips again. *Dang, why do I like that so much?*

"Yeah, I figured." Silis turns away from me, settling into his seat. "I'm good at the friend-zone anyways. It will be nice to have a friend like you around school."

"A friend like me?" I ask. That seems like a weird way to phrase that.

Alden glares back over at Silis, and the boy sighs in defeat. "Yeah, you know…A pretty girl that can up my street cred."

"Right." I nod, feeling awkward all of a sudden. Alden doesn't seem too happy to join in on the conversation, and something about his rejection hurts. I've never cared much about what other people think of me until now.

I settle into the soft leather of my seat, pulling in that delicious scent that makes me feel at home. I shoot off a quick text to Lorelei, hoping she's not worrying too much back at home.

ME: "Look up Alta, CA. That's where the asylum is. Don't worry too much about me, okay? I'll call you tomorrow."

LOR: "I'll try, little bear. If you don't call, I'm going to drive across the country to rescue you."

I smile and my heart aches from missing my big sister already. I don't know what awaits me at Wolfe Asylum, but it can't be worse than juvie…right?

CHAPTER 4

"Wow," I say in a breath. The huge iron gate opens ahead of us with a sign above that reads "Wolfe Asylum".

The mansion that towers above this remote area of the Tahoe National Forest is nothing like I could have imagined. I've seen some big buildings back home, but nothing even compares to this chateau-style behemoth. I could fit at least ten of my houses inside this place.

"It's cool, huh?" Silis says, flashing a smile over his shoulder.

Night has fallen, so the view around the mansion is dark. I have no idea how much forest stretches beyond Wolfe Asylum, but I can feel the desire inside of me to explore. To run. *To conquer.*

I blink at that last thought that flashed through my mind. I don't know what I would want to conquer. I must be sleep deprived after traveling.

Alden parks the Jeep beside the incredible front steps of the huge building. A few lights shine down at us from what I can only describe as the front porch. Lights from some of the many windows also show that people are still up and moving around inside, and nervousness starts to churn in my gut.

I climb out of the Jeep, my eyes glued to that insane front door. "So, uh…do I need to check in somewhere? Will the guards need to search me before we go in?"

I receive no response, so I spin around to look at the guys who each now have their brows pressed together in confusion as they stare back at me like I came from outer space.

Silis is the one who speaks, *of course.* "Ivy, this isn't a prison. We have grounds-keepers, but not *guards*. And why on earth would you need to be searched? Are you carrying weapons?"

My face heats up. I glance from Silis to Alden, and I swear there is pity in his dark eyes as he watches me. My mouth dries up and I pry my eyes away from them both.

"Oh," I say, trying to act like everything in my life hasn't been incredibly screwed up. "No, of course I don't have weapons. That would be crazy. I just thought…" What *did* I think?

Alden clears his throat and moves past me with my bag in his large hands. "You're right. The place does look like some sort of jail." He turns to me with the slightest smile, and *damn* it's perfection. "Don't worry about it, though.

It's just a glorified boarding school." His deep voice softens. "You're free here. *Safe.*"

Free? When have I ever been free, or felt any sort of safety? It's too good to be true. Alden's smile falls as he sees the uncertainty on my face. Or maybe he just doesn't like smiling. He walks up the steps with my bag in tow.

Silis links his arm with mine, dragging me with him after Alden. "My brother is an odd duck, isn't he?"

"What?" I look over at Silis and realize he's talking about the large, broody man ahead of us. "Alden is your brother?"

Silis chuckles, squeezing my arm a little tighter. "Yeah. I didn't get a say in the matter." He laughs again, so light and carefree. The very opposite of the vibe his brother gives off.

"You guys look nothing alike. I never would have guessed." Not that Lorelei and I share many similarities.

Silis leads me through a two-story high doorway. "Not all of us can have my devastating good looks. Poor guy. He got all the crap genes."

I hold back my laughter at the adorable boy. He's cute, no doubt about it. I imagine age will only do him good. But Alden is…indescribable.

The massive lobby of the asylum is dimly lit, but I don't need bright lights to see its beauty. The molding around the walls is elaborate, needing much more attention to appreciate than a glance. Paintings of fierce animals and incredible landscapes adorn the tall walls all around us. A grand staircase curls up in two directions ahead, with huge brass statues of twin howling wolves resting at the base of each. I make a mental note to spend some time appreciating this room one day.

"This is…"

"It's pretty sweet, eh?" Silis answers for me.

I shake my head. "Something like that."

"You'll be on the third floor," Alden says, craning his neck toward the stairs on the left. "All of the girls take the third floor, and Stella assigned you to Fay's room."

"Ooh, I love Fay." Silis's eyes go all wide and dreamy as he says her name.

Alden scoffs, already headed up the stairs. "You love all of the girls, Sy."

I turn toward the boy still holding onto my arm with my jaw hanging low. "Oh, I see. And I thought I was special." Alden pauses in front of us, but he quickly continues forward.

Silis turns to me with wide eyes. "I'm sorry, Ivy. I can't help it! I'm a teenage boy, for crying out loud!"

I smile back at him, gently shoving his shoulder. "I'm just kidding. Us girls *are* pretty great."

Silis sighs, relaxing against my side as we climb higher and higher. "Alden doesn't get it. He's only eighteen, but it's like he already forgot what it was like being so hormonal all the time."

"Silis!" Alden spins to glare at his younger brother. His eyes flick to me so fast that I nearly miss it, and then he just continues forward.

Alden is eighteen, just a little older than me. That wouldn't even be considered inappropriate if we…*oh lord.* What am I even thinking right now? I don't have these kinds of thoughts, especially about guys I barely know!

Everything about this night is like living in the twilight zone. I'm joking and smiling, moving into a mansion in the middle of nowhere with hopes of freedom. And now I'm daydreaming about some guy's lickable lips against mine, roaming across my body. Holy hell, how is this my life?

"Here you are," Alden says, his voice rougher than before.

I shake away my thoughts and look at the closed door in front of me. I was so lost in my panicky thoughts that I had no idea we even made it to the third floor.

Silis is stopped a few doors down, flirting with some girl who looks to be his age. Alden hands over my suitcase, his eyes darker blue than they were downstairs. I grab the handle of my bag, accidentally brushing my fingers against his warm ones.

A heat spreads up my arm and throughout my body, making me gasp from the intensity of it. My eyes find Alden's, and he steps so close to me that I'm sandwiched between him and the door, his fingers still touching mine.

"Shit," Alden whispers harshly, his breath fanning my face. He closes his eyes and leans into my hair, breathing in deep as if he's smelling me.

I should be immensely freaked out by his actions, but all I want to do is move closer, maybe smell him back. What on earth is wrong with me? Alden releases his hold on my bag and pulls back quickly, his dark blue eyes burning into me.

He licks his lips again, suddenly looking wild, and maybe even *miserable*. "Be careful, okay?"

I blink rapidly, more confused than I have ever been in my life. Be careful? Why would he even say that to me? I'm literally in the doorway to my new room. What kind of trouble could I get into here?

I open my mouth to respond, to ask him what he means, but the door swings open behind me and I fall backwards into small arms. I right myself with the help of whoever caught me, and when I look back to where Alden was standing, he's already gone.

I turn around to find a girl smiling back at me. "Well, if this isn't a meet-cute, I don't know what is." She sticks her multi-ring-adorned hand out in front of her. "You must be Ivy. I'm Fay, your new roommate."

CHAPTER 5

"Come on in," Fay says, stepping aside so I can enter our shared bedroom.

I try to smile back at her, but after the weird moment with Alden, my heart is still pounding wildly. I glance around the room and I freeze. No freaking way is this my room. The place is huge, much bigger than my shared cell back at juvie. Just this one room has to be double the size of my parent's old master bedroom.

A full-sized bed rests against the far left wall, opposite one beside the right. It's clear where Fay sleeps, because the entire right side of the room is decorated in neon pink and black. Almost emo, but also very girly. Flowers are painted all over the wall, behind a pink dresser, a fluffy black comforter, and a bright pink shaggy rug.

The left side is mostly bare, with just a blue comforter on the bed and a plain white dresser. A window sits at the back of the room, wide and dark this time of night. I can't even imagine the amazing view from here.

"Here," Fay says, dragging my suitcase over to the blue bed. "I'll help you unpack. I'm sure you're exhausted."

I shake my head, realizing I haven't said a single word to this girl. "Oh, you don't need to worry about that. I don't have much in there." I gesture to the room. "I wasn't expecting this place."

Fay smiles, and she really is beautiful. Her hair is wavy to her shoulders, colored jet-black to purple in an ombre style. Her violet eyes match her hair, and they are so unnatural that they have to be contacts. She has a piercing on one side of her nose, and at least three on each ear. Her style sticks out, and I love it.

She leaves my bag on the bed and walks across the room to a door in the corner. "I'll leave you to it, then, but let me give you a quick tour. This is our private bathroom. I made room in the cabinets for your stuff. It has a shower and a tub, which is great." She crosses the room again to swing open a closet door. "Here is where we can store our backpacks and clothes. It's not a walk-in closet, but it has plenty of space."

Backpack? Private bathroom? What on earth is this place?

Fay plops down on her bed with a whoosh of air. "And, obviously this is my bed. I'm really into art, so you'll see me constantly doodling or painting over here. What do you like to do?"

I move to the blue bed, trying to look as comfortable as she does in our shared space. "I like to write, I guess. I'm no good at it, but I do enjoy it."

She claps her hands together. "That's great! We aren't so different then. Writers and artists are kindred spirits."

I shrug. "I'm not sure what I'm supposed to do here. It was probably stupid of me to not ask more questions, but that woman, Miss Wolfe, was very convincing. Will I need a backpack?"

Fay grins again. "Ah, you mean Stella. She...has a way with people. I figured you were up to speed, but I don't mind filling you in." She waves her hands to everything around us. "This is Wolfe Asylum, a strange name to you maybe, but it really should be called Wolfe Academy. It's a school for..." She looks up as if searching for the right word. "*Gifted* students, I guess. All of us are special to Stella, for different reasons. But, it's a lot like normal school. We have classes, and we have cliques. A cafeteria with sub-par food, and a principal. That's Stella, our headmistress."

I can feel my eyes widen as I listen to her, and I try to calm my reaction. I'm in a boarding school. Somehow, I was picked out of juvenile detention and dropped into a massive academy in the middle of nowhere. Holy crap, I do not have the money for this.

I rub my palm against my chest, feeling something thick pressing against my ribs. Stress, maybe. "I don't understand. Boarding, meal plans, uniforms. I can't afford all of that. I didn't realize what I signed up for." How could I have been so stupid and just left without asking questions? Lorelei is going to freak.

Fay shakes her head, leaning forward. "Hey, it's not like that, Ivy. I know it sounds unorthodox, but this school is completely paid for by a trust. All students have a full-ride, no bills at all."

"How is that even possible?"

She shrugs. "It's great that there are rich people out there that want to see kids like us succeed."

I sigh, and rub a hand down my face. "I need to somehow get my hands on a bag, notebooks, pens. And a uniform, somehow."

Fay chuckles. "No uniform, thank the goddess." She gestures to her purple tank-top and poofy skirt, very much not a school uniform. "As for that other stuff, we'll get all of that settled tomorrow. You'll have a day to settle in before classes start, anyways. And then we graduate in just three months!"

"Wait, what?" I stand from my bed. "School lets out in a week."

Fay's eyes go wide, and then realization hits her. "Oh, right. I forget that hu–normal school gets out in spring. That sucks." She grimaces. "Our school lets out in the fall, which means three more months until grad for us seniors."

Well, great. I groan, and shake my head. Honestly, how can I even complain? This place is wildly better than juvie, and I can handle a few months before experiencing freedom. I know I can.

I look over at the bedroom door and think about Alden. I have a feeling that boy won't easily escape my thoughts. "So, what about that guy who dropped me off? Is he a senior?"

Fay looks confused. "I didn't even see who dropped you. He must've left before I got a look."

I chew on my lip. "Uh, Alden I think. He and his brother picked me up from the airport."

Fay's eyes widen, and she smiles dreamily. "Oh, you met Alden, then. Isn't he smokin' hot?"

I blush and shrug, but who am I kidding. "He's cute I guess."

Fay laughs. "Cute? His brother is cute, sure, but Alden is definitely not *cute*." She sighs. "Either way, he is a senior, yes. He's also very off-limits, sadly. He refuses to date any girls at the school, and it's probably for the best."

I shrug, nonchalant, or at least hoping I look that way. "Why is it for the best? Is he a jerk?"

"I wouldn't really know. He doesn't say much. All I know is that he's complicated. Some say he's dangerous, or borderline sociopathic. I think he's just shy." She climbs into her bed and tucks herself under the black comforter. "I wouldn't worry about him, though. Our school has some cute boys that will love having a new girl around."

"I'm not interested in all of that." I yawn as tiredness tugs at me. "I'll let you sleep though. I am pretty tired."

Fay nods, her own yawn following mine. "I hope we can be friends, Ivy. I'll help you get whatever you need tomorrow, so try not to worry."

"Thanks." Maybe I really could be free here, and make friends. If they're all as friendly as Fay, I could really like Wolfe Asylum.

CHAPTER 6

I woke up this morning feeling uneasy. I don't remember having any nightmares, though it's not uncommon. After my parents died, I dreamt about them a lot. Images of their mangled bodies, or what I imagined their bodies looked like. I never got to see them because it was supposedly a terrible sight. Apparently plane crashes aren't pretty.

Fay had already gone to her classes when I got out of bed, but she left a note on my nightstand with just two sentences written on it.

Ivy, I've got classes til 2pm. Have fun roaming, but watch your back. -Fay AKA New Bestie

I don't know when "besties" started warning their friends to watch their backs, but it has been a while since I've had any good friends. What do I know?

I'm wearing skinny jeans and a simple t-shirt today, hoping to stay under the radar while I explore Wolfe Asylum. I don't necessarily like being a loner, but it's easier than trying to pretend for a bunch of strangers.

So far, the third floor is empty, aside from me. This place is incredibly well built, with high ceilings on every floor and famous paintings adorning the halls. At the end of what seems to be the girl's hall, I find a staircase smaller than the one Alden and Silis brought me up last night.

I grab the railing and plan on heading downstairs when I stop mid-step. A slick oil of some sort coats the top three stairs, making them shine back at me. If I had stepped forward, I would have fallen on my ass.

"What the hell?" I mumble, looking around for whoever oiled up the stairs. Nobody is around. I take a long step over the wooden stairs, avoiding the mess. It's likely a prank, but a potentially deadly one that I want no part in.

I reach the bottom floor and land right outside of the cafeteria. The smell of food drags me inside, making my stomach rumble since I haven't had breakfast yet. I stop short again, somehow still amazed at this place.

When Fay mentioned a cafeteria, I couldn't have imagined this huge restaurant-looking ballroom. Round tables litter the polished wood floor, with high-backed chairs placed around each. Four elaborate chandeliers decorate the rounded ceiling high above, and long counters around the room hold a huge assortment of food.

Just a couple of women are working behind the counters, bringing out food or cleaning up leftovers. I follow the counter, finding a white plate and a roll of silverware. I begin to load up my plate with everything I can find. So much for mediocre food. This is sweet.

I look at one of the women, expecting her to ask me for my student ID or a credit card, but she just smiles and heads off. I sit down at an empty table, ready to dig into some bacon, but a group of students files into the room.

It's immediately obvious that these are the popular kids, unless all of the students here are drop dead gorgeous. Honestly, after meeting Silis, Alden, and Fay, it could be the truth. A girl about my height at the front of the group has a long blonde braid over one shoulder and a very low-cut blouse over her double-Ds.

Behind blondie, another girl a little taller with dark curls and almond-colored skin, and a beefy guy with muscles the size of my head are holding hands. The couple both look my way and their eyes narrow as if they found an enemy. Blondie follows their gaze and looks me up and down with a sneer on her face. She scrunches up her petite nose before whispering back at her friends. The six kids behind her all chuckle, giving me a once over, and then they veer off to the opposite end of the room. *Great. Bullies.*

One guy at the back of the group looks my way, only he doesn't glare like his buddies. His lips curl up in a sexy smirk, and his eyes take me in slowly. I squirm in my seat, not sure if I should return his smile or focus on my food.

He's hot, but in a different way than Alden. Alden is all mystery and calming heat, where this guy could melt the clothes off a girl in seconds. There is definitely no mystery in his brown gaze. His hair is dark, nearly black, and his smooth skin is probably three shades darker than my pale complexion. He's muscular, toned, but not as wide as his buddy from before.

He doesn't look away from me, so I break eye contact first and take a bite of my toast. I can feel the heat of someone standing beside me, but I try to ignore it.

"We don't get a lot of new people here," a deep voice says.

I finally look up at the guy, realizing how big he really is at this distance. "I'm sorry to disappoint."

His grin widens and he sits down in the empty chair beside me, his knees nearly touching me. "Trust me. It's not a disappointment." He looks me up and down again as he sticks a hand out. "I'm Gabe."

I take his hand and he holds mine without shaking it. "Nice to meet you, Gabe. I'm Ivy."

Gabe doesn't release my hand. His skin is warm, almost feverish, and his dark brown eyes are piercing.

He scoots closer to me, invading my personal bubble. "Ivy, right. I think I heard about you. I wasn't expecting…" he breathes in deeply and I swear his eyes darken.

I nearly shiver, but I can't tell if I'm creeped out or turned on. "You weren't expecting *what*? The plain girl with a hearty appetite?"

He chuckles and releases my hand. "Not exactly. You'll realize that a lot of the students here are big eaters. I like a girl with an appetite."

He says it like he is hoping to be on the menu, but I have no plans on devouring the guy, no matter how sexy he is. I just smile kindly and nod.

"Good. Shouldn't you be joining your friends?" I dip my head toward the mob at the end of the cafeteria.

Gabe shakes his head. "You know, I would much rather stay right here, but I do have a class." He sighs sadly. "Hopefully we will see one another again soon, Ivy."

I nod. "I'm sure we will. There are only so many spots I can hide in this place."

Gabe stands up with a wicked grin on his handsome face. "You'd be surprised how easy it is to disappear around here."

With that, he saunters off as if he didn't just say something incredibly weird.

It's nearly two o'clock and I want to be back in the room to see Fay. I'm hoping she can help me get a bag and some supplies for my classes tomorrow. The day has gone by relatively smoothly as I've explored the halls and parts of the garden out front, except for the strange glares I keep getting from passing students. It seems like Wolfe Asylum is not such a welcoming place.

"Oh, Ivy! I'm so glad you're here!"

I spin toward the familiar voice and find Miss Wolfe walking toward me down the second floor hall. "Hi, Miss Wolfe."

She shakes her head as she pulls me into a soft hug. "No, everyone here just calls me Stella."

I nod. "Okay, Stella. Thanks again for inviting me to your school. The place is incredible."

Stella smiles happily. "I'm so glad you like it. My father really hoped students would feel at home here." She looks around. "What exactly are you doing in the boy's dorms, though?"

A blush floods my cheeks. "Oh, I'm sorry. I had no idea where I was. I've just been exploring."

She giggles and waves a hand at me. "No worries. I should have had someone give you the grand tour." She glances past me and her face lights up. "Ooh, like this handsome man. Alden, come here."

My heart skips a beat at his name, and I turn slowly as Alden walks toward us. Somehow, he looks even better in the daylight. He's dressed in a simple pair of jeans and a form-fitting t-shirt. His blue eyes scan me once before turning to Stella.

"What do you need, Stella?" He asks, stopping just inches from me.

She touches his muscled arm tenderly, and something inside of me clenches. "I want you to give Ivy a tour of the house this week. She has been wandering around all alone."

Alden nods to the headmistress and smiles kindly at her. "Sure. I can do that."

Stella leans forward and kisses Alden on the cheek fast before grinning at me. "It's really good to see you, Ivy. Please let me know if you need anything."

I nod, but anger rolls through me. I shouldn't be mad, but what kind of teacher kisses her students? Of course she is attracted to him, and he's eighteen, so it's not technically illegal.

As soon as Stella turns down the hall, Alden grabs my arm and spins me toward him. "What are you doing running around by yourself? Are you crazy?"

I'm so shocked that my throat dries up and I lose all sense. The heat from his hand on me and the darkness in his blue eyes makes me realize what he just said, and fury replaces surprise.

"Excuse me?" I try to pull out of his grip, but he tightens his hold, strong but not painful.

Alden leans in, his eyes scanning my face. "Who have you talked to today? Did anyone threaten you?" His free hand touches my cheek for a moment before he drops it again.

I blink, completely flabbergasted. "Let go of me, Alden." He looks down at his hand on my arm, and he pauses as if confused. "Let me go," I say again slowly, and he finally listens.

He steps back, running a hand through his hair before licking his lips. "I'm sorry. I don't know…" he closes his eyes briefly, and then meets my gaze again. "Are you alright?"

I scoff, feeling like I just imagined his whole crazed attitude from a moment ago. "Am I alright? Really? What the hell is wrong with you?"

Alden steps toward me, his hands down this time. He looks at where he had a hold of my arm and he frowns. "There are a lot of things wrong with me, I think." He meets my eyes again. "I didn't mean to scare you."

I shake my head. "You didn't scare me. I'm not weak, Alden."

He almost smiles, and I want so badly to see what a true smile from him looks like. "No, you're definitely not weak, Ivy."

The way he says my name is like a caress, slow and gentle. It takes concentration not to gravitate closer to him. *Gah, I've lost my damn mind.*

Alden steps closer again, his chest nearly touching mine, and something like desire stirs inside of my belly. Suddenly, the air is too warm in this hallway, and I can't breathe properly. Alden's eyes fall to my lips, and the desire inside of me flips in an instant, turning to fierce anger.

I shove at his chest with a strength I didn't know I had, and he stumbles back a few feet before righting himself. My fists clench at my sides, against my own will, and I have the urge to pounce on Alden and beat him to a pulp.

"What's happening, Ivy?" He watches me like I'm an entirely different person.

I honestly don't know what is happening. I just feel rage at the idea of Alden touching me and kissing me, which is the opposite of what I felt moments ago. I take a deep breath, trying to calm my temper.

"I've got to get to my room," I say, trying not to look back at him as I run to the staircase and leave him behind.

CHAPTER 7

Yesterday evening ended better than I thought once the strange interaction with Alden was over. Fay was late to our room after her classes, which wasn't surprising considering she showed up with her arms loaded with shopping bags. I had asked her how she found the time to go shopping, but she assured me she had nothing to do with it.

I guess Fay ran by Miss Wolfe, Stella's office after class and Stella had already ordered everything I needed to finish the school year out; and then some. The bags had a new backpack for me, a few notebooks, pens, a binder, and even a week's worth of clothes. Stella also included some bathroom items, all high end brands.

I have never been spoiled like that in my life, and I still don't know how to possibly thank the headmistress for her kindness. Looking down at my busy schedule, who knows if I'll even have the time to thank her.

"Nature studies?" I whisper to myself as I scan the pink piece of paper that Fay picked up for me.

I look over to Fay as she snores softly in her bed. I want to ask her so many questions about my new teachers and the classes, but she has a free day today and she made it perfectly clear that she would be sleeping in.

Oh well. I tuck the schedule beside my phone in the back pocket of my jeans and toss the new backpack over one shoulder. My long black hair is tied up in a loose bun and I tighten it quickly before quietly opening the door to my room.

I freeze, backing away as I look at the red liquid dripping from the outside of the door. *Another prank?* I lean in to sniff the red substance, and it makes my stomach bottom out. It smells like blood, but that would just be insane.

"Uh, Fay?" I move to her side and gently shake her shoulder. "Fay. I'm sorry, but I need you to see this."

She slowly peels her eyes open and groans as she looks up at me with cloudy violet eyes. "Why would you ever wake a sleeping teenager? Have you lost your damn mind, woman?"

I would normally laugh at her reaction, but I can't help the uneasiness in my gut. "There's something on our door. I know this sounds crazy, but I think it might be…blood." I cringe, realizing how I sound.

Fay's eyebrows scrunch together as she sits up, tossing her comforter to the side. "There's no way," she mumbles, making her way to the door.

Fay looks up and down where red covers nearly every inch of the wooden door. She sniffs it like I had, and she even sticks a finger out to swipe some of the stuff away. I swear the girl growls a little as she quickly wipes the goop off of her finger.

She turns to me with her face incredibly pale. Her purple eyes have turned so dark that they could be black, but she quickly shakes her head and returns to normal again. "It's just paint. Some idiot's idea of initiation for the new girl." Her voice is strained, but she forces an eye-roll.

I blink, feeling like I just imagined her strange reaction now that her eyes are bright again. "Are you sure, Fay? It's not like any paint I've seen."

She waves a hand at me. "Trust me. Art is my thing, and it's paint." She lays a small hand on my arm with a fake smile. "Just get to class, okay?"

I nod, but I can't bring a smile to my face. "I'll help you clean it up later."

She ushers me out the door and waves goodbye as I make my way toward the stairwell. "Oh, Ivy," she calls, making me turn around. "Just, lay low for today. Don't get yourself noticed."

My eyebrows bunch up out of confusion. "Okay, sure," I say back, and then I hurry to my first class. What's with all of the constant worrying over me?

I'm glad that my first class is "Creative Writing". I love to write, and I'm hopeful that I'll learn something new in such a prestigious school. I step into the class just minutes before it's meant to start, and the chairs are already full.

So much for not getting noticed.

I grimace under the many eyes on me as I move through the large classroom. Two people sit at each table, and there are at least twelve tables. A lot of the students glare at me, just like the kids from the cafeteria yesterday, but a few of them don't seem to care much about my existence. I find the back row, and I recognize one pair of eyes in particular beside the only empty seat in the whole room. *Figures.*

Alden watches me approach, but he doesn't glare like the other students. "Hey, Ivy."

I settle into the chair beside him, trying not to let our skin touch. I don't want another reaction like I had yesterday. "Hey," I say, taking out a notebook and popping the little plastic ball off of the end of a brand new pen.

"Good morning, writers!" The teacher, Mr. Hale steps into the classroom. His smile is warm, surrounded by a brown beard that matches his short brown hair. He's incredibly tan, and looks to be in his thirties. His eyes find me, and they crinkle up with his smile. "Ah, Miss Hart! I'm so glad that you are in my class."

I nod to him, my face becoming tomato-red as the students all turn to glare once more. Mr. Hale turns to his white board and begins writing the key components of a plot, so I open my notebook and scribble down some notes.

The hairs at the back of my neck begin to stand on end, and I shiver, feeling like I'm being watched. I glance to the side, and my eyes meet Alden's. He quickly looks down at his own notebook, and I realize he hasn't been writing anything down.

"Do you already know all of this stuff?" I whisper to him.

"Oh," he says, following my gaze to his empty paper. "I wasn't really paying attention."

I look into his eyes and his pupils dilate as they look back at me. I try to smile, but I'm sure it falls short. Everything about Alden makes me feel lost, and a little too flustered. I swallow hard, my mouth suddenly feeling dry.

I twirl my pen in my fingers. "Are you not a fan of writing?"

He shrugs. "I don't really know what I'm a fan of. I never thought this far into my life."

I sit back, shocked at how honest his answer is. I was beginning to think the guy had a limited vocabulary. "Why wouldn't you think about your future? I don't think I ever *stop* thinking about where I'm headed."

His blue eyes search my face for a moment before he looks ahead at nothing in particular. "The future isn't something that has ever felt promised, I guess. You never know what's around the next corner."

"Woah," I say softly. "That's kind of dark."

His lips curl up into a small smile, and I stop breathing at the sight. "You're right. It's incredibly depressing." He turns back to me, licking those lips like he does.

I have to stop myself from copying the movement, and I turn my attention back to Mr. Hale. "I should pay attention."

I can hear Alden release a slow breath before clearing his throat. He shifts in his chair, scooting a little closer to me, and his scent floats up to my nose. I nearly lean closer to the smell, realizing that the amazing pine tree and spearmint smell from the Jeep was just him all along. How will I ever learn a damn thing in this class?

CHAPTER 8

I've survived the first three days of school, and I have finally settled into a sort of routine. The classes for seniors are separated into lettered days. A days, and B days. I like A days because I get to have Creative Writing, even though I can barely focus with Alden's scent so close to me. Thankfully, he hasn't tried talking to me since the first day. It's like the rest of the world disappears when he's giving me attention.

B days aren't bad, especially because we get to go outside. Fay is in my Nature Studies class, so we get to study plants and bugs together. I never thought I cared much for the outdoors, but it's quickly becoming a new passion.

The Nature Studies teacher, Mrs. Granton is an odd duck. She's barely five feet tall and reminds me of a pixie with her pink hair and delicate features. She is clearly passionate about nature, but she won't let us go past the main grounds of the Asylum, even though I'd love to explore the woods.

The grounds of Wolfe Asylum are nearly as impressive as, if not more than, the interior design. The lawn is always lush and green, and pavilions litter the yard for students to gather together. Gardens encircle the entire building as well, filled with more flowers than I could name.

I step into the lunch room which is filled with students. I still don't know how many students go here, but they all seem to agree on one thing. I am apparently the enemy. At least, it sure seems that way. I get constant glares everywhere I go, but I'm beginning to just get used to it. None of them seem to want to approach me, and I'm fine with that.

"Ivy!" Silis's voice calls after me as I gather food onto my plate.

I turn toward him and a grin covers my face. "Hey, Silis. I haven't seen you around all week."

"Did you miss me?" He asks, stopping at my side and filling his own plate with cooked vegetables.

I chuckle. "Of course I missed you. I think you and Fay are the only two who actually want me here."

Silis scoffs. "That's not true! Have people not been welcoming?"

I shake my head and point to the rest of the cafeteria where a few people are staring and pointing my way. "Just look at them. It's like I have the plague or something."

Silis follows my gaze to the gawkers and he glares right back at them. "They're all crazy. Maybe they are just jealous. Have you seen you, Ivy?" He winks at me.

I laugh at him and have to cover my mouth as we leave the food line. "You are insane, you know that? Are you ever *not* hitting on someone?"

Silis pulls an empty seat out for me, and I take it as he settles in beside me. "You know what? I don't think I ever do stop. How will I ever find the love of my life if I don't put myself out there?"

I take a bite of my turkey sandwich. "Isn't fate supposed to do that for you? You know, drop you in front of your soulmate and tell you she's the one."

Silis's eyebrows raise high. "You believe in soulmates, Ivy? I never would have thought that."

I shrug. "I don't, really. I just thought you might."

"Of course I do!" He practically yells it with his bright green eyes shining. "Everyone has a soulmate, Ivy. I just feel like fate needs a helping hand now and then. Why wait for that fated encounter, when I can do the work and find her now?"

I shake my head with a smile. "Well, good for you, Silis. You deserve to find the perfect person for you. I'm just not sure I'm made for that."

I continue scarfing down my sandwich after missing breakfast this morning, and something starts to feel tingly across my skin, like I'm being watched. I don't think much of it, because I'm always being watched nowadays, but the feeling intensifies. I look around the room, realizing most of the students aren't even paying any attention to me, but one younger boy across the cafeteria is staring hard in my direction.

I look back at him with a question in my eyes. He has to know I caught him staring, but he doesn't even blink. The boy has curly brown hair and a young-looking face.

He's likely Silis's age, maybe slightly older. I wave a hand at him, but he doesn't show any sign of noticing the movement. Maybe he's spaced out.

The boy's face turns dark, like a shadow passes over him as his eyes close tightly and his jaw clenches, and then something cracks beneath me and I'm falling. I cry out as I fall, and my head slams against the polished floor so hard that my vision goes fuzzy.

"Ivy!" Silis yells and his face moves in front of me. "Are you oka–" He's cut off as someone slams into his side and shoves him out of the way.

Alden's blue gaze latches onto mine as he bends to pick me up. "What the hell happened?" He growls the words out at someone, maybe me.

His face is spinning too much for me to focus on him fully. "Let me go," I say, trying to break out of his arms.

Alden growls again, like some sort of animal as he lifts me off the ground. "Stop fighting," he says, his eyes searching mine intensely.

"Her chair just snapped, Alden." Silis's voice speaks from somewhere behind me. "Nobody even touched her."

My vision starts to straighten out, but the pain at the back of my head makes me wince as I try to look around me. Alden is carrying me across the cafeteria and students are gawking at me, some even snickering as we pass by.

"Put me down." I push against Alden, but he only tightens his hold on me. "Alden, I'm serious."

"Don't fight him, Ivy," Silis says as he follows behind Alden. "You'll just make it worse."

"Make *what* worse?" More kids laugh as they watch Alden carry me away. "People are staring. Just let me go. I can take care of myself." I wiggle again, with no luck.

"She wants to be let go, man. Just put her down." I recognize that voice, and I turn my throbbing head to find Gabe standing at the cafeteria doors.

"Back. Off." Alden's voice is dark and clipped. I look up to see fury in his dark blue eyes as he glares back at Gabe. His jaw is clenched tight, and he's grinding his teeth together. *So, not friends then.*

Gabe steps closer, holding his arms out. "Chill out, Alden. She's not your property, so hand her over and I'll take care of her."

Alden's arms tighten around me, and his scent is overwhelming as I breathe him in. "I don't need anyone taking care of me. Just let me go to my room!"

I shove against Alden hard, and he finally puts me back on my feet. "You hit your head, Ivy," Alden says, his eyes softer as he looks my way. "You could have a concussion."

I step back from him, needing to breathe properly. I feel the back of my head and hold my hand up. "Look, I'm not even bleeding. I just want to go to my room."

Gabe's hand reaches out and grabs gently onto my arm. "Let me walk you upstairs," he says, tugging me toward him.

Alden growls low and deep, making me jump as he grabs Gabe's wrist and shoves him away from me. "Don't touch her," he roars, bumping my shoulder as he pushes past me.

Gabe stands tall, glaring back at Alden, and I groan in frustration. "Knock it off!" I yell, stepping between the two raging men. They don't even look down at me as they practically breathe fire at the other with their angry breaths.

"For the love of…Silis," I turn toward the only sane boy in the vicinity. "Will you walk me to my dorm?"

He looks nervously up at Alden before nodding and placing a hand on my back. Alden spins toward him, and Silis quickly takes his hand away. "Yeah, let's hurry upstairs before I get killed."

I follow after Silis as he leads the way, and it takes all that I have not to look back as they both call my name.

"What's wrong with those guys?" I hurry up the grand staircase, taking two steps at a time and struggling to not get dizzy.

Silis sighs, looking ahead as he walks. "Haven't you ever had guys fight over you before?"

I pause on the landing at the third floor, my eyebrows pressing together. "Fight over *me*? Of course not." I shake my head and immediately regret it as pain flows through me. "That's not what they were doing. They must just not like one another."

Silis lays a comforting hand on my arm. "Come on, Ivy. Can't you see it? I think Alden is…"

"He's *what*?"

He rolls his green eyes in an adorable way. "To put it simply, he has the hots for you. And, maybe Gabe does too." He looks at me like *I'm* the child in this conversation. "But, no. Those guys don't get along great anyways. They also don't normally growl at each other in the cafeteria."

I groan, ready for bed already. I don't want to be the girl that skips her classes, but I can't imagine running around with this pain for much longer.

Silis nudges me toward my dorm room and releases my arm. "Get some rest. I'll let Stella know that you hit your head and won't be in class for the rest of the day. She'll understand."

Gosh, this kid can read me like a book. I smile at him with a nod. "Thanks, Silis. You're a great friend."

He grins from ear to ear, his face flushing red. "Then, as your friend, don't mind my stupid brother. He's not normally like that, okay? He…" Silis clicks his tongue in thought. "Alden can't help the way he acts around you right now. Try to understand."

I shrug, not understanding even slightly. "I can try. Guys here seem different than they were at my old school. Even you, but it's a good difference in your case."

He chuckles with that big grin. "Make sure you tell your roommate that." He winks.

"Will do."

CHAPTER 9

A knocking sounds at my door and I sit up so fast that I pull a muscle in my neck. I've been laying in bed texting Lorelei back and forth since Fay left for her early physics class half an hour ago. It's nine in the morning. I don't have a class until ten-thirty on B days and I haven't talked to Lor in a couple of days. Luckily, she's too busy with her own finals to worry about me.

The knock comes again, so I pull my door open just slightly, having no idea who would be visiting me this early. "Oh, hey."

Alden dips his head to me in hello, and his blue eyes scan me from head to toe, taking in my fuzzy pajama bottoms and my too-tight tank top. "Good morning, Ivy. I'm sorry if I woke you up." *Oh, so it's nice Alden today.*

I tug my top higher over my cleavage. "No, you didn't. I just haven't gotten ready for the day yet."

He smiles softly, and my heart flutters at the image. "Good. So, Mr. Hale sent out a text last night with a list of the student partners for our writing project. It turns out that you and I were paired up."

I run to my bed and grab my phone, checking for any missed messages, but finding none. "Oh, I wonder why I didn't get a text."

"He probably doesn't have your number. He got the rest of ours at the beginning of the year." Alden reaches into the pocket of his loose jeans and pulls out his phone. "Let me get your number and I'll send it over to Mr. Hale."

I nod and tell him my phone number. "So, since we're partners, are we supposed to sit down and start brainstorming?"

"I thought I could take you to a spot out on the grounds. It's quiet out there." He almost looks shy as he says it.

"I'll hurry and get dressed."

I close the door and change my clothes so fast that I have to double check that everything isn't backwards and inside out. I'm going to go somewhere alone with Alden, and I don't know what to think about that. The guy is regularly in some sort of silent rage, but he also draws me to him for some reason. Maybe some part of me is super into psychopaths.

I grab my backpack and meet Alden in the hallway. We walk silently through the school, side by side, and no students are around to glare at me this morning, thankfully. Alden keeps looking around, almost nervously, like he is waiting for someone to jump out and scare us. It makes my nerves a little wild, but I don't comment on his behavior.

He leads me out the main doors at the front of the Asylum, and we walk through the beautiful gardens to a little gazebo that I didn't know existed.

"This is gorgeous," I say, breathless as I stare up at the vines that wrap around the old wood.

He climbs the small steps and sits on a bench at the center. "I thought it would be a nice place to go over some story ideas." He dips his head, gesturing for me to sit. "Have you ever written a fictional short story?"

I sit down on the metal bench and try not to get close to Alden. His scent is already floating around us, and I might do something stupid if I get too close. Mr. Hale has been talking about the keys to writing fiction, and how to make a story out of imagination. I've always loved to write nonsense scenes and parts of stories that I never seem to complete, but I'm not about to share one of those with Alden.

I shrug. "Not really. I've written down my thoughts and dreams, but nothing that made a complete story."

His eyes meet mine, and he lets his gaze stay there. "I don't know if I believe that."

I blink, my mouth opening in surprise. "You think I'm lying?"

He chuckles warmly, sending vibrations through me even though we aren't touching. "I think you really enjoy writing. It's why you feverishly take notes in class without even breathing sometimes."

I squirm, feeling all too seen. "I'm just a good student, and how would you know if I'm breathing or not?"

Alden tilts his head like I can't be serious for asking him such a ridiculous question. "All I'm saying is that I don't believe you haven't written stories before."

"It's just not that easy to come up with things worthy of writing about."

He suddenly leans in close to me, and I really do stop breathing. "Look," he whispers, his breath close to my cheek.

"Look?" I instinctively lean into him, my breath coming out shakily as I lick my lips in preparation.

Alden's blue eyes flick to mine, turning dark like the ocean in a storm. A strand of hair falls over his eyebrows and I want to reach up and push it away, but his voice stops me. "That bug next to you." He reaches over me to pick a fuzzy caterpillar off of the arm of the bench before sitting back again.

"Oh, yeah." Heat floods my entire body as I realize he wasn't actually trying to kiss me. And I leaned into him too. *Oh, dear lord. Maybe he didn't notice.*

Alden holds the caterpillar out in the palm of his hand. "Something as small and vulnerable as this little furry thing has had countless stories written about it, and it's incredibly worthy of the hype."

I raise my eyebrows. "Why do you think people are so crazy about caterpillars?"

He smiles, and I wonder why he doesn't do that more. It's intoxicating. "They're capable of magic."

I scoff. "Magic? Like spells and unicorns?"

Alden puts the caterpillar on a vine that runs along the bottom boards of the gazebo. "No, not unicorn magic. But, think about it. A caterpillar is just this slow, un-remarkable creature for the first part of its life." We watch the bug disappear between the floorboards. "Then, knowing exactly how to do it without any training, it transforms its entire person into something extraordinary, a butterfly." He meets my gaze again. "I'd say that's magical, and more than worthy of a good story."

I watch him, the small tick in his jaw, the glimmer in his eyes as he looks back at me. He's worthy of a story, and one that I could lose myself in easily. At least, when he's not being a crazy rage guy.

I open my mouth to tell him we should write a story about a butterfly, but the ground begins to shake. I grab the metal bench in fear, looking around for any place to hide. I've never been in an earthquake before, so I have no training other than what my second grade teacher told us. *And, there isn't a damn desk anywhere to hide under!*

Alden's hands grab onto my arms, pulling me to my feet. He looks around us and a deep growl leaves his throat. "Who's there?" He calls out, his eyes turning almost black.

"What?" I try to get out of his hold, but he pulls me to his chest.

The sound of cracking wood comes from all around us, and in a moment, the entire gazebo begins to fall on top of us. Alden dives with me in his arms, flipping himself around in the air so that he lands on his back with me on top of him. His breath comes out in a whoosh, and his back lands on my wrist, causing it to crack from his weight.

I cry out in pain as I roll off of Alden's body, and I sit up to lean over him. "Alden, are you okay?" I feel his chest and his head for any wounds.

He sits up fast, his dark eyes roaming over me and landing on my wrist. "It's broken," he says, slow and rough.

I shake my head. "I'm fine. You broke my fall, so you should be hurt too." I look him over again, finding not even a scratch. "Are you hurt?"

He shakes his head, looking around us again. The gazebo is in pieces, just a pile of old wood, but the earthquake is over. "You need to get back to your room."

My eyes widen in panic. "Will there be an aftershock?"

Alden grips my shoulders and drags me with him until we're both standing. His eyes glare down at me, angry and cold. "Your wrist is broken, Ivy. You need to go to your room and I'll send the nurse to check on you."

I shake my head. "Let's go to her office together. You need to get checked."

"I'm fine."

I groan, frustrated. "Stop, Alden. I landed on you. You could have cuts on your back, or a broken rib."

He clenches his jaw. "I said I'm fine."

"You are just so damn tough, aren't you?" There goes my anger. "Just come with me!"

Alden spins to me with so much fury in his eyes. "Go to your room, Ivy! *Now!*"

I flinch at the dark growl in his voice, and my heart aches from the coldness in his eyes. I blink and then turn to run back to my dorm. So much for a nice time alone with Alden.

CHAPTER 10

A long howl wakes me from my nightmare. I was dreaming of flying through the air with my parents beside me. My mom always had the best smile, especially when my dad kissed her on the cheek and told her he loved her. Only, in the dream, when my father flew toward my mom and kissed her cheek, the three of us began falling from the sky. They fell faster than me, the ground coming too fast, and I could do nothing to reach them.

The howling reaches my ears again, and I sit up in bed. I pull back the curtains over mine and Fay's shared window. I've never seen a real wolf before, but it sounds like it's far off in the woods. Hopefully it won't get too close to campus.

I'm amazed at the brightness of the stars. I lean against the cool glass of the window, and my mind wanders to an image of me lying back in the grass and staring up at the night sky. It sounds heavenly, and what could it hurt? I haven't had a chance to explore the asylum at night yet, so this could be fun.

I hurry and slip on my black slipper-socks and throw a small hoodie on, careful to not jostle my hurt wrist too much. It's nearly summer time, but it still gets cold at night. I shove my phone in the pocket of my pajama pants and sneak out the bedroom door, trying not to wake Fay. She isn't much of a morning person so I can only imagine how she handles being woken in the middle of the night.

The halls are empty and quiet, exactly what I needed. I don't like the constant stares from the other students, even though a very small part of me likes that they all leave me alone. Even a smaller part of me is itching for a fight, and I hate that part.

I push gently on the doors that lead out to the front of the school. They aren't locked, which seems odd for a boarding school. A lot of things about this place seem odd, though. The cool night air brushes across my cheeks and through my wild black hair. It's refreshing, and I close my eyes to just enjoy it for a moment.

Walking through the grass, I search for a perfect spot to lay out and watch the stars. My parents used to love stargazing with me, and Dad always made sure we had the perfect viewing spot, which was usually the back of his old pickup truck.

I settle onto the grass and lay my head back. The moon is nearly full, but not quite yet. Laying here like this makes me think about Alden. I wonder if he likes to watch the stars like I do, or if he's asleep right now, dreaming of caterpillars. He probably doesn't even dream. Maybe he has nightmares like I do.

I sigh, wishing my mind could focus on anything but a stupid boy. Why him? I could be daydreaming of the sexy Gabe. He certainly acted like he liked me, even though he did get all macho against Alden.

Another long, low howl floats through the air, and this time it feels close. "Crap," I mutter, sitting up in the grass and looking out at the treeline. *Wolves don't come near people, right?*

Coming out here at night may have been a bad idea. I flinch at the sound of crunching leaves and feet padding against dirt. It's coming from just beyond the forest. Who would be out here at this time of night? *Oh, right. Me.*

"Hello?" I call out, slowly getting to my feet in case I need to run.

Nobody answers, but the steps come closer until a curly head of brown hair pokes out from the woods. It's the boy from the cafeteria two days ago. The one who was watching me from across the room.

I sigh, relieved it's not a wolf coming to eat me alive. "Oh, hey," I say, waving to the boy. "You probably shouldn't go out in the woods after dark. I heard a wolf howling."

The boy's brown eyes land on me and he hisses. "Why won't you get the hint, demon?"

My eyes go wide. "Uh, what? Are you okay?"

He narrows his eyes at me as he steps closer, just a few yards away now. "You need to leave. You are an abomination, a trapped soul that should be rotting in hell."

I hold my hands up, backing away now. His voice doesn't sound young, and now that he's closer to me, he definitely looks to be at least eighteen. "I think you're sleepwalking. Let me help you get back to your room."

He shakes his head, his curls swaying. "No!" He screams at me. "I know what you are. Some half-human girl with no knowledge of our people? Ha! It's laughable how easily you trick them all." He grins with long fangs jutting out from his mouth.

I gasp, nearly falling backwards as I try to slowly retreat. "Stop right there! I don't want any trouble from you. I haven't tricked anyone, okay? I'm nobody."

"You are only partially nobody. The demon makes you so much more." He chuckles evilly. "I thought she'd awaken and take the hints. I tried a little stumble down the stairs, or a little broken chair, and she did nothing. Even the blood on your door and the earthquake couldn't bring her to the surface. She feeds on *real* fear, so let's give it to you."

"Who are you talking about? Who is *she*?" Panic bubbles up in my chest, threatening to choke me.

The guy's eyes turn completely black under the glow of the moon. His arms sprout new hair, dark and curly like the hair on his head, and those fangs seem to stretch even longer. I have to be dreaming. This is just crazy.

He crouches slightly, his back hunching over as horns grow atop his head. He growls at me, still inching closer. "Fight me," he says, a rumble in his words.

I shake my head and the backs of my legs hit the asylum steps, knocking me onto my butt. The creature in front of me lunges, but he's hit in the air from his side. Something bigger than him, and covered in light brown hair tackles him to the ground.

It's a wolf. A huge, out of this world type of wolf with pointed ears and pitch-black eyes. The wolf bites down on the other creature's neck, making blood pour out from the wound, and my stomach rolls. I lean over to vomit, but nothing comes out as I remain glued to the scene in front of me.

I don't know who I should be rooting for in this fight as the creature rolls on top of the wolf and bites into its shoulder. Either way, both of them could choose to kill me. I push up on my hands, trying to crawl backward up the steps, but I wince as pressure tweaks my broken wrist.

"Dammit," I cry out, cradling the sore spot.

The brown wolf spins in my direction, its black eyes moving to my bandaged wrist. I didn't let the nurse worry over my wrist, but now I might need her to. If I can get out of here alive.

The wolf is too busy watching me to notice the other creature lunging at it. The creature lands on the wolf's back, but it hardly phases the furry wolf. The wolf pushes off the ground, throwing the horned beast in the air, and then the wolf spins to latch onto the creature's throat once more. It's one hard snap that takes down the creature, and then the wolf finally releases him to turn back in my direction.

I gulp, not sure if I should run or try to stay frozen in place. Where was wolf encounter training when I was in elementary school? The wolf howls into the night and then its body starts to contort in front of me.

I try to scream as it stands on its back legs and the sound of bones snapping pierces my ears. My scream is lodged in my throat, and then I nearly start running when my eyes take in the sight of what was a wolf only seconds ago. It's Alden.

He's watching me, just in a pair of basketball shorts, his thick muscles slick with sweat. His eyes are blue again, and his breath is heavy as he takes a large step toward me. I hurry backwards, stumbling up a few steps, and Alden freezes in his spot.

"I'm not going to hurt you, Ivy. I promise." His voice is tender, caring.

"W–what…" I don't even know how to speak. "Y–you killed him." What did I just see? A horned beast attacked me, and then was killed by a…what? A *werewolf* who just happens to be the cute boy in my writing class?

My head spins and the stars begin to dance around the sky behind Alden's head. I open my mouth to speak, but I can't find any words to say. The last thing I see is Alden moving toward me with his hands out as darkness drags me under.

Read a chapter from Alden's point of view on the next page!

CHAPTER 11

ALDEN

"Wow," Ivy says, her breath a whisper as I pull through the Wolfe Asylum main gate.

I glance in the rearview mirror at her. She's breathtaking. I knew Stella wanted me to pick up some new girl from the airport today, but I wasn't expecting it to be her. It has been a hell of a few days at school, helping Stella organize the new girl's stay.

Ivy is supposed to be part wolf shifter, and she was raised in the human world without knowledge of the supernatural. I warned Stella that taking in a human girl was a bad idea, but Stella wouldn't shut up about how much promise this girl has, and how she needs this in her life. I don't know what Ivy's life has been like, but being a wolf shifter teen among humans couldn't have been easy.

Hell, it's hard enough going through it at a school for the supernatural.

"It's cool, huh?" Silis says, flashing a smile over his shoulder at Ivy. I want to hate him for hitting on her, but I don't even know the girl. Besides, he's my little brother. I couldn't hate him if I tried.

I park my Jeep out in front of the building. I'm nervous about taking Ivy inside. I don't know if I trust the other students to keep their mouths shut about our gifts. They could really freak her out if we don't introduce her to our world gradually. Stella is out of her mind for this.

I try not to stare at Ivy as she looks wide-eyed at the massive building. It'd be intimidating for anyone. It was for me when I first saw it seven years ago. "So, uh…do I need to check in somewhere? Will the guards need to search me before we go in?"

Silis and I both look at Ivy in confusion. I knew she had been to juvenile detention, but I figure Stella would have told her that this isn't like those places. My heart aches for her as I watch the fear in her eyes. She's expecting a jail cell and a cot.

Silis shakes his head. "Ivy, this isn't a prison. We have grounds-keepers, but not *guards*. And why on earth would you need to be searched? Are you carrying weapons?"

I want to slap my brother for making Ivy's face blush. She's ashamed of where she came from, but I wish she knew that we didn't care about that.

"Oh," she says softly, her beautiful crystal-gray eyes shifting to the ground. "No, of course I don't have weapons. That would be crazy. I just thought…"

I heft Ivy's bag into my arms and clear my throat, needing to stop her embarrassment. "You're right," I say.

"The place does look like some sort of jail." I try to smile at her, but she's looking at me like I'm crazy. "Don't worry about it, though. It's just a glorified boarding school. You're free here. *Safe.*"

I hope I sound reassuring, and not like some nut-job welcoming the girl into a cult.

Silis links his arm with Ivy's and I have to clench my teeth in order to not growl. "My brother is an odd duck, isn't he?"

"What?" Ivy says quietly, imagining I can't hear her. If only she knew I could hear the squirrels in the trees right now. "Alden is your brother?"

Silis continues to joke back and forth with Ivy as I lead them through the main floor of the building. I've gotten used to this place over time, not caring much for the details, but it's clear that Ivy is enthralled.

She sighs. "This is…"

"It's pretty sweet, eh?" Silis answers for her.

She giggles sweetly, but I fight the urge to turn and look at her. "Something like that."

"You'll be on the third floor," I say, realizing I'm being creepily quiet. "All of the girls take the third floor, and Stella assigned you to Fay's room."

Fay is an odd girl, but probably the most trustworthy of the students. Seers are all a little eccentric.

"Ooh, I love Fay." Silis sighs behind me. *Figures.*

I scoff as I keep my eyes on the steps in front of me. "You love all of the girls, Sy."

"Oh, I see," Ivy says to Silis. "And I thought I was special."

I pause, jealousy rippling through me, but I shove that thought away. If she wants to flirt, she can. I don't own the girl, and Silis is still just a kid.

"I'm sorry, Ivy. I can't help it! I'm a teenage boy for crying out loud!" Silis shouts in defense.

"I'm just kidding. Us girls *are* pretty great." *Sometimes.*

Silis sighs, and I have to shake my head at him. "Alden doesn't get it. He's only eighteen, but it's like he already forgot what it was like being so hormonal all the time."

"Silis!" I shout back at him. I didn't choose to be a part of this conversation, dammit.

I try to focus on taking the last few steps onto the third floor, but Ivy's scent changes. Since she climbed into my Jeep, that scent has taken hold of me. It's like french vanilla and honey, only somehow like nothing I've ever smelled before. But now, her scent is mixed with the telltale scent of desire. I have picked up on that smell a lot in a school full of hormonal teens, but this time it's affecting me, washing over me.

Silis wanders off toward one of his classmates who is standing in the hall. She's a cute girl, so of course he got sidetracked.

I clear my throat, hoping Ivy doesn't pick up on the change in my mood as I stop beside Fay's bedroom. "Here you are."

She looks up at me, her gray eyes piercing as she tries to take the bag from me. Her fingers brush against mine, and it's like the world stops spinning. Ivy gasps, feeling the same heat as me, and the feeling is intoxicating, addicting.

I can't stop myself from leaning toward her, crowding into her space as she stares into my eyes. Her cheeks flush red and her minty breath blows against me. Desire fills my belly, and I want to grab her, to lift her into my arms.

"Shit," I whisper, realization dawning on me. *She's my fated mate.* I close my eyes, needing to stop looking at her before I do something to scare the hell out of her. I draw Ivy's scent into my nose, reveling in it. I never knew finding my mate could feel like this.

I look down at her again and let go of her bag. A feeling of overwhelming protectiveness pours over me for this girl. Like I would die for her anytime, anyplace. "Be careful, okay?"

Shit, I sound like a psycho.

The door opens behind Ivy, and she gasps as she falls backwards into Fay's arms. Fay's eyes widen when she spots the look on my face, and I take that moment to disappear, running away to clear my mind. I just found my fated mate, and she has no idea what that even means. *Goddess help me.*

PART

2

CHAPTER 12

I'm wrapped in the most delicious scent as sleep fades away and my mind brings me back to consciousness. "Mmmm." I can't hold back the yummy noises as I snuggle deeper into the warmth of my bed that smells like spearmint and pine trees. *So warm.*

I don't want to open my eyes just yet. It's Saturday, so sleeping in is very much on the table after my first week at Wolfe Asylum. It's a strange name for this boarding school at the edge of the Tahoe National Forest, but I've come to feel at home here already. At least, much more at home than I felt in juvie.

Something shifts beneath me, and my mind jumps into gear. Beds don't move. I let my eyes slowly open to take in a dimly lit hallway. It's the hall on the third floor of the school that houses the girl's dorms. *What the hell?*

I turn my head, feeling that warmth against my cheek, and I freeze when I realize that the warmth is a bare chest. A very muscular, delicious-smelling bare chest. I'm wrapped in large arms, being held like a cradled child on someone's lap. I hesitate to raise my head, somehow knowing exactly what I'll find when I look up.

"You're awake." Alden's rich voice is barely a whisper, rough and low.

I force my gaze upward and lock onto those deep blue eyes. Alden is looking down at me with so much concern on his handsome face. This close to him, I can see the lines of detail in his irises and the fast-growing stubble on his square jaw. He licks his lips like I've seen him do so many times. A nervous habit. As if someone as gorgeous and built as him could ever be nervous.

"Uh…" I struggle finding the words. What does a person even say when they randomly wake up in a sexy guy's arms in what looks to be the middle of the night? "What's going on?"

He shifts his arms, hoisting me higher on his lap so that our faces are on the same level. His eyes slightly darken, turning into a dark, stormy blue as he scans my face for some sort of answer. "Do you remember what happened before you…fell asleep?"

I think back to going to bed last night. It was like any night, nothing out of the ordinary. "I said goodnight to Fay and read a little on my kindle before falling asleep." Fear fills my body for some reason, but I push that down. "That's it."

Alden sighs, his warm breath blowing a few strands of hair from my face. "Oh, I uh…" Something like guilt crosses his face. "I found you sleep-walking downstairs.

You were afraid, like you had a nightmare, and then you passed out. I thought I'd sit here until you came to, so I didn't wake up Fay."

I can feel my face screw up in a twist of confusion. I've never wandered around in my sleep before, *ever*. Alden raises one of his hands and touches the side of my face, stopping my breath. His thumb is slow and soft as he strokes my cheek. His eyes fall to my lips, and I can feel the fast beat of his heart beside my shoulder, keeping pace with my own.

"Just push me away," he says, pain layering his voice.

My breathing comes out ragged as I'm pulled tighter against Alden's chest, and then an image flashes through my mind. It's Alden, with sharp fangs and black eyes, leaning toward me under the stars. He's telling me he won't hurt me as the lifeless body of a horned creature lies behind him. A creature he killed.

I gasp, scrambling out of Alden's arms and landing hard on the polished wood floor. He drops to his knees beside me, his eyes wide with worry as I scramble away from him. I remember everything. I *did* fall asleep in my bed last night, but I woke up to the sound of howling.

I went outside of the school to stargaze and ended up nearly attacked by one of the students after he transformed into some horned beast with dark eyes and long claws. A wolf saved me. It attacked the creature and killed it before suddenly turning into Alden. He's an actual friggin' werewolf!

Alden reaches for me. "Hey, Ivy. It's okay." His hands grab mine and he pulls me to my feet. "It was just a nightmare. I've got you."

He tries to pull me back into his arms, but I step away from him. He's dressed exactly as he was in my so-called "dream". Shirtless, wearing black basketball shorts. It wasn't a nightmare at all.

"Ivy?" Alden's voice is soft, but he doesn't try to grab me again.

I watch him, the gentleness in his eyes and the strength of his body. How can he be a monster? Why did he carry me up here instead of killing me when he had the chance? Is it all a game?

I straighten my shoulders and run fingers through my messy hair. "You're right. I must've had a really bad nightmare." I try to smile reassuringly, but I know it falls short. I can't tell him that I know what he is. Not until I'm sure of what I'm dealing with.

Alden nods, a slow, relieved breath leaving him. "I'm sorry about your dream, Ivy." His words sound sincere. "But you're safe now. I won't ever hurt you. I promise you that."

I wrap my arms around myself, needing comfort, and I turn toward my bedroom. "I uh…I should get back to bed." I meet his gaze again, and his body twitches like he wants to move closer. "Thanks for bringing me up here."

He nods again. "Of course. I'll always be here for you."

My heart aches from his words, and even more from the truth in them and the unwavering of his strong voice. Maybe Alden really won't hurt me like he says, but he has proven that he'll lie for his benefit. Things aren't what they seem at Wolfe Asylum.

CHAPTER 13

Who needs sleep after getting attacked by a mythical creature and saved by another? Not me. I have been up all night since leaving Alden in the hallway. Fay was still fast asleep when I came into the room, and I've had way too much time on my hands to do an immense amount of research on the laptop that Miss Wolfe, Stella provided to me.

I have found more information on horned creatures than I thought possible. Some are demons, others are just folk stories passed down from grumpy elders. I have no way of knowing what that guy really was, without asking Alden, the werewolf or wolf shifter, according to the internet.

Just the thought of walking among demon and animal shifter students has me ready to run and hide somewhere, but I don't exactly have anywhere else to go. Fay turns over in her bed with a loud groan, very much not a morning person.

Her purple and black ombre hair is sticking up in all directions, and she has a red mark on the side of her face that she slept on all night. I smile at the image of my quirky roommate, but my smile falls as I imagine her being some creature too.

Two beasts in a school doesn't mean the whole student body are mythical creatures, unless young adult fantasy books are to be believed. Still, even Fay has seemed eccentric since I arrived here a week ago, and I can't help but wonder if she has been keeping something from me.

My phone dings loudly and Fay groans again. "Ugh, stupid phones. Kill them all!" I raise my cell to see a new text from my older sister.

LOR: "I miss you already, little bear! I def don't miss your dirty clothes strewn all over the house, but I'm sure I will soon. How r u? Picked any fights yet?"

ME: "No fights yet, but u know me. Any day now."
ME: "And I miss u too...mostly."

I smile as I lay my phone down on the bed. My big sister has always been my rock. She has raised me from the day my parents died when I was only fourteen and she was nineteen. We were just two teens with no idea how to survive without Mom and Dad. Now, she is building her career as a nurse back in Colorado, too far away.

"Shoot, are you crying?" Fay is sitting up in her bed, watching me with worry on her dainty face.

I wipe away the single tear on my cheek and shake my head. "No, sorry. I'm fine."

Fay stands up and runs to her dresser, opening up the top drawer to pull out a candy bar. "Here." She tosses the chocolate to me and plops back onto her bed. "It's said that chocolate cures breakups, periods, and any old blues. I'm sure you're missing home, so eat the candy and cheer up."

I smile back at her and she gives me a big grin. No way is this girl some hideous monster. I open the chocolate bar and take a big bite of the delicious milky flavor. "Mmm, best breakfast *ever*."

Fay giggles and stands up to bow dramatically. "Anytime, my friend." She moves to the bathroom and I let my smile fall.

I look around at her side of the room for any sign of weirdness, officially paranoid. She's into art and incredibly girly, while also somehow pulling off that goth look. Fay did act pretty weird last week when I woke to the color red painted all over our bedroom door.

"Ugh." I shiver, remembering what the kid with the horns said to me last night.

"Even the blood on your door and the earthquake couldn't bring her to the surface."

It was *real* blood, just like I thought, but Fay was certain it was paint. And I still don't know who this woman is that the boy was trying to bring out. Maybe he was targeting Fay.

I groan and throw my head back. Fay comes out of the bathroom and stops beside my bed. "What's up, Ivy? I know we're new friends, but I'm here for you."

I look up at her concerned violet eyes. "I had a long night. I think I need some more sleep." Fay nods with a soft smile before heading back to her bed. "Fay," I say, wanting so badly to ask her if she's some beast.

She whips her head around. "Yeah?"

I hesitate. *Just ask her!* "Do you believe in fairytale creatures? Like… fairies, or goblins or… *werewolves*?"

She tilts her head to the side, her sparkling eyes studying me for a second, and then she scoffs. "Nah. Maybe when I was younger, but not anymore." Her eyes stay on me for a long moment before she turns away.

I've spent two days in bed, being too afraid to leave my room. Thankfully, Fay has a life and left me alone to sit and freak out in peace for most of the weekend.

I don't know what it is, but I didn't believe her when she told me she doesn't believe in the supernatural. Call it intuition or whatever.

I got a text yesterday from an unknown number, and it turned out to be Alden. I was both excited and upset by it, so I chose not to reply. It didn't stop me from staring at the screen until I fell asleep though.

UNKNOWN: "Just thinking about you. I hope you're feeling better. -A"

It's Monday and I can't avoid my classes if I want to graduate. I have calculus this morning, the hardest of all of my classes. At least I will have something to focus on.

I quietly toss my backpack on and step out into the hall, trying not to wake up Fay. It's a free period for her this morning and she practically commanded me not to wake her. If she is a creature of some sort, it's certainly one that needs their rest.

"Hey, Ivy," a deep voice calls for me from down the long hallway.

I jump, my heart racing with panic as I turn toward the voice. I'm clearly not handling things well. My body relaxes when I see the gorgeous guy jogging toward me with a big grin.

"Oh, hi Gabe." I smile up at his golden-brown eyes. "What are you doing up here?"

His thick pecs strain against his blue polo shirt that's unbuttoned at the top. "I came to walk you to class, actually." His sexy grin could melt a glacier.

I look behind me as if he could be speaking to someone else. "Me? Ivy Hart? The weird new girl who is prone to injury?" I hold up my wrist that's wrapped tightly in an ace bandage.

Gabe takes my wrapped hand in his large, dark ones. He lays my fingers against his chest and the heat from his skin through his shirt is insane. "Good thing I am certified in first aid and CPR." He steps closer to me. "Will you let me walk you to class? At least with me by your side, I can catch you before you stumble down the stairs."

I giggle, falling for his charm even as I compare his good looks to those of another guy that I can't get out of my head. "Sure. I don't see a problem with some company."

Gabe somehow even grins wider as he laces our fingers together and drags me toward the stairwell. "Sweet. Mr. Anderson's calc class, right?"

My eyebrows raise. "How do you know my schedule? Are you a stalker, Gabe?"

He laughs, the sound bouncing off the high ceilings. "Not really. I saw Fay at breakfast yesterday and asked her about your morning class. I did have to do some begging to get her to cough it up, though."

I smile. She is a good friend. I needed one of those. "You really are a charmer, aren't you?"

He glances back at me with a wicked gleam in his eye as we hit the first floor and turn toward the math wing. "Beasts like me are good at getting info out of people."

My heart leaps. *Beasts?* "What, uh… what kind of beast are you, exactly?" I blurt out the question with a quiet voice, hoping he isn't actually some creature.

Gabe's eyebrows press together in question. "Why, a sexy beast of course." He growls teasingly at me and I laugh, much too relieved.

"Ah, well. That's quite the image you have of yourself, Mr. Beast."

He shrugs, but his smile is confident. "It's my burden to bear, but I do it for the good of all."

I can't stop the laughter that bubbles up out of me again. He really is a charmer, and much too cocky.

Gabe stops just outside of my calculus class and places a quick peck on my cheek. "See ya later, Ivy. Thanks for letting me walk with you."

My face flushes red, and Gabe runs off before I can respond. A sudden heat flashes across my skin and I shiver against the feeling of eyes on me. I look around the hall, and my eyes land on Alden's back as he walks away with stiff shoulders.

My heart sinks. Did he see Gabe kiss my cheek? I really hope not. I shake away the ridiculous thought. Why do I care what Alden saw or didn't see? Man, I need my head fixed.

CHAPTER 14

I walk quietly along the wall from calculus class, watching the students as they mill about and chat with their friends. *So normal.* Nobody seems to be paying me any attention, and I'm taking this opportunity for some spying.

Three girls laugh together as they walk arm-in-arm. Two of them are tall and blonde, practically model-types, while the girl at the center is shorter with black hair, dark skin, and turquoise eyes. The smaller girl turns toward a group of boys and her eyes darken and shift to an emerald green.

One of the blondes nudges the darker friend and whispers in her ear which causes her eyes to return to their normal color. I blink a few times, but I know I hadn't imagined that. Pupils widen, eyes may darken or lighten based on lighting, but they don't just change color.

I swallow hard, searching the other kids for abnormalities, until my eyes land on Fay. She's standing at one of the few drink machines that sit around the school.

She pulls out a stainless-steel thermos and places it below a nameless option. They all have a blank option beside the sodas, but I figured that meant nothing came out of those spots. Fay fills her thermos and takes a big drink of it before looking around her.

Her head turns in my direction, but she doesn't see me. A red liquid coats her upper lip, so she hurries to lick the drink away before closing her bottle and heading off to the right.

I look from side to side for any eyes on me and then hurry across the hall to the drink machine. I press the button for the blank option and a thick red liquid pours out. I stick my finger below the stream and bring the fluid to my lips.

A metallic taste coats my tongue and I shiver at the flavor. I know that taste after getting punched in the face by a girl in middle school and cutting the inside of my lip. *Blood.*

"What in the actual hell?" I mutter, horror filling my bones.

I can feel a presence crowd in behind me just before a male voice causes me to jump. "It's nasty, right? But I figure we all gotta try it once."

I spin toward the sound and come face-to-face with a medium-height guy, ruggedly handsome with insanely broad shoulders and skin the color of milk chocolate. His dark brown eyes match his curly brown hair perfectly, and he's watching me with curiosity.

"Uh, you know what this drink is?" *Please say it's not blood.*

The guy raises a single eyebrow at me and crosses his arms. "Come on. I was watching you after calculus, and it's clear you're not as naive about this school as people say." He points back to the red drink that's pooled up in the drain. "And you know that's blood."

I swallow hard, taking a step back from the stranger's knowing eyes. "Why would someone drink blood? It's crazy, right?" He looks at me like I'm stupid. "Or maybe I'm the crazy one. This school has a lot of secrets."

He shrugs. "We don't normally hide the more...interesting parts of ourselves, but Stella told us we needed to for your sake." He sighs, looking almost sorry. "I can see that you're figuring some stuff out, and I wonder if it has anything to do with the attack the other night? I heard that a krantus demon attacked a student out front Friday night. Was that you?"

My eyebrows shoot to my forehead and it feels like the air leaves my lungs too fast. "A *what* demon? I tried doing some research, but I couldn't narrow it down." I lower my voice to a whisper. "You...*know* about the weird, supernatural stuff going on here?"

To his credit, he doesn't outright laugh at my ignorance. "Yeah, I'm sorry to tell you this, but you are the only one who *doesn't* know about the supernatural 'stuff' around Wolfe Asylum."

I close my eyes, ready to wake up from this crazy dream. "I'm so lost," I whisper.

The guy gently touches my shoulders and I open my eyes to look up at him. "You'll find your way, Ivy. Sneaking around and spying on students may not be the way to go, though." He chuckles warmly. "By the way, I'm Sebastian. I'm in your calc class, but I normally fade into the back. And just so you are aware, it's not my place to out Fay, but *I* am a dragon shifter."

I take a big step back and look him up and down in shock. "What the hell does that mean?"

Sebastian laughs again before shaking his head. "I'm not allowed to shift in the school and damage crap, but I can turn into a dragon whenever I want. I'll show you sometime."

I sigh, feeling like this whole thing is a big prank. "I'm going to head to my next class and pretend the world is a normal place for a few more hours. But, thanks for your openness, Sebastian. You are probably the only person to treat me with any honesty in this whole place."

"Like I said. The boss told us to stay quiet, so I'm technically the only person to break the rules." He smiles. "Either way, I'm happy to help…or hinder. Whatever way you take it."

ALDEN: "Can we meet up and talk? -A"

I stare down at the text message, fighting between my heart and my head with how to respond. Alden wants to talk, but I don't want anything to do with him if he's not ready to tell me the truth.

I take a deep breath and choose to tell him just that.

ME: "That depends. Are you going to lie to me again?"

I chew on my bottom lip as I enter the cafeteria. I've struggled eating all weekend, and I'll wither away if I don't get some food in me. I have an hour lunch break before my last class of the day, and then I'm going to confront Fay.

I need to learn about this place and the creatures that go to school here. I'm beginning to realize that I might be the only human of them all, which terrifies me. My phone buzzes as I stand in line for a cheeseburger, stomach rumbling.

ALDEN: "I never wanted to lie to you. Please believe me."

ME: "I don't know if I can…"

ALDEN: "I'll do anything."

I take a slow breath and stuff my phone away, choosing to ignore it for a bit. My heart doesn't need to be tugged in Alden's direction. He showed me the wild part of himself, and then acted like I dreamt it all up. I can't handle that right now, and my trust is wearing thin.

I turn with my burger-filled plate and nearly slam right into the beautiful blonde girl that glared at me on my first day in the cafeteria. She's not surrounded by her posse, but she is no less unimpressed by me.

"Excuse you," she says, her voice a sharp hiss.

I glare back in her direction with very little patience for school bullies. I've dealt with girls like her too many times in my life. "I didn't even touch you. I have no need to be excused."

She raises one well-manicured eyebrow and flips her long braid over her shoulder. She steps into my personal space and a light fills her blue eyes, making them look like two glowing orbs. "You have a demon in you, girl. I wonder how easily she can be squashed."

"Xena, back off." Alden steps between us and places his hands on the girl, Xena's shoulders. "What's up with you?"

Xena's eyes continue to glow as she looks up at Alden and sinks against his body. "Something about our new girl screams *danger*, Alden. Kill her for me." Her voice is practically a purr, and I want to either gag or start running.

Alden growls low. "Are you serious, Xena?" He shakes her and the glow in her eyes disappears.

Xena blinks as she looks up at Alden, still leaning on him. "What?" She looks almost confused as she glances over at me. "What do *you* want?"

Alden looks over his shoulder at me with concern on his handsome face. It has been three days since I saw him last and I can't believe how much I missed that face. *What is wrong with me?*

"So," I say, finding a small bit of bravado, fed up with this girl's act. "She's like you, then?" I look into Xena's glaring eyes. "What do you turn into? A wolf? A dragon?"

Xena scoffs and strokes her hand along Alden's arm. "No, baby. I'm a faerie. Much better."

My eyebrows raise at that and I take a step back, not being able to look away from the way Xena touches Alden. *Intimately.*

Alden follows my gaze to the hand on his arm and he steps away from the clinger. "I don't know what's going on with you, Xena, but you and I need to talk. *Later.*"

"Ivy," he says gently, turning to move closer to me. "I wanted to protect you from all of this. I never wanted you to see how dark the world could be."

I look long and hard into his blue eyes, and I know he means what he says. "But Fay isn't dark. Silis isn't dark, and neither are you." I pause, sure that this guy in front of me could never be a real monster. "*Are* you, Alden?"

His face seems to take on extreme sorrow as he drops his hands by his sides and shakes his head. "Ivy, you have no idea how dark I am."

The last thing I hear is Alden's voice calling my name as I leave my food behind and run to my bedroom. I can't have this conversation. Not with him. And standing in a room full of gawking teenagers isn't the place I want to be when I break down.

CHAPTER 15

I run through the halls, letting myself truly see the things around me. There are so many clues and hints, and I've been an idiot for missing them all. The paintings of wolves and dragons, proud and supernaturally strong. The gargoyle statues with watching eyes, and the intricate designs along the walls of creatures changing, shifting as they go.

I burst through my bedroom door and toss my backpack across the room. I don't care that I have another class today. The teachers have probably been lying to me too. Anger rolls through me, like no anger I've felt before, and fury is a feeling I know well.

I grab my hair and cry out in frustration as I throw myself face down onto my bed. A bitter voice in my mind speaks to me. *They're all hateful liars. Evil monsters with a penchant for blood.*

I swallow the sour taste on my tongue that seems to be a side effect of that voice. It's not my voice, and the thoughts don't belong to me, but I know I heard it inside of myself.

I shake my head, trying to rid myself of that hateful feeling. I know that I've been kept in the dark since arriving at this school, and I have every right to be pissed, but I don't hate these people. In truth, Stella Wolfe saved me from the hellhole I was trapped in. I could never hate that bit of kindness.

"Am I interrupting a mental breakdown?" Fay's voice floats to me from behind, and I jerk up out of bed. She's standing just inside the doorway with deep worry in her violet eyes, and her hair wild atop her head like she just finished running a mile or ten.

I stand, wringing my hands together nervously. It's now or never. "Close the door, Fay. We need to talk."

She cringes at my words and chews on the inside of her lip as she shuts the bedroom door and gently sets her backpack to the side. "Okay, we can talk. No biggie. We got this." It's as if she's talking to herself, calming herself. She keeps her eyes on me as she moves to her bed and sits with her dainty hands resting on her poofy, poodle skirt. "What's up, girl?"

I half-snort, half-scoff as I eye her like she can't be seriously asking me that question. "Really, Fay? What's up?"

She groans and rubs a hand through her tangled, purple hair. "Shit, you know, don't you?"

I open my mouth to tell her what I know, but the bedroom door flies open and Silis practically falls into our room, yelling. "Don't kill her, Ivy! She had no choice!"

Fay and I both stare at the boy with wide eyes, and I hold my hands up in question. "Who exactly was I going to kill?"

His bright green eyes land on mine, and he hurriedly glances between me and Fay, letting out a long sigh before rambling like a maniac. "Oh, thank the goddess. I walked by a group of kids gossiping, and they said the new girl was attacked in the cafeteria by Xena. One of them said the school's secret is out and you were dangerous and you went running to your room all angry like you were about to murder someone! I hurried up here as fast as I could to stop you from acting out at Fay for lying to you because she didn't have a choice!"

Fay gasps. "You were attacked, Ivy?"

I gape at the panting boy, absolutely flabbergasted by the way high school drama filters through the school. "Okay, first of all, I am not going to murder anyone. Xena did act all crazy to me in the cafeteria, but I wasn't attacked because Alden pulled her back. Not that I would have let that *witch* touch me anyways." I look between my two friends. "Oh, right. Wrong term. The *faerie*."

"Shit," Fay says again, at the same time Silis says, "Oh boy."

I sit back on my bed, my eyes flicking from Fay to Silis and back, waiting for them to start talking. My stomach growls in the silent room and I curse under my breath at its timing.

Silis claps his hands together before pulling a cellphone from his pocket. "Okay, we need to have a long talk, but not while my girl is starving. I'm ordering pizza."

My mouth waters at the idea. "Wait, we can order room service?"

Fay rolls her eyes. "*We* can't, but the headmistress's son can do whatever the hell he wants, right Si?" He grins and then starts chattering through the phone, ordering enough pizza for ten people.

I look wide-eyed at Fay. "Silis is Stella's son?" She nods. *Which means Alden is also her son...* I think back to that kiss that Stella dropped on Alden's cheek, and shame tugs at me. I was so jealous for no reason. Another thought strikes me. "Woah, does that mean Silis and Stella can shift into wolves like Alden?"

Fay's violet eyes go wide this time, and Silis hangs up the phone, turning to me. "It's a long story, Ivy. Do you really want to know everything? After this, your life is going to change."

I swallow hard, contemplating his question. "Yes, I want to know it all. My life got flipped around when I was fourteen, then again just a month ago, and all over again when Stella pulled me from juvie. I can handle change. Plus, what's a few more nightmares?"

Silis looks at Fay, and she pats the bed beside her for him to take a seat. He obeys, a sheepish grin on his freckled face. "Okay, first of all, tell us everything you know. Including how you found out that my brother is a wolf shifter."

The pizza arrives as I'm finishing up my story about the incident in the cafeteria at lunch. There's enough for us each to have our own full box of pizza, so we settle on the floor and dig in.

I've been talking for a half hour about all of the crazy things that have happened over the last week. About the times I was hurt, or nearly hurt by the boy who turned out to be a krantus demon, I still don't know what that is. How Alden jumped in and saved me, and I passed out only to wake up in his arms where he told me I was sleepwalking. About the moment I saw Fay drinking blood and my encounter with Sebastian by the drink machine. And then my cafeteria run-in.

Mouth full of pepperoni pizza, Silis shakes his head. "What a week, huh?"

"And you really saw me drinking blood?" Fay asks, picking pineapples off of a pizza slice. "Ugh, I'm so bad at being sneaky."

I sit back, already on my third slice of pizza, and I let my eyes land on my roommate. "So, you drink blood, and you eat food. There are faeries, wolf shifters, dragon shifters, and demons in the school that I know of. What are you?"

Fay sits up straight and flips her hair back. "Well, I am part seer, and part vampire. A straight-down-the-middle mix."

I stop chewing, looking my friend up and down. "What? There are mixed supernaturals? And did you say *vampire*? Like a walking-dead creature of the night that sucks blood and lives for eternity?"

Silis laughs and nearly chokes on his food, but Fay nods and shrugs at the same time. "Yes, and sort of. Supernaturals used to stay within their own species, but they started to mix over four hundred years ago. My dad is a pure-blood vamp, and my mom is a full-blood seer. Vampires were never dead to begin with, but they did used to live for thousands of years. Since I am half, I will live longer than humans, but not forever. And I can eat food, but I still need blood in my diet to keep from getting sick."

"I need to write all of this down," I say, but I don't reach for my notebook. "So, what about the seer side of you? Can you see into the future?"

She shrugs again. "I'm working on that, but I haven't had my first vision yet. Seers are what humans know as witches. I can do a little bit of magic, and I can sense things that others can't. Sometimes it's approaching danger or knowing when the weather will change. Nothing crazy."

I shake my head, in awe. "Wow, I don't even know how to process this information. I mean, you seem so…human. Sorry if that's an insult."

Fay laughs softly. "Not an insult. I've had to hide the magical sides of myself from you. Stella knew that you grew up in the human world, so she asked the students and faculty to act human until she could teach you about us. I don't think she expected you to get attacked and start snooping on your own."

"Yeah," Silis adds. "I still don't know why the krantus demon targeted you. He wasn't a student here, so he must've sensed something in you that he didn't like. They can track people from a long distance, without ever meeting the person to begin with. He had to have caught your trail in Sacramento."

"Right, explain what a krantus demon is. I know he had these crazy curved horns and hair all over his body. His teeth were sharp and large, seriously scary."

Silis thinks for a moment. "Have you ever heard of the scary Christmas story of the Krampus?" I shake my head. "Well, Krampus was a legend, supposed to be a creature that attacks naughty kids at Christmas time, sometimes eating them or stealing them away from their beds. This is basically our krantus demon."

I balk at that. "So, I was attacked by a Christmas demon who thought I was on the naughty list?"

Fay and Silis both chuckle, and Silis shakes his head. "No, not exactly. That was just the human legend. The krantus demon does detect darkness in a person, but they don't hunt children at Christmas time. They hunt year-round, and they only hunt supernaturals, specifically those with evil souls that the krantus demon can feed off of."

"But, why me then?" I ask, more confused than ever.

Fay shrugs. "We don't know. I can sense danger, but I don't feel that when I'm around you."

"And I'm not a supernatural," I say. Both of them look at one another with worry. "What? I'm *not*, right? I would know."

Fay leans forward and lays a hand on my knee. "Actually, Ivy. You are half wolf shifter, and half human."

It's about time to freak out. I jump to my feet and hold my hands out, even though I don't know why. "Hold on a damn minute. I'm a human, guys. Born in Colorado to two ordinary *human* parents. Raised in a school of ordinary *human* people."

They both stand up with me. Silis takes a step toward me. "I know it sounds crazy, but this happens sometimes. Your parents were probably human, but at least one of them had wolf shifter blood in their lineage that they passed to you. Stella is a wolf too, so she saw it in you the moment

111

she laid eyes on you. She says you're a wolf shifter, hands down."

I think about that strange voice in my mind. Maybe they're right. I've always felt different, wilder and more temperamental than other kids. Maybe that voice in my head is that wolf side of me. I close my eyes, really feeling for that entity for the first time. It's like another being lives within me, squirming behind the human part, trying to break free.

I open my eyes. "Holy crap. *Holy crap!*"

CHAPTER 16

"I'm sorry, Ivy." Fay says, watching my mental breakdown. "Maybe I shouldn't have said anything."

I shake my head. "No, don't be sorry. I will just need time to process, I think." I steady my breathing and turn to Silis. "So, wait. You said Stella was your mom, and she's a wolf shifter. Doesn't that mean you're a wolf too?"

Silis grimaces. "Well, that's another story altogether." He pauses. "I'm a faerie. I was orphaned when I was five. My parents were killed, and Stella found me in a human orphanage. She knew I was fae, and she had no hopes of having kids of her own, so she adopted me. She brought me to the school to live with her and her father, the headmaster of the school at that time. They treated me like I was their own, and Stella has ever since." He smiles sweetly, and I'm so glad for him.

"That's incredible," I say. "Stella really has a way with us orphans, huh?"

He chuckles. "It's her calling, I guess. She has made it her life goal to find supernatural kids in the human world and rescue them. She doesn't usually bring them here, though. You and I are lucky in that way."

"And Alden," I say, figuring he has a similar story.

Silis shakes his head. "Alden is actually Stella's blood nephew, her late sister's son."

I draw my chin back. "But you said you were brothers."

Silis smiles wide. "We call each other that, but we are technically cousins on paper. Alden didn't come to the school to live with me and Stella until he was twelve. I was nine at the time."

I shrug. "Why, though? What happened to his parents?"

Silis and Fay share a look that I don't understand, and Silis bites his lip. "That's not really my story to tell. If you want to know more about my bro, you can ask him. I can't promise he'll answer because he's great at being all mysterious, but maybe, for *you*–" He stops what he was about to say and shakes his head. "It's getting late."

I flip my phone over to check the time. It's nearly seven PM. "Yeah, I guess. I have another question though."

Silis starts cleaning up pizza boxes, and Fay touches my arm. "What is it?"

"So, why this school? What's the real purpose of Wolfe Asylum?"

Fay waves her hands around. "Well, that's the one thing that we never lied about. It's a boarding school for kids to learn and have a good start to life. Those kids just happen to all be supernatural."

I nod, feeling good now that I have a few answers. "I'm half hoping that I'll wake up in the morning to a normal life, and this was all just a dream." I laugh. "And the other half of me really wants to accept all of this and be a part of this world. I think I need to have a talk with our headmistress."

Silis groans, his arms full of pizza boxes. "Oh, she is going to ground me till the end of the earth for discussing all of this with you without her."

"Fine. I'll tell her a different, flirty, red-headed faerie boy told me all of her secrets."

Silis fake laughs. "Har, har. Very funny. But I just spent an entire afternoon in the dorm of the two hottest girls in school. I'll go down as a legend."

Fay shoves his shoulder with a scoff. "If you're going to spread rumors, at least tell people that I'm a good kisser."

"Fay!" I shout, laughter bubbling up out of me. "He's a freshman!"

"A very popular freshman," Silis adds. "And no worries. I got you, babe." He winks at Fay before scurrying out of the room in a hurry, leaving the two of us in fits of giggles.

It wasn't just a dream. I sit, spaced out at the edge of my bed, dressed and ready for class as I remember the conversation with Fay and Silis last night. After Silis left, I asked Fay to show me her vampire side. She flashed me some extremely sharp fangs, which retracted with a single thought.

"You're not going to drink my blood while I sleep, right?" I had asked her.

She just laughed and assured me that she preferred her blood cold, not from the tap. I should have been freaked, but I wasn't. I was amazed. I couldn't bring myself to ask her any questions about my wolf shifter side. I don't think I'm ready for that just yet.

A pinging sound brings me out of my spacey moment, and I lift my phone.

ALDEN: "Good morning, Ivy."
Ping.
ALDEN: "Silis told me about your conversation."
Ping.
ALDEN: "Can we talk later?"
Ping.
ALDEN: "Please?"

I stare down at my phone, my heart beating out of control with just a few text messages. I forgave Silis and Fay so easily, so why can't I forgive Alden? Something about his lies feels like such a deeper betrayal, and it makes no sense. Or maybe I'm avoiding him for other reasons.

ME: "I'll see you in class, Alden. Maybe we can talk after?"
ALDEN: "It's a date."

My body shivers at the idea of a date with Alden, even if it is just to talk about his lies. A small smile tugs at the corners of my lips, and I put my phone away just as a knock comes to my door.

I tuck my long black hair behind my ears and pull the door open to see Gabe grinning at me with a single rose in his hand. "Hey, beautiful."

"Hi, Gabe." I blush, accepting the rose from him as I shut the door behind me. "What's this for?"

He reaches over to touch my cheek softly, his eyes searching my face. "Can't a guy give the girl he likes a flower, just because?"

He likes me. My face flushes with warmth as I stare down at the red rose. "I don't think a guy has ever liked me before."

"That's impossible." Gabe scoffs, and I look back up at him. His golden-brown eyes always hold such humor, but I can't seem to get lost in them like I do when I look at Alden.

Don't think about Alden right now, Ivy!

Gabe grabs my hand and starts to tug me downstairs. "It's Creative Writing this morning, right?"

I nod. "Yeah, with Mr. Hale. Are you going to walk me to class every morning, Gabe?"

He looks down at me with a huge, sexy grin. "If you'll let me. I'd like it if we can do more together than just walk to class, though." His eyebrow raises in question.

I'm not naive enough to misunderstand that look. Gabe doesn't want to start a book club with me. He wants to date me.

"Gabe," I say, my eyes looking at the ground as we walk hand-in-hand.

He stops me at the bottom of the stairs, his fingers gripping my chin to make me look up at him. "I really like you, Ivy. You're incredibly beautiful, and I was struck dumb the moment I first spotted you. I want us to go out. I want to be able to kiss you." His golden eyes drop to my lips, and I suck in a sharp breath.

I blink rapidly, feeling so torn about this boy. He's sexy as all hell, and he is so open. *Honest.* But, when he's not around me, I don't think about him. I don't crave him. "Gabe, what are you?"

He drops my chin and his eyebrows press together. "What do you mean?"

"I mean," I pause. I wish I knew supernatural etiquette. "What kind of...*species* are you? I'm really sorry if that's an inappropriate question." *Gosh, I wanna die.*

Gabe makes an "O" face and laughs. "Ah, right. I did hear that you had figured some things out." He checks his watch and starts tugging me toward the classrooms again. "Most of us can sense the others, so we don't usually have to ask. My father is a full-blooded dragon shifter, and my mother is part vampire, part fae. I don't have any faerie tendencies, but I do have the others."

I look up at him, and it makes sense now that I've met a few shifters. The shifters are all huge, but the faeries seem to be smaller, daintier. "So, do you drink blood?"

He shrugs, his eyes kept on the hall ahead of us. "For me, blood is more like Tylenol. If I get sore muscles or headaches, the blood is an instant fix, but it's not something I *need.*"

"But you can shift into a dragon?"

He nods with a grin. "Oh, yeah. One hundred percent."

We stop outside of Mr. Hale's classroom, and Gabe steps close to me, his gaze on my mouth again. He dips his head, but I turn so his lips touch my cheek. He doesn't seem to care, though.

He rises again, drawing my eyes back to his. "Hey, can I give you a bit of advice?"

I nod. "Go for it. I could use some advice on a lot of things lately."

"Good. Then, I think you should stay away from Alden." I draw my chin back in confusion. Where did that come from? He continues, "Alden is a great wolf shifter, but he's also part demon. And his dad was one of the worst of their kind. He's no good."

I try to imagine Alden as a demon, but it makes no sense. "He doesn't seem dangerous to me."

Gabe shrugs. "I can't tell you what to do, but I thought you should know. He smiles and releases my hand. "I'll see you later, Ivy."

I watch him walk away and turn to go into the classroom, but my eyes find Alden watching me with a fury in his dark blue eyes. He looks down at my hand, and then back up at my eyes. Hurt crosses his face, and he doesn't say a word as he shuffles back to the table we share at the back of the class.

I look down at the rose still clutched in my fingers, and I silently curse myself for not putting the damned thing in my backpack. Well, there goes my fresh start with Alden, the demon apparently.

CHAPTER 17

Alden ignored me all through class. I opened my mouth to talk to him, just to close it about a hundred times, chickening out. As soon as the bell rang, he stood from his chair so fast that I barely saw the movement, and then he left without a single word. My heart wanted to break, but when was it ever whole to begin with?

I step into the massive library that I've only seen once before now. It's like no library I've ever been in, and I feel like Belle from Beauty and the Beast just standing at its center. I laugh at myself for the thought. I really am a simple girl surrounded by magic and fairytale.

The room is shaped like a pentagon, with two stories. A staircase leads up to the second floor which is lined with books on each of the five walls, just like the first. A balcony wraps around the huge room, so that from the bottom floor, the second is clearly visible. Tall glass windows rise above where the third floor would be, bringing in rays of sunshine.

I pass along shelves of books that are labeled by genre. I remember seeing a Paranormal & Supernatural Beings aisle when I first visited this room, but I didn't think much about it.

"Aha," I say softly as I find what I was looking for.

I browse the shelves, finding more non-fiction than fiction books, which is exactly what I hoped for. I pull out everything I can see on demons, loading my arms high before heading to one of the empty tables at the center of the room.

I'm the only person in here, and it's nice to not be watched for a moment. After being attacked by that krantus demon, my mind has been running wild. Then, hearing Gabe say that Alden is a demon too, I can't *not* do my research. I open up the first book that gives a history of the tales of demons.

"Demons are believed to be spawned from hell, born of evil thoughts and intent on terrorizing mortal souls. Some demons will drag mortals to hell and feast on their souls."

My nose scrunches up and a chill creeps down my spine. Maybe looking into demons is a bad idea for a girl prone to nightmares.

"Don't believe everything you read," a voice says behind me. I'd know that voice anywhere.

I spin in my seat and look up at Alden's stoic face. His hands are in his jean pockets, and his pecs look like they might break through his plain blue t-shirt. My throat dries up, as well as every thought in my head.

Alden pulls out the chair beside me and he sits, his blue eyes searching mine. "Can I join you, Ivy?"

I look down at where his knees are nearly touching my right thigh. "I think you already have."

He shrugs. "I wasn't going to take no for an answer this time." He looks down at the pile of books on my table, and then back at me. "I heard what Gabe told you about me."

I swallow a lump in my throat, suddenly feeling like a total ass for not asking Alden to explain and coming here instead. "I wanted to know more. You haven't exactly been forthcoming with information."

He nods. "You're right. I lied to you, and I'm so sorry for that. I just…" He closes his eyes for a moment, looking like he's in complete agony. "I don't know how to act around you." He opens his eyes, blowing out a long breath.

His scent floats up to me, and the muscles in my belly clench with need. That pine tree, spearmint scent is a drug. I clear my throat. "You could try acting, I don't know, *normal?*"

Alden almost smiles, but it doesn't get far. "Normal, huh? You just found out that I'm part demon and you think I'm capable of being normal?"

My heart races. "So, it's true, then. You're one of these." I point to the image of the goblin-like creature in the open book.

His eyes go wide and he slams the book shut with a low growl. "I already said not to believe everything you read." He leans forward with his elbow on the table, and my senses go on high alert. "Demons can look like the one you saw the other night, but they can also look human. I'm always in my demon form, unless I shift into a wolf."

I watch him lick his lips and have to pluck my eyes away from his mouth. "So, you don't drag souls to the underworld and eat them?"

He shakes his head. "No, I don't."

"You're a good demon, then."

Alden shakes his head again. "Not necessarily."

I hold my breath. "But you aren't bad either?"

"I don't think any demons are capable of being purely good, or purely evil. It's like…" He pauses, his eyes looking up before locking onto mine again. "There is this constant pull in me that goes two ways. One way is to fiercely protect the things that are mine, and the people I love." His eyes fall to my lips, and then rise back up. "And the other way is the urge to destroy everything in my path and cause utter chaos and death."

I sigh, but a strangled noise tags along with it. "Which way normally wins out?"

"Neither," he says sadly. "I usually choose to shut my emotions off and feel nothing."

I can't help but lean closer to him with the urge to wrap him in my arms and tell him everything will be alright. "That sounds like a miserable way to be. I would know." *I'm used to shutting off my emotions.* He laughs humorlessly, his jaw clenching with the motion, and I accidentally lunge forward, wrapping my arms around his neck.

Alden gasps, but his arms encircle my waist and he drags me onto his lap, squeezing me tightly. His body is hard and so warm. His face is in my hair and I can hear his deep intake of breath as he smells my neck. I hold him like

124

this for a long moment, feeling parts of myself click into place, perfectly content.

Alden's rough cheek slips along mine as he slowly pulls back until he's looking into my eyes again, his hands firmly on my hips, holding me still on his lap. His eyes are black, like they were when he was the wolf, and he licks his lips in that way that I love, his breath mingling with mine. Every inch of me shudders.

"I don't want you to let him touch you, Ivy. I can't take it." His voice is rough and deeper than normal.

"Okay," I say breathlessly. I know he's talking about Gabe, and I oblige much too easily.

Alden's fingers dig into me, and his black eyes fall to my lips. For a second, all I want is his mouth on mine, but in an instant, that dark voice inside of me takes control. *Stop! Hurt him, kill him!*

"No," I whisper as my hands shove against Alden. I jump to my feet.

His eyes fade to blue again and he stands with me, his hands reaching out to grab mine. "Ivy, what's wrong?"

I slap his hands away, a complete loss of control over my own body. A growl leaves my throat and I have the urge to pounce on Alden in a very un-sexy way. To pummel my fist into his perfect face.

I shake my head. *No, no, no! Get out of my body!* I turn away from Alden and run, afraid that I'll hurt him if I stay, and I don't stop until I reach my bed. That voice can't be my wolf, and if it is, I don't want anything to do with her.

CHAPTER 18

I feel like crap. Worse than crap. Alden probably thinks I'm a tease, or a psychopath. I launched myself at him and then pushed him away for no reason. I wanted him to kiss me more than anything I've ever wanted before. *Maybe I am a psycho.*

I spent the rest of the afternoon in my room, shame-ridden, until Fay texted me to meet her in the cafeteria for dinner. I can't sulk in my room forever, even if I would love to avoid the student body of supernaturals staring at me.

I fluff up my hair in the hall before stepping into the busy cafeteria. Everyone is here getting dinner and chatting with friends, like any normal horde of teenagers. I smile when I find Fay waving wildly at me from a table by the far window.

"Hey, roomie," she says as I sit beside her. "Why'd you miss class this afternoon?"

I shake my head. "You don't want to know."

Her mouth drops open. "Uh, now I *have* to know. Come on, I'm a drama addict!"

I giggle and wipe a hand along my face. "Fine. I went to the library to do some research on demons." I look around and lower my voice. "Gabe told me that Alden is half demon, and to steer clear of him. I wanted to know what that meant."

"Why was Gabe telling you anything? Are you guys friends?"

I shrug. "I guess. He sorta asked me out, and he tried to kiss me…before the warning about Alden."

Fay's eyes are so wide that I worry about them drying out. "*Gabe Foster* asked you out? And he tried to *kiss* you? Holy shit!"

I hold my finger to my lips for her to shut the hell up before the whole school overhears. What am I even worried about? They all probably have super hearing anyways. "Fay, it's not like he's a king. He's just a boy."

Fay scoffs. "Uh, he may not be a king, but he is sort of a prince. He's the dragon alpha's son. That's basically royalty in our world."

Now my jaw drops. "Are you serious?" I cover my mouth. "Am I going to be assassinated for turning him down, then?"

"You turned him down? I'd say you're crazy, but I guess I can't blame you. The guy is pretty pretentious. Either way, he has enough ladies lined up to marry him at a moment's notice that I'm sure one rejection can't hurt."

128

I shake my head. "Yikes. I guess I haven't really turned him down yet. I didn't let him kiss me, so I'm sure he got the hint, but I'll just talk to him later."

Fay opens a bag that I hadn't even noticed, and she starts to pull out tubs of Chinese food. "I got us all the goods." She grins, opening a box of fried rice and takes a big whiff. "So, that was the drama? You were studying up on demons?"

I shake my head and open my mouth to tell her about the incident with Alden, but Sebastian interrupts by sitting loudly in the empty chair beside Fay. "Hey ladies. Mind if I join you?"

His beefy arms are so wide that he's practically bumping into Fay, and I catch a small blush on my friend's cheeks. She drops some chopsticks in front of him and shoves food his way. "Dig in, dragon boy."

"You two are friends," I ask, pointing between them both.

Sebastian smiles, already stuffing his mouth full of noodles. "I've known little Fay since we were freshmen, when her head was too big for her body."

Fay gasps and smacks Sebastian on one of his thick arms. "Shut up, and don't call me *little*, you buffoon!"

I smile at their interaction. "So, I'm guessing Sebastian told you I was stalking you in the hallway yesterday morning, Fay?"

Fay smiles warmly at me. "Sorry, but yeah. He was worried about you and wanted to make sure I filled you in on some things."

"So," I say, flicking my gaze between them both. "Are you two an item or something?"

Sebastian laughs so loud that I jump. "Fay wouldn't date me if I was the only guy in the school. She *loathes* me." He takes another huge bite of food, still chuckling.

"I don't *loathe* you, you imbecile," Fay says, her cheeks even redder than before. She doesn't make eye contact with me, and I can't wait to ask her what the deal is later. She changes the subject. "Anyways, Bast, Ivy was just telling me about her afternoon in the library when you interrupted."

My eyes widen. "Oh, it's not important. I don't think Sebastian wants to hear my boy drama."

He shrugs. "I've heard it all, Ivy. We're friends now, so shoot. Maybe I can explain guy behavior to you."

I smile back at him, amazed that I have real friends in such a crazy place. "Fine. I was in the library, and Alden showed up." I glance around to make sure nobody is listening. "He was explaining to me about his demon side, and I sort of threw myself at him. I hugged him, and I don't know why, but I couldn't stop myself."

"Hon," Fay says. "A hug is not throwing yourself at a guy. When you start stripping clothes off of him, then you can call yourself desperate."

"Whew," Sebastian says, wiping fake sweat off of his brow. "I bet Alden was flying high. Did you kiss him?"

I blush, lowering my voice even more. "No, but I think he was going to kiss me, until..." I chew on my bottom lip, still feeling the violence in me. "Some part of me took over and shoved him away, then I freaked out and ran." *Dammit, I left my backpack in the library.*

Fay and Sebastian share a look and then Fay shrugs. "What do you mean a part of you took over? Was it your wolf side?"

130

I shake my head. "I don't think so. I mean, unless my wolf side is violent. I wanted to hurt him."

Sebastian looks at me with his dark eyebrows pressed together. "It could be that your first shift is coming. Wolves shift for the first time on their eighteenth birthday, and if they're anything like dragons, the months before can be pretty up and down emotionally."

I nod, relief flooding me. "Maybe you're right. My birthday is three months from now. Does everyone shift? Like, since I'm half human, will I even shift into a wolf?"

Fay reaches out and touches my shaking hand. "It's more than likely that you will have to shift, but don't worry. We'll help you through it. It sounds like Alden likes you, and he's the most powerful wolf in the school. He'd be a great help when the time comes."

"Oh shit. Is Alden a prince too?"

Sebastian's eyebrows raise, but Fay gives him a "shut up" look. "Alden's grandfather was the wolf alpha, but he passed away a few years ago. Technically, the title is being held by Stella right now, so Alden is the alpha's nephew. It's…"

"Complicated," Sebastian adds.

I rub my temples. "I don't understand anything."

"You'll get there," Sebastian says gently, his mouth full of orange chicken. Dragons can really eat.

A group of kids walks past us, and I look up to see Gabe with Xena and her followers. Gabe winks at me, and Xena practically shoots daggers into me from her glare.

"Here's something that you should understand," Sebastian whispers. "That crowd is no good. Even human schools have bullies, and those ones are ours."

I look at Sebastian's broad chest and muscular neck. "I can't imagine you've been bullied. Have you seen yourself?"

He flexes his arms, but his eyes are serious. "I can hold my own, but I'm at the bottom of the dragon hierarchy. A peasant. And if my alpha or his family give me crap, I have no choice but to take it."

"That's dumb," I mutter.

Fay shrugs. "It's the same as the human world, hon. Some people are on top, and some are on the bottom. I'm somewhere in the middle, but I still don't treat others like dirt."

"That's cause you're an angel, Fay." Sebastian smiles down at my friend, and then promptly snatches the biscuit out of her hands before shoving it in his mouth.

"Pig," she mumbles, and Sebastian and I both laugh.

CHAPTER 19

I stop Fay at the top of the stairs, just beside the girl's dorms. "Okay, I have to know what the deal is with you and Sebastian. I'm not normally one for gossip, but I've become invested. So, spill it."

Fay scoffs at me, her violet eyes avoiding mine. "Come on. There is no deal between Bast and me. We're friends."

I shake her shoulders so she'll look at me. "Fay, seriously! I am literally asking for gossip for the first time in my life, and you're going to deny me?"

A few students filter past us on their way to bed. It's dark out now, and we spent so much time talking at dinner. It was actually really nice joking with Sebastian and Fay, but I'm not an idiot. Fay is clearly crazy about the guy.

She looks around and drags me against the wall so we aren't in the line of traffic. "Okay, I sorta like the big, goofy dragon." Her eyes seem to sparkle. "I had a huge crush on him when we were fourteen, but he always treated me like a buddy. I never told him how I felt, so we got stuck in the friend-zone, and now it's four years later. The zone has been sealed."

I shake my head. "No way. I don't think the friend-zone can be sealed. I think friends actually make the best couples. You like being around one another, and he looks at you like you walk on water. Do you still like him?"

Fay sighs and her shoulders sag. "I more than like him, Ivy. I'm freakin' head-over-heels for the idiot."

Awww. When did I become such a softy? "I know I'm new here, and new to the best friend gig, but I don't think you should have to miss out on being in love. My parents were crazy about each other, and that's something amazing."

Fay grabs me and pulls me into a warm hug. "You're really good at the best friend gig, especially for a newbie. Thanks, Ivy."

Xena's high pitched voice breaks into our moment. "Awww, how sweet. The human trash and the goth."

I turn toward the bully and her band of followers with my fists clenched. "Knock it off, Xena. Nobody ever asks you to speak, yet you still seem to say things."

She glares hard at me, and her two girlfriends gasp at my comment. "I think it's time for you to leave, new girl. You don't belong here."

Fay steps beside me. "She belongs here just as much as you do, Xena. She's smart and can probably kick your faerie ass, even without her wolf."

One of the tall blondes behind Xena growls. "You're dark, new girl. I can feel it." She flashes sharp fangs at me and her eyes turn black. *She's a wolf shifter.*

Xena steps closer to me, sniffing the air around me, and suddenly butterfly wings pop out the back of her shirt. She raises long, sharp nails at me and her eyes begin to glow like they had the last time.

"Back off, Xena," Fay shouts, tugging me backward. "Fighting is against the rules, and so is shifting in the school." She looks at the wolf girl behind Xena. "Put the fangs away, Tori!"

The wolf girl, Tori, growls again, crouching with a hunched back as she eyes me. She's lost her mind, and I am utterly unprepared for this kind of fight.

"I don't want to fight. Just let me go and I'll leave you guys alone."

Xena raises her claws and charges toward me, but Fay jumps in the way, faster than lightning, receiving a long scratch across her chest. I gasp, but Fay recovers fast. She shoves Xena backwards, knocking her to the ground, and then she leaps on Tori's back, biting into her shoulder with razor-sharp teeth. *My friend is a total badass.*

The third girl looks around wildly, much less deranged than her friends, but she still turns in my direction and whispers something under her breath as she touches just a finger to my arm. My hair starts to rise on my head, and my whole skin sparks with electricity. Small shocks pierce my skin, as if I'm being tazed on different spots of my body.

I yelp with each shock, and I realize this must be some sort of spell that the girl placed on me. I step toward her and have to fight the pain along my body as I swing a fist into the girl's surprised face. The electricity stops as the girl drops like a sack of potatoes.

I don't have time to celebrate my hit, because nails dig into my arm, and I cry out in pain. I turn to see Xena with her eyes bright and her fingernails cutting into me. Her wings flutter behind her, and in the next moment, she's ripped from me, thrown across the hall.

Alden stands over me with black eyes and his breathing heavy. Behind him, Stella is holding onto Tori's arm with one hand and Fay's arm with the other, looking like a warrior princess with her brown eyes exceptionally dark and her hair sitting wildly on her head.

"What in the ever-loving goddess's name is happening here?" Stella shouts, flicking her eyes around the hallway.

I wince as pain filters through my arm and down to my fingers. Alden drops to his knees and grabs my arm in his warm hands. "Xena's nails poisoned her." His voice is deadly calm, and a low growl rumbles in his chest.

Stella sighs loudly and calls to a group of girls that have gathered around to watch the fight. "Someone please carry Eliza to my office, and someone else escort Xena." She looks down at Alden. "Get Ivy fixed up, and then I will need to speak to her."

Alden nods, helping me to my feet before tugging me toward the stairs. I turn back to Fay. "Wait, you got scratched by Xena too. Are you going to be okay?"

Fay smiles at me. "I'm a vampire, Ivy. I'll heal from a little faerie poison much easier than you."

I let Alden continue to lead me away, but I turn back once more. "I'm sorry, Stella."

The headmistress shakes her head at me. "We'll talk later."

CHAPTER 20

Alden is silent as he laces his thick fingers through mine and continues to pull me through the Asylum. I'm struggling focusing on anything but the feel of our hands tangled together, except for the continuous jolts of pain in my arm.

We pass by the library, now bathed in darkness from the night hanging over the walls of windows. Alden opens a wooden door that I don't recognize and pulls me up a short staircase that leads to a huge bedroom. The room is decorated in dark wood and warm reds.

A king-sized bed sits along one wall, covered in a deep red comforter. The floor is made up of slabs of shining stone, making the whole room feel medieval, aside from the modern things like a mini fridge, and a huge flat-screen T.V. with an intricate sound system. A circular window sits opposite the bed, bathing the room in moonlight and framing a comfy-looking leather couch.

Alden walks me to the couch and gently grasps my shoulders to help me sit, which is unnecessary, but I'm not about to complain. "Wait here," he says, his eyes a stormy blue again now that he has calmed down.

"Is this your bedroom?" I ask, watching him move toward the fridge that has an attached freezer at the top. He pulls out an ice pack and wraps it in a paper towel.

"Yeah. I live here year-round, so I don't have to stay in the dorms." He walks back toward me and sits on the couch with his thigh against mine, setting the ice pack on the coffee table in front of us.

"Is the cold all that it takes to heal poison?" Seems simple.

Alden shakes his head. "The ice will only help with the pain and swelling if it doesn't go away instantly." His eyes look deep into mine, and the heat where our legs touch becomes almost too much to handle. "I'll need to heal you, but it's a little unorthodox."

He licks his lips, and I start to sweat. "So, wolf shifters can heal each other?"

He shakes his head. "This particular ability is thanks to my demon side. Probably the only good thing my father ever gave me." He looks away as sadness fills his eyes.

I lay my hand on Alden's clenched fist, and his head whips back around. "What do I need to do for you to heal me then?" I ask.

He swallows and lets out a shaky breath. "First, you wanted to know what type of demon I am, and I have two answers for that. I am a warrior demon, made with strength and speed. Paired with my wolf shifter blood, that makes me a bulldozer. But I also come from a line of...Incubi."

Where do I know that word from? My brain fights to remember and then it hits me. "Oh." An incubus is a sex demon that has sexual magic over women, making them their slaves.

Alden grimaces. "Yeah, I don't dip into that side of myself much, but the incubi can be healers. Only, the way they heal is through intimate acts. Like, touching, kissing...sex."

I'm definitely sweating now. I swallow audibly, ignoring the stinging pain that's spreading toward my chest from the poison. "Okay, so what do we need to do, exactly?"

Alden shifts on the couch so he's turned toward me. "I'm hoping that I can touch you." He grimaces again. "I mean, not inappropriately, but in a non-sexual intimate way. I think it'll do the trick. But, if it doesn't, would you be okay with me kissing you, Ivy?"

I squirm under his gaze, but I nod slowly. "Yeah, if you have to."

Alden nods as well, and his pupils dilate as he leans close to me. "Just, try to relax, and tell me if you want me to stop."

His large hands rest on my arms and begin softly stroking upward. His left hand skims over the wound on my bicep, and he continues his caress over my shoulders. My breathing is heavy, and even though his touch is supposed to be non-sexual, my entire body aches for more already.

I'm lost in his dark gaze as his eyes track every movement his hands make along my skin. He gently touches my neck, the fingers of one hand dipping into the hair at the base of my neck but not pulling me closer. His other hand strokes upward to my jaw and his thumb slips so close to my lips as he strokes my cheek.

I'm practically panting as Alden's forehead rests against mine, and my eyes flutter closed. It's a struggle to not make a move, to not climb onto his lap. The hand that was in my hair slides down my spine, making me shiver. He moves his hand to my thigh and then my knee, where he grips me and pills until my leg is draped over his lap.

He lifts my body, causing me to gasp as he places me on top of him so I'm straddling his thighs. My eyes fly open and Alden's head is still against mine. His eyes are closed tightly, wrinkled at the edges from the strain. His hands slip to my back, stroking upward again, along the fabric of my tight shirt, and then he takes his forehead off of mine.

His eyes open and they're completely black now. "How are you feeling?" He asks, his voice raspy and thick.

"Incredible," I whisper before I can stop myself. *Oh, lord kill me now.* My heart is pounding and my chest rises and falls with fast breaths.

Alden looks down at my wounded arm and I follow his gaze. The skin is perfectly healed and smooth, and the stinging has disappeared completely. But all I want to do is tell him that it still hurts.

He shifts me slightly on his lap so that my chest touches his, and he licks his open lips. "Is the pain gone, Ivy?"

I hesitate, wanting nothing more than to lean forward and kiss him. It's like I crave Alden's touch, and I would die without it. But that's absolutely absurd. It has to be the demon magic. *I'm drugged.*

I nod, and the heat in Alden's eyes fades. He lifts me off of his lap and sets me on the couch again before standing up and running fingers through his thick sandy-brown hair. "Good. I'm glad my demon side is good for something."

I try to compose myself and I stand too. "Thank you, Alden. I think your demon side is amazing, actually."

He turns to me with a look of disbelief. Maybe nobody has ever appreciated the darker sides of him. "Why did those girls attack you? Did they say anything?"

I scoff. "That's just bullying girls for you. They don't need a reason to be assholes."

Alden shrugs. "I've known Xena for a long time, and I'm not exactly a fan of hers, but she has never been violent before."

He's defending that witch? A sharp pang of jealousy shoots through my heart. "I guess you don't know her as well as you thought. She just called me names and then her friend went all wolf crazy and said she felt darkness in me. Whatever that means."

"Tori said that?" I nod and he continues. "Tori's mom is a Seer, like Fay. One of her abilities is to sense danger."

I shake my head. "But I'm not dangerous. I'm barely even supernatural, if at all."

Alden looks at me for a long moment. "You'll be eighteen at the end of July, right?"

My eyebrows raise, but I don't ask how he knows that. "Yeah, why?"

"Well, you'll have your first shift then. Maybe you're a really powerful shifter. Extreme power can be seen as dangerous. And maybe the girls are on edge because they see you as a threat." He almost looks proud.

I cross my arms. "They'll be real shocked in July then, because I'm no threat." *We're more than a threat, darling. They should be quaking.* The voice in my head croons at me. I flinch at the sound and look back at Alden. "Could I be like you, Alden? Is it possible that I have a demon in me too?"

It's the only possibility I can think of. Alden said he feels split in two, prone to extreme protection and extreme violence. If I'm part demon, maybe it's the violent kind.

Alden takes a single step forward, his blue eyes really seeing me and making me feel split open. "No, Ivy. You're not a demon. It's impossible."

I try to smile, but my heart feels too heavy. Alden could be wrong. And if there is a part of me set on destruction, how will I get rid of it?

Read a chapter from Alden's point of view on the next page!

142

CHAPTER 21

ALDEN

Watching that damn dragon kiss Ivy's cheek nearly broke something inside of me. When Ivy texted me back earlier, agreeing to talk with me, I felt like there was hope for us. If hope is even possible for someone like me. And when her mesmerizing gray eyes met mine while she held Gabe's rose in her hand, I wanted to rip the flower away and demand that she chooses me.

I've been an idiot on too many occasions lately. Being a coward and texting her instead of going to her room. I was afraid of scaring her. The way she looked at me that night after I shifted in front of her, now *that* broke me. I've always worried the people I care about would one day fear me, and I was right.

I know Ivy wanted to say something during writing class, but she kept it to herself. I would've preferred that she yell at me than say nothing. And my damn ego made me a jealous ass who doesn't even deserve Ivy's attention.

I'm being a creep, watching her as she moves through the library, those fierce eyes on the hunt for something specific. She already moves like a wolf shifter, smooth and silent, but she probably has no idea she's doing it.

"Aha," she whispers excitedly as she dips into the paranormal aisle.

It takes her just a minute to have her arms overflowing with books and hurrying back to an empty table in the middle of the room. I slink back behind a shelf of books and she doesn't even look in my direction. We'll need to work on her observance of her surroundings

I walk quietly across the room as Ivy starts rifling through her stash of books, and I peer silently over her shoulder. *Demons.* She's studying types of demons, and I know exactly why. I read the text on the page in front of her.

"Demons are believed to be spawned from hell, born of evil thoughts and intent on terrorizing mortal souls. Some demons will drag mortals to hell and feast on their souls."

I have to say something. "Don't believe everything you read."

Ivy spins in her seat and looks up at me with those wide, gray eyes. Her gaze scans down my body and I pretend I don't notice the way her pupils dilate. She can feel our connection just like I can, but she doesn't

144

understand the gravity of it. She doesn't know what a fated mate is.

I pull out the chair beside Ivy and sit as close to her as I can, still wanting to be closer. "Can I join you, Ivy?"

"I think you already have," she says, her eyes looking down at where our legs almost touch.

I shrug. "I wasn't going to take no for an answer this time." I should have manned up and done this sooner. "I heard what Gabe told you about me." *Which he had no right to do.*

Ivy swallows hard and a look of guilt flashes across her beautiful face. "I wanted to know more. You haven't exactly been forthcoming with information."

Well, shit. I nod. "You're right. I lied to you, and I'm so sorry for that. I just..." I close my eyes. *Why is honesty so hard?* "I don't know how to act around you." *There, I said it.*

Ivy's scent suddenly becomes tinged with desire, stirring all sorts of mess inside of me. She clears her throat. "You could try acting, I don't know, *normal?*"

Damn, she's feisty. "Normal, huh? You just found out that I'm part demon and you think I'm capable of being normal?"

"So, it's true, then. You're one of these." She points to the image of the made up thing in the open book.

I can't help but growl. I can't let her think I'm something like *that,* so I slam the book shut. "I already said not to believe everything you read." I lean forward with my elbow on the table, unintentionally. "Demons can look like the one you saw the other night, but they can also look human. I'm always in my demon form, unless I shift into a wolf."

She watches my mouth for a moment before speaking. "So, you don't drag souls to the underworld and eat them?"

I shake my head. "No, I don't."

"You're a good demon, then."

I shake my head again. "Not necessarily."

She holds her breath. "But you aren't bad either?"

"I don't think any demons are capable of being purely good, or purely evil. It's like…" I pause, searching for some way to explain my cursed existence. "There is this constant pull in me that goes two ways. One way is to fiercely protect the things that are mine, and the people I love." I try not to tell her she's one of those things. "And the other way is the urge to destroy everything in my path and cause utter chaos and death."

She makes a tight, wheezing noise as she sighs. "Which way normally wins out?"

"Neither," I say. I imagine my father, before my mom was killed. The kindness in his eyes and the devotion he had for her. He felt that pull to protection and love, until the moment he lost her. From that day on, his eyes held only hate and anger for everything, including his son. "I usually choose to shut my emotions off and feel nothing." *It's easier that way.*

Ivy leans closer to me, her eyes so full of emotion. "That sounds like a miserable way to be. I would know."

I laugh, but there's no humor in it. She's completely right, and I hate that she knows the feeling. I'm about to tell her that when she leaves her chair and throws her small arms around my neck.

A gasp leaves my lips, but I can't stop my own arms from clinging onto her and dragging her onto my lap. I've craved this, the feeling of her soft body against mine, the

146

heat from our bond connecting us. I burrow my face into her silky black hair and breathe her vanilla scent into my hungry lungs. Nothing in my eighteen years of life has felt this damn good.

I grip onto Ivy's hips and slide my cheek along her smooth one, needing to look into her eyes, to kiss her waiting lips. My incubus magic surges to the front, but I stop it in its tracks. I won't use that power without permission. *Never.*

Our eyes meet and I feel like I'll die without Ivy's lips on mine. She shudders against me as if reading my thoughts, and my control nearly snaps.

That controlling wolf mate part of me comes around as the image of Gabe touching her cheek fills my mind. "I don't want you to let him touch you, Ivy. I can't take it."

"Okay," she says without any hesitation, and I want to howl to the moon.

I drop my gaze to her parted lips and I grip onto her hips for dear life as I'm about to take what's mine.

"No," Ivy whispers, just before her hands slam into my chest.

She jumps to her feet and my heart sinks. I follow her, needing to feel her again. To understand. "Ivy, what's wrong?"

Ivy slaps my hands away, and guilt floods my mind. I was too forward, too possessive. She growls at me, that small bit of wolf leaking in, and I freeze. She's not scared. She's *angry*, and she looks like she wants to rip my head from my body. It's the same way she looked at me last week when I got too close.

Ivy spins and runs from the library, leaving her bag and books behind. I run a hand through my hair and shake my head. I've never wanted anything as bad as I want Ivy Hart, but if she won't have me, I will need to accept that. She'll be better off anyways, which is what I told myself from the beginning. I won't become my father. *I'll die first.*

PART

3

CHAPTER 22

I push open the heavy wooden door to Stella Wolfe's office. The room is cozy, decorated in dark-colored walls and soft leather furniture. A large, plush couch rests against one wall, facing Stella's solid mahogany desk.

My body feels charged after leaving Alden in his room. My mind flashes through the feel of his fingers on my skin, the way he seemed to breathe me in when he dragged me onto his lap. It was just him helping me, healing me with his magic, but I can't get over how well we fit together.

Stella smiles up at me from behind her desk. "Thank you for coming to see me, Ivy. I hate to keep you up so late."

I blink away the images of Alden, realizing I'm looking right at his aunt. She's a beautiful woman with delicate features, dark hair and eyes that always look welcoming. Not at all like the principals and teachers that I grew up with who always felt stern and rigid to be around. Of course, they may have just not liked me. I've never been a great student. Stella could easily blend in with the student body, thanks to her young looks, but I know she's old enough to be Silis's adoptive mother. Mid-thirties at the least.

Stella gestures to the high-backed leather chair in front of her, and I settle myself into it. "It's alright," I say. "I'm not sure I could sleep right now anyways."

Stella's eyes turn sad as she looks at my arm. "You're all healed. I'm happy Alden got you to the nurse's office so quickly. Jacob really is a miracle-worker, isn't he?"

Jacob? I haven't actually met the school nurse, but I've heard his name and seen him in the halls in his blue scrubs. He's young, and I had assumed he was just out of college, but now that I know about the supernatural, I'm thinking he might have magic healing like Alden. He probably never even went to med school.

After the fight with the mean girl, Xena and her minions, Alden took me back to his bedroom where he healed me with his demon magic. Xena is a faerie and I learned the hard way about her poisonous claws after getting them lodged into my arm.

From the expectant look on Stella's face, she's convinced that Alden must have taken me straight to the nurse, and not to his bedroom where his touch took away my pain. Why didn't he take me to Jacob?

"Uh, yes. I'm much better. How many types of healing magic are there?" Would the nurse touch me the way Alden had, slow and sensual? I don't think I'd like that nearly as much.

Stella holds up three fingers. "Let's see, there is Jacob's seer magic that makes him able to create healing elixirs and remedies." She drops one finger. "Very few vampires are capable of healing with a bite, but there are still a few around." She drops the second finger. "And incubus demons can heal with intimacy, though they are just as rare as the healing vampires." She drops the final finger.

I nod. Alden is part incubus, and I wonder if Stella knows this. She's his aunt, so she has to know everything about him, right? Of course, the guy is about as closed off as Fort Knox. He's impossible to read half the time.

"So, Ivy. Do you want to talk about what happened outside the girl's dorms? I spoke to your roommate, Fay, and the three girls that you had the disagreement with."

"Disagreement?" It sounds so simple. Maybe that stuff happens around here a lot. "Fay and I were minding our own business when Xena started calling us names." I sigh. "It has been like this since the day I got here. People see something in me that they don't like. I don't know if it's because they've been forced to hide themselves from me. Maybe they resent me. I'm not like them."

Stella stands from her chair and moves around her desk to lean back against the wood, her brown eyes searching mine. "Ivy, I can't imagine what it's been like for you here. I never…I never meant to make you feel isolated or lied to. I expected you to find friends and settle in before I scared you with the truth."

I raise my eyebrows. "I guess you couldn't have predicted I'd be attacked as the only human in a school full

153

of *beasts*." I don't mean it. I have nothing against the friends I've made so far who range from faerie to dragon shifter. Still, I can't help but feel betrayed.

Stella sighs, all of her usual cheeriness gone. "Okay, I'm not going to pretend I don't deserve that sarcasm. I run a school full of teenagers with more than the average level of hormones and mood swings." She scoffs. "I was one of them less than twenty years ago, you know. A young wolf shifter trying to grow up. Trying to push down the heightened emotions that come to people like us. That flicker of rage that sits constantly at the edge."

I shrug, not meeting her eyes. "But I don't think I'm a wolf shifter, Stella. What if I'm something worse? Something evil?" I look up into her eyes, wanting to open up to someone. "For as long as I can remember, I've constantly felt on the brink of losing it. Of snapping and hurting everyone who ever looked at me in the wrong way. It's more than teenage angst and rage. I feel like a bomb just waiting to go off."

Stella is silent for a moment as she gnaws on the inside of her cheek. "I knew you were a wolf shifter the moment I laid eyes on you the day you walked into that juvenile detention center. I watched you that evening, and then the next day in that cafeteria. I looked into your file, and your student record. You've had a hard life, Ivy. Who can blame you for feeling trapped inside of yourself when you never knew half of who you were from the very beginning. And then to lose your parents, your lifeline..."

I blink back the tears that want to come. "What about that demon outside the school that called me evil? Or that girl, Tori telling me there's darkness inside of me? Could I be broken? Can wolf shifters be bipolar?"

Stella kneels in front of me. "Wolf shifters cannot have mental illnesses. Whatever those others said they saw in you, I don't see it. I see tenacity, strength, incredible will-power, but you are *not* bad, Ivy. You are good."

I nod, choosing to believe her, at least for now. "Are Fay and I going to be in trouble for the fight?"

Stella shakes her head. "Xena and Tori both admitted to starting the fight, but neither one of them are sure why they chose to lash out. It's as if they blacked out for a moment. The other girl, Eliza, said she was just following her friends. She seemed really sorry for how she reacted."

"So, I'm not getting sent away for fighting?" It's the question that has been in the back of my mind all night. To be honest, I don't want to leave Wolfe Asylum.

Stella's eyes widen. "Oh, of course not. I told you that supernatural emotions run a lot higher than human emotions. You aren't the first girls to fight in this school, and you won't be the last."

I sigh, letting myself relax. "Thank you, Stella."

She grabs my hands. "What are you thanking me for, hon? I'm sorry for bringing you into this world blind. All I want is your forgiveness."

It's my turn to scoff. "I'm not even upset about any of that. You saved me, you know?" I blush. "Maybe it sounds crazy, but I finally feel a sense of home here that I haven't felt in a really long time. It shouldn't make sense that being surrounded by mythological creatures is where I feel settled."

Stella grins and stands back up. "You're one of us, Ivy. It makes perfect sense to me."

I stand with her, and before I can stop myself, I wrap my arms around her waist. "I forgive you, by the way."

155

She squeezes me tight and it feels like the way my mom used to hug me. "Maybe don't forgive me so fast. I'm signing you up for shifter training and shifter pack history now that you're all caught up. Your schedule is about to fill up."

I laugh and pull away from her. "No worries. I can handle it."

"I know you can." She walks me to the door and opens it up. "Oh, before I forget, family visitation day is in three weeks. I already got your sister a plane ticket."

I gasp. "Lorelei is coming here? To a school full of shifters and faeries?"

Stella laughs. "Yes, but I will make sure everyone is on their best behavior, so don't worry."

I nod and exit her office. Stella waves goodbye to me and I make my way back to the girl's dorms. Lorelei is coming here. I should be terrified, but my heart aches from missing my only family. Maybe I can tell Lor the truth someday. I let myself hope for the future for the first time in a long time.

CHAPTER 23

After my visit with Stella last night, I arrived back at my bedroom to find my backpack sitting on the ground outside the door. I opened it up and found an envelope inside that wasn't there before. Fay was already fast asleep in her bed, so I used my phone light to rip into the envelope and read the letter.

Ivy,

You left your backpack in the library while you were studying up on demons. None of those books had any insight into what it means to be what I am. If you're ever curious, come to me and I'll answer your questions.

Yes, I know I haven't been a great friend so far, but I'll do better. Ivy, you deserve the world. You're the only light when the darkness bleeds in. Shit, that sounds stupid, but I hope you know what I mean.

We haven't had a chance to talk about our creative writing assignment, so I wrote up an outline for our little caterpillar friend. Names and settings included. I named her Ivy, but you can change that if you want. I'm leaving the writing portion to you. You're the creative mind, and it's your story to do with what you wish, just don't kill off the big, ugly moth. He might seem scary, but he has good intentions.

Sincerely yours, (is that what people write in these?) Alden

P.S. If your arm starts to hurt again, you know where to find me.

I read through the letter for the tenth time, watching the sunlight slowly pour through my bedroom window. I've hardly slept, replaying the last twenty-four hours in my head over and over again. It's Friday, which means I have to get off my butt and get to class, but I need to text Alden first.

ME: "Thanks for the story outline, and my backpack. I'll start writing Ivy's story tonight."

I wait, staring at my phone for way too long. It's barely seven in the morning, so why do I expect him to respond right away? I roll my eyes at myself and jump out of bed to start getting ready for the day. I'm slipping on my tennis shoes just as my phone alerts me of a new text.

ALDEN: "I've never written a letter to someone before. I hope it wasn't weird."

ME: "It was perfect."

"Ugh," I groan, wanting to unsend that last text. My phone pings again and I'm smiling.

ALDEN: "Perfect, huh? Maybe I've found my calling."

ALDEN: "Also, how are you feeling today, Ivy? I'm happy to help if you're in any more pain..."

I swallow hard. What am I supposed to say to that? *No, I'm not in any pain, but if you want to come touch me again, I'm all for it.*

ME: "No pain, but thank you for last night. Your healing magic is incredible."

ALDEN: "Incredible, but not perfect? I'll take it I guess."

I'm staring down at my phone when Fay's voice makes me jump. "Why on earth are you grinning like that, Ivy?"

I blush and look over at Fay. She's sitting on her bed, watching me with raised eyebrows and a sly smirk. "I'm not grinning."

She laughs. "You absolutely are, literally from ear to ear. Who are you texting?"

I sigh and give in. This is what friends do, right? Talk about the opposite sex? "I'm texting Alden. He wrote me a letter."

Fay jumps out of bed and runs over to pick up the piece of paper folded on my bedside table. I don't protest as her violet eyes scan the paper. She looks up at me with a massive grin. "Okay, that's the most adorable thing I have ever seen. He's into you, like really, really into you."

I shake my head. "He called me his friend. It's not anything more than that."

Fay plops onto my bed beside me, an incredulous look on her heart-shaped face. "Oh, girl. I love how innocent you are." I shove her shoulder, but she only giggles and holds the letter up. "What's this about him helping you with your arm? Is arm just an innuendo for something else?"

My mouth drops open. "Stop! He healed me last night." I hold up my arm, showing smooth skin where Xena had stuck her nails into me. "See? No more poison."

Fay's eyebrows rise. "Wait, *Alden* healed you? Not the nurse?"

"Yeah."

"How is that possible?"

I start to blush. "Alden's demon side has healing magic. I guess you didn't know this?"

Fay's jaw drops. "Wait, Alden is part incubus? Holy shit! You guys had sex!"

Yup, my face is practically a tomato now. I hold my hands up. "No, we did *not* have sex! He just touched me." I close my eyes, mortified at the way that sounds. "I mean, not in *that* way." *Oh, dear lord.*

Fay's sparkling purple eyes stay glued to me as I explain going to Alden's room last night. The way he seemed so nervous when he told me about being an incubus. The way he slowly touched my arms and my neck.

How he lifted me onto his lap and breathed me in as his hands explored my back and slipped into my hair.

When I finish talking, Fay groans and throws herself back onto my pillow. "Oh, my. Ivy, I would kill to be you right now. How on this green earth did you not take that boy right then and there?"

I scoff. "He was helping me, Fay. That's it. One friend helping another." My words sound like a lie, *and maybe they are.*

She stares at me in disbelief and shakes her dark head of hair. "Whatever you need to tell yourself, girl. Either way, I am invested in this thing between you two. Consider me your wing-woman."

I roll my eyes at her just as a knock comes at our door. Fay runs to open it up and Silis bursts through, shoving past her. "Where's Ivy?" He sighs once his eyes land on me, and he grabs my arm, inspecting it.

"Um, Silis. Can we help you?" I ask.

He drops my arm and he pulls me into a hug. "Alden told me about what happened last night, and I was so worried! Are you feeling alright?" He shakes his head. "Oh, that Xena may be super hot, but I will punch a girl for you, Ivy. I swear!"

I laugh. "I'm fine now. No need to be worried, and please don't punch Xena."

Fay scoffs. "What the hell, Si? I was in that fight too. Aren't you worried about me?"

Silis looks at my friend like she's being ridiculous. "Come on, Fay. I've seen you when you go all vamp and that's terrifying. Xena doesn't stand a chance."

I hold up my hands. "But you think I'm weak? Thanks a lot."

Silis shrugs his shoulders. "You're half human and haven't connected with your wolf side. So, yeah. You're super weak."

I shove his arm hard and he grunts. *See, not weak, faerie boy.* "Is that why you came, Silis? To check on me?"

He shakes his head. "Yes and no. I wanted to see if you girls are going to the party tomorrow night."

I shrug. "I don't know about any party."

Fay touches Silis's shoulder. "Yeah, we're going. I'm not about to let Ivy miss her first Wolfe Asylum kegger."

"Kegger?" My eyes widen. "Uh, is that allowed?"

They both laugh at me like I'm an idiot. "Since when is a high school party allowed? The seniors throw these parties every year down in the basement. The faculty has no idea."

"And it's the first time I'm actually invited! No way am I going without my girls." Silis throws an arm around both of our shoulders, making Fay and I giggle.

"Not your girl, Silis, but I'll be there." I don't ask the question that's burning in my mind as Fay and Silis discuss the party details. *Will Alden be there?*

CHAPTER 24

"Ivy, my darling. Come here, baby girl." The gentle voice drifts to me in the wind. *Why is there wind in my bedroom?*

I blink, realizing my eyes have been closed, and I look around at the surrounding forest. *Where am I?* Another cold breeze brushes past me and I look down at the flowy nightgown swaying around my body, delicately brushing my skin.

I don't wear nightgowns, and I don't remember coming outside. Last I remember, I was going to bed in my dorm room Friday night. Is it still Friday night? The moon is high in the sky, and the wind rustles the branches of the trees that surround me. I don't know which direction the school is.

"Sweetheart," the voice calls to me. It's achingly familiar, slicing through my heart.

I spin around, finding only darkness all around. "Hello? Who are you?"

A soft giggle reaches my ears and it instantly brings tears to my eyes. I know that laugh like I know my own reflection. "Mom?" My voice cracks on the word.

A rustling from behind has me spinning around. My mother, barefoot and in a nightgown matching mine, glides out of the forest and smiles at me. I fall to my knees, too weak to stand in her presence. Her dark brown hair flows in the breeze and her cheeks are pink against the cold night.

"Hey, darling. I've missed you." She stands only a few feet from me, but I can't move.

I'm shaking, blinking rapidly as I try to make myself see the truth. This can't be real. "Mom, you're not really here. You d–died."

She kneels in the dirt in front of me, her gray eyes so much like my own. "I'm here, Ivy. I need you to do something for me."

A sob leaves my lips. "I'll do anything for you. *Anything.*"

She grins back at me, but her face starts to morph. Her gray eyes become blue and her smooth face grows a prickly blonde beard. Her shoulders widen, and she's no longer my mother, in jeans and a collared shirt.

"Dad?" I whisper, my heart aching more by the second.

"Hi there, baby girl." His voice is exactly as I remember it. "I need to talk to Sage. Can you let me do that?"

I shake my head, my hand vibrating as I try to reach out for my father. "I don't know who that is. What's happening, dad? I'm so confused."

He sighs, and when my hand reaches him, it passes through like swiping through smoke. "Baby girl, I know you can bring Sage to me. Just close your eyes and focus on her."

My eyebrows scrunch together. The dirt beneath my knees is too cold. "You're not real. I can't even touch you." I look around, my stomach feeling heavy. "Where's mom?"

He growls angrily and my eyes fly open. That's not my dad. "Ivy, I need to speak with Sage. Now!"

I crawl backwards, not caring about the rough forest floor against my hands. "No, you're not my dad. I don't know a Sage." I launch to my feet and start to run, hoping I'm headed in the direction of Wolfe Asylum.

"Stop, Ivy. You can't run from me!" The voice is dark now, masculine and thick with rasp that my father never had.

I force myself to keep running, ignoring the creature behind me. This isn't real. This is not real! *Wake up, Ivy!* I scream at myself. "This isn't real!"

"Ivy!" My eyes fly open and I jump out of my bed, needing to keep running, but soft arms wrap around me. "Ivy, it's me! It's Fay. You were dreaming."

I gasp for breath, my eyes landing on my surroundings. I'm not in the woods. I'm in my bedroom. Sunshine leaks into the room from the window, and I'm wearing the pajamas I fell asleep in last night.

I turn my head and my eyes meet Fay's violet ones. "Fay?"

She nods, her hand gently running through my hair. "Yeah, girl. I'm right here. It was just a nightmare."

I take a deep breath and let it out shakily. Fay releases me and I rub my palms along my face. "I was in the woods, outside the school, I think. I saw…"

Fay drags a chair from across the room and sits in front of me. "What'd you see?"

I blink back the tears that want to come. "My mom, and my dad. Well, first it was my mom, but her body shifted and it became my dad."

"That doesn't sound scary at all. I know you miss them."

I nod. "I really do, but it wasn't really them. I mean, of course it wasn't. It felt so real though, but they were asking me to speak to someone else and then my dad's voice changed and he was really angry. He started chasing me, telling me he needed to talk to this other person."

Fay's eyebrows press together, making a peak between her eyes. "Who did they want to talk to?"

I shrug. "Someone named Sage. I don't even know a Sage." Fay's eyes widen slightly but she hurries to calm her surprise. "Wait," I say. "Do you know a Sage?"

Fay chews on her bottom lip. "Well, Sage is kind of a cursed name around here. There was this super evil demon chick named Sage back in the day who killed a whole bunch of people and became sort of a scary bedtime story for a lot of supernatural kids."

A sick feeling rests in my belly. "What happened to her?"

"She was actually a student here with my parents and Alden's parents. I think Xena's mom went to school here too. A lot of the kids here are children of Wolfe Asylum alumni." She pauses. "Anyway, the story is that Sage was a normal teen, but she got into trouble a lot. No big deal. She had this huge crush on Alden's dad, who is also a demon, but Alden's dad fell in love with the headmaster's daughter, Alden's mom of course. Apparently, Sage got super jealous and went all demon crazy, giving into her darkness. She left before graduation and started killing wolf shifters left and right. Nobody could catch her, especially because she built this band of evil followers who had a grudge against shifters. It didn't matter if they were wolf, dragon, tiger, eagle, whatever."

"Did anyone ever stop her?" I ask, feeling sick for those poor shifters.

Fay nods. "Yeah, it was when I was just a baby, years after she started her killing spree. The leaders announced that Sage had been killed, and her small army was either killed or captured. Everything became mostly peaceful after that."

"How did they get her?"

"I don't know the specifics." Fay shrugs her shoulders. "All I know is that she's gone. Thank the goddess."

I sigh, already tired again after that crazy dream. "It's weird that I would dream of her name. Maybe I heard it around the school since she's some scary legend."

"Probably," Fay says. She stands from her chair. "Well, you're finally awake and it's like ten-thirty. We have a party to get ready for."

I laugh, choosing to forget about that nightmare. "Wait, it's ten in the morning and we're going to start getting ready for a party that doesn't start until after dark?"

Fay looks at me like I'm slow. "Yeah, of course. It's your first Wolfe Asylum kegger, Ivy. You need to make an impression." She runs to the closet and immediately starts shuffling through her wardrobe. "And now that I've admitted to you my feelings for Sebastian, I need to look scorching hot when we see him tonight."

I smile, grateful to have this crazy vamp girl in my life. "Okay, let's do it then."

CHAPTER 25

"There's no way a party is going on down here. I feel like I'm about to be murdered." I rub my sweaty palms on the extremely tight jeans that hug my hips perfectly, stopping around my belly button. My shirt feels barely-there, just a thin piece of silky fabric that's tied around my neck and hangs a few inches below my breasts. A small strip of bare skin shows between my top and jeans and the silk is tied into a bow at my back.

I shiver at the cool air that drifts through the dark basement, but Silis drapes his arm around my bare shoulders. "We're almost to the door, Ivy. Stop worrying and just let loose." He winks at me, and it's more comforting than suggestive. I trust him completely.

Fay stops at a plain brick wall. She knocks on the brick four times, and calls out, "It's party time!" Her voice is high and girly, like she has already had a few drinks.

I'm sure I look lost as I stare at the wall, finding no door in sight. "Uh, guys–" I stop talking as soon as the wall starts to shift. One by one, the bricks drop into the floor, making a door-sized opening in the wall. I can see students dancing and lights flickering in the open room, but no sound filters toward me.

Fay turns around with a wide grin. "Let's do it."

She and Silis laugh, tugging me through the wall, and as soon as my body crosses the threshold, noise blasts at me. The music is pumping, like any dance club, and people cheer and laugh together in the large space.

"What the hell just happened?" I call out over the noise. I spin around to find the door closed up once more and I shake my head in disbelief.

Sebastian runs over to us, dressed in a black collared shirt and tight blue jeans. "What'd you think of that, newbie? I watched you guys come in and had to laugh at the look on your face!"

I blink a few times, looking from Sebastian, to Fay, and then to Silis. "I think I might be dreaming. How did that door just appear, and why didn't the sound reach into the basement hall?"

Silis nudges my shoulder. "You're so cute, Ivy. It's called magic, you know, that thing that we had to hide from you. The wall is spelled each year to open up to a number of knocks and a certain phrase. This room is spelled to keep the noise within its walls."

"How else would we keep it from the faculty and Stella?" Fay smiles, scooting a tiny bit closer to Sebastian.

"So, the phrase was 'It's party time'?" I can't help but giggle.

"Hey, it wasn't our idea," Sebastian shrugs. "Thank Gabe's squad for that gem." Sebastian turns to smile down at Fay, his eyes taking in her extremely tight dress that's a sparkly purple, perfectly matching her eyes. She looks gorgeous, and I know Sebastian is in awe.

"Ooh," Silis croons, looking across the room toward some girls dancing. "I see my future wife. I'll see you guys later!" He doesn't even look back as he runs across the room.

I laugh, and Fay shakes her head. "That boy is a handful, I swear," she says. She looks between me and Sebastian. "Shall we drink?"

"Yes," Sebastian bellows.

I smile as I shake my head. "I'm going to snag a moment to breathe and take in all of this. I'll find you two in a bit."

"You do you, girl." Fay links arms with Sebastian. "Come on, dragon boy!" Fay smiles knowingly at me. She knows I want her and Sebastian to connect.

They both run off to a long table along the far wall. It's lined with snacks and bowls of what looks to be punch. A keg sits beside the table, tapped for the flow of students who run past and fill their plastic cups. A muscular boy grabs the hose from the top of the keg and sprays beer directly into his mouth. His friends laugh as they each take turns.

I didn't want to tell Fay, but I've never been invited to a party before. I never made good friends at my old school, so I haven't actually tried beer or any hard liquor. Lorelei let me have a glass of white wine for New Years Eve last year, but I didn't care for it. My nerves are running wild as I watch the students party and enjoy this night.

A voice clears beside me and I'm torn from my nervous thoughts as I look up at Gabe. "Oh, hey. I should've known you'd be here."

He smiles that dashing, white grin that makes girls swoon. "Hey, beautiful. Why are you all alone over here? You should be having fun."

I shrug. "I'm new to this whole thing."

"To what thing? Partying?" He raises his eyebrows.

I nod. "Yes, exactly." I chuckle.

Gabe reaches a hand out to me and I realize each of his hands has a drink in them. "Here, to calm the nerves."

I take the cup and look down at the dark liquid. "What is it?"

"Does it matter?" Gabe asks like my question was ridiculous. He downs his cup in one gulp and smiles wider at me. "Toss it back, Ivy. Live a little."

I shrug, figuring if this is going to be my only high school party experience, I might as well enjoy it. I put the cup to my lips and toss my head back, letting the alcohol slip past my tongue and burn my throat. I cough like I'm on my deathbed and Gabe laughs louder than the booming music.

"Nice!" He yells, taking my empty cup. "Stay right here."

Gabe runs off to the refreshments table and I take a moment to try and breathe past the burn in my esophagus. If that's what drinking is like, I don't think I'm a fan. I watch Gabe smile at a few people as he makes his way back to me with two more full cups.

"Ready for round two, beautiful?" He asks, waggling his thick eyebrows as he places the cup in my hands again.

I look down at the dark liquid and shake my head. "If round two is like round one, I think I'm good."

Gabe laughs, his golden eyes shining in the dim lights. "The second time is way easier, trust me. And this will be the one that stops your nervousness." He winks at me. "Maybe it will get you away from the wall and on the dance floor with me."

I smile shyly, not sure I'm ready to be thrown into the sweaty throng of people. But, if the second time's the charm, maybe it could feel good to relax for once. I take a deep breath and down the drink before I can second-guess myself, and Gabe was right. It goes down much smoother than the last.

"Yes!" He yells, finishing his own drink. His arms encircle my waist and he lifts me up to spin me around. He tosses our cups into a garbage can behind me before whispering in my ear. "Dance with me, beautiful."

My body heats up, but not from Gabe's breath on my neck. I can feel the alcohol work through me and cause every inch of me to relax. I step back from Gabe, though, remembering what Alden told me in the library last week.

"I don't want you to let him touch you, Ivy. I can't take it."

I agreed with him, basically promising that I won't be with Gabe. Even through the increasing fog in my mind, I know I don't want to break that promise.

I look up at Gabe and shake my head. "I can't dance with you, Gabe. I'm sorry, but you wanted me to be your girlfriend and I don't want to lead you on. I just want to be friends."

Gabe slouches a bit, but his smile is still glued to his handsome face. "Fine, you don't have to be my girlfriend if you don't want to, but friends dance all the time." He sticks out his bottom lip. "One dance, please?"

I would love to have more good friends at this school, and Gabe seems sincere. I nod and let him take my hand. He drags me to the center of the moving crowd and the heat from the dancing students touches my skin. Gabe bounces side-to-side with the rest of the group, tugging me close but not too close.

I smile, letting myself enjoy this moment as I move to the beat. I look around, hoping to find Alden here, but I can't exactly imagine him at a place like this. His familiar blue eyes are nowhere to be seen, but I do see Fay and Sebastian dancing close together. His arms are around her waist, and she toys with the hairs on the back of his neck as they move fast to the thumping music.

I can't help but feel elated, though maybe that's the alcohol warming my body. My heart races and the flickering lights make me feel like I'm moving along with them instead of the song. A thrill courses through my blood and I feel invincible, wild. This is my wolf; I know it is. It's a primal side of me that I haven't ever fully felt, and I want to fall into it.

My body is so hot and I can feel sweat drip from my hairline. Hands stroke along the bare skin of my back, and I'm pulled tightly against a wall of warmth. I sigh at the contact, my body still swaying to the *thump thump thump* all around me.

I can feel lips press to my neck, kissing along my damp skin, and my eyes fly open. I hadn't even realized they were closed. My head is thrown back and I'm staring up at the flashing lights along the ceiling. I drop my chin, my gaze clinging with Gabe's. His eyes are completely

174

black and his arms are wrapped around me so tight as our bodies rub together to the beat.

"Gabe?" I ask, my mind foggy.

He leans in close, his lips touching my neck again as he whispers. "You're so sexy, Ivy."

This isn't right. I shove against his chest, putting some space between us. "I told you I don't want to be with you, Gabe." My voice slurs as I speak.

He chuckles. "You could've fooled me, babe." He tries to pull me back and I want to sink back in.

I want to feel that wild feeling again, but just as I start to give in, large hands drag me away from Gabe's arms. Gabe shouts something, but the sound fades quickly as I'm tugged through the dancing crowd. I fight against the hold until I'm flipped around to face Alden's fierce glare. He looks beyond pissed as he holds onto my shoulders and stops in a dark corner of the party room.

"What the hell are you doing, Ivy?" His voice is livid, his chest rising and falling too fast.

I know he looks terrifying right now, but my whole body reacts to him in the most primal way. I sink against his broad chest, purring as I let my hands lock together behind his neck. "You want to dance with me too, Alden?"

I start to move against him, the music slower and more sensual than before. Alden's hands fall to my hips and he grips me hard, stilling my swaying movements. "Stop," he groans, his voice more animal than man. "You shouldn't be here like this, Ivy."

"Mhm," I mumble. "Like what, Alden?" I press my chest against his and fight against his grip, trying to dance like I so badly want to. "Don't you want to dance with me?"

Alden's eyes are dark and angry. His hands lose their grip a little and he lets me move my hips against him. "You're drunk. Why did you drink so much?" His fingers cling onto me again and I groan in frustration as I'm forced to be still. "Why were you dancing with *him* like that?"

I shrug, resting my chin on his chest as I look up into his dangerous eyes. "I've never been drunk before; did you know that? Gabe gave me two drinks. That's not a lot." I smile up at him. "I'm glad you're here, Alden." His eyes soften. "I told him I didn't want to be his girlfriend. He said we were going to dance as friends, but I think he lied. He wants to kiss me."

Alden growls and I can feel the rippling fury through his body. "I'm taking you to your room, Ivy. If I stay, I might kill him."

I shake my head. "Nooo, just dance with me. Maybe you can kiss me instead of him."

"Dammit, Ivy." Alden's eyes close tightly and he groans as he throws his head back. In a movement too fast for me to process, he bends to loop his arm around my waist and then he hoists me over his shoulder.

"Alden!" I squeal. "What are you doing?"

He carries me out of the room and into the dark hallway of the basement. "Party's over."

CHAPTER 26

"Ugh," I groan, my stomach turning in the worst ways as I roll out of bed. I'm still wearing my skin-tight jeans and I hate them, so I peel them off of my legs and throw on some soft cotton shorts and an oversized t-shirt. "Much better," I mumble to myself.

Fay hasn't returned to the room yet, and I have no clue where my phone is to even call her. I stumble across the bedroom, remembering that Alden told me he was going to wait outside my door all night. It was right after he tossed me onto my bed and grumbled curses under his breath as he walked out and slammed my door shut.

I can't sleep, though. My body is still wired from my first drunk experience, and I don't want to lay in bed all night. I want to see him, to talk to him.

I pull my bedroom door open slowly, having to hang onto the frame so I don't fall over. I only had two drinks, but I am clearly a lightweight. I lean my head out the doorway and see Alden sitting up against the wall. His eyes are closed and his breathing is steady as he sleeps soundly. I don't understand how a person can sleep sitting up like that, but he looks so good doing it.

I tip toe toward him, wanting to touch his stubbly jaw as he rests. He looks more peaceful than I've ever seen him, and I love that I get to ogle this gorgeous guy without him noticing. I sit down beside Alden, letting his moment of calm bleed into me. I lay down on the hardwood floor, resting my head on Alden's lap.

If he were awake, he'd probably push me away, but I don't care. This is much better than sleeping alone in my bed. I let my eyes flutter closed, feeling peaceful with Alden's scent surrounding me and his slow breaths soothing my mind. It's mere moments before I drift off to sleep.

"Ivy, come here," a voice calls.

I don't want to get up, but my body moves anyways, feeling drawn to that voice. I crawl to my knees and look from one end of the dim hallway to the other. Nobody's there. I look down and realize that even Alden has left. I wish he would have woken me to say goodbye.

"Come on, Ivy. I'm waiting."

The voice comes from the stairwell. It sounds familiar. Maybe it's actually Alden playing a game with me. I smile and stand up, moving slowly toward the winding staircase.

"Alden?" I whisper, looking down into the dark.

The voice chuckles warmly. "I'm right here. Can you find me?"

I giggle, loving this little game already. I have to hold tightly to the railing as I descend the stairs. My body feels weak and wobbly. It gets darker the further I go, until I can no longer see anything.

I feel along the walls. "Alden, where are you?"

"Ivy, stop!" Alden yells, and this time it's really his voice, unmistakable.

I spin around, looking for him, and that softer voice speaks again. "Sage, come out my queen."

"Who are you?" It's so dark now and I don't know which way to turn. My heart is pounding as I spin in all directions.

The real Alden shouts for me again, but when I take a step in his direction, I suddenly start falling. It's too dark to see what I've fallen into, but within seconds, my body lands hard against a solid ground. My head aches from whatever I landed on.

"Sage!" The voice yells one more time before I'm jerked upward and suddenly being cradled in warm arms.

It's no longer pitch black, and Alden is carrying me up a flight of stairs. "Alden?" I ask, so confused and incredibly dizzy.

He looks down at me and he sighs, so much worry in his blue eyes. "Christ, Ivy! I'm so glad you're finally awake."

I shake my head, but the movement makes my vision go fuzzy and I flinch from a stab of pain. "I've been awake since you left me in the hall. I was looking for you."

Alden looks down at me again, his eyebrows drawn together. "I never left you in the hall. I woke up to you stirring in your sleep. You were laying your head in my lap and I tried to wake you, but you just got up and started walking away." Alden pushes my bedroom door open and sits me on my bed. Fay still isn't back. Hopefully she's off with Sebastian.

Alden drops to his knees in front of me, his eyes searching my body. "I followed you, and you went downstairs to the second floor. I called for you to stop, but you were sleepwalking, I think. You ignored me, and then you threw yourself down the damn stairs. You just started falling and hit your head at the bottom." He touches my face, turning it from side-to-side to look over my hurt head. "I picked you up and that's when you finally woke up and looked at me."

I place my hand against the back of my head, feeling a large bump and wincing at the pain. "Shoot, that hurts."

Alden gently touches the same spot I had and his face looks as pained as I feel. "I should've tried harder to wake you, but people say to never wake someone who is sleepwalking." He sighs. "I'm so sorry, Ivy. I stayed outside your door to make sure you were safe and I failed."

I think I'm still drunk because I rest my palms against Alden's cheeks, needing to soothe the wrinkles of worry around his eyes. I run my thumbs along his forehead. "You didn't fail, Alden. I've been having crazy dreams. I guess they've evolved into sleepwalking." I giggle in a weird way.

Alden's hands rest beside me on my bed and he is so still as he kneels between my legs. He looks deep into my eyes before licking his perfect lips. "You might have a concussion, Ivy, and you're probably still drunk. I need to get you some ice. Some water too."

180

He moves to stand, but I grip onto the front of his white shirt, tugging him back between my legs. "I'm not drunk," I slur. *Yup, definitely inebriated.* "I don't want you to go."

"Ivy," Alden whispers. "I can't be here like this. You're not yourself." He lays his hands on mine that hold tightly to his shirt. "I don't know what you drank, but Gabe shouldn't have given you what he did. The liquor is stronger at these parties, for the shifters and vampires. It takes a lot more alcohol to affect us, but you haven't shifted yet. You should have had the human stuff, and Gabe is a moron who needs his ass kicked."

I smile like an idiot, unable to control it. "You're jealous." Alden's eyes go wide, but I guess I'm not done yet. "You don't want that guy touching me, because *you* want to touch me." I walk my fingers up his chest, letting them land on his plump lips. "Did you know that you lick your lips a lot?" I stroke his bottom lip with my finger. "It drives me *crazy.*"

Alden lets out a heavy breath. "Ivy, *please.*" His voice sounds pained. He reaches up and takes my hand in his, dragging it away from his mouth. "You need to be taken care of. You could be really hurt."

I shrug. "I don't care. You can just heal me, remember? You have *sexy* magic."

Alden groans, closing his eyes. "You're too drunk to consent to me using my magic on you. It's not right."

I nod, understanding, but the movement of my head makes me dizzy and I start to fall backwards. "Ow, that's not fun." I can hear myself whimper from the pain.

Alden's hand moves behind my neck and he keeps me upright. He looks at the way my face scrunches up in pain and then he growls again.

"Screw it," he snaps, and then his lips are on mine.

CHAPTER 27

It takes me a moment to realize that Alden is kissing me, *like really kissing me*, but then heat floods my body, reaching all the way to my toes. I let my eyes flutter closed and I move my lips against his. His hand rests at the back of my neck, holding me steady, and his other arm snakes around my waist, pulling my body close to his where he still kneels before me.

Alden's lips are slow and soft. His hot breath warms my cheeks and I breathe in his exhales as I open my mouth to gasp from the electricity that sparks across my lips. I throw my arms around Alden's neck, needing to feel more of him, wanting to drown in him. He groans, his lips pushing harder and sliding faster across mine.

His tongue barely touches my bottom lip, but I take it as an invitation. I open my mouth to him, letting my tongue stroke his once, twice. I push myself off the edge of my bed, dropping onto Alden's lap.

"Ivy," he whispers, pulling away from me.

I know he only kissed me to help fix my head, but I'm beyond that now. I'm going to take what I want from this man that drives me wild every time he looks at me.

I don't let him retreat. I slip my fingers into his soft hair and pull his mouth back to mine. Alden's hands splay across my back, holding me against his chest as he takes my mouth like he has been starving for this, *craving* me.

We're both breathing so fast that it feels like time is fast-forwarding. My head is clear and the pain from falling is completely gone. All I feel now is so much desire for Alden. A need like nothing I've felt before.

Suddenly, a thought pops into my mind. *This is wrong. He's not mine, none of this is mine. Stop!* I gasp at the invasive voice in my head and I suddenly bite down on Alden's bottom lip, anger flowing through me.

Alden pulls back, flinching from my assault. He stands up and deposits me back on my bed as blood drips from his bottom lip. *I just bit Alden, and not in a sexy way whatsoever.* He turns away from me, running a hand through his hair.

"Alden, I'm sor—"

He turns with his hands up, cutting me off. "No, it's okay." He licks the blood off of his lip. "I got carried away. I shouldn't have…"

My heart sinks. "Either way, I *am* sorry. I didn't mean to hurt you. I wasn't myself." *Myself* wanted to keep kissing Alden, to never stop feeling his body against mine. This other thing inside of me isn't a part of me at all.

Alden's chest rises and falls fast as he looks at me, his eyes trailing along my bare legs. He blinks fast before turning to grab the bedroom door handle. "Get some sleep, Ivy."

"Wait," I call after him. He pauses to look back at me, but I don't even know why I stopped him. I look over at Fay's empty bed and remember that voice in my dreams. "I don't want to be alone tonight. Can you...stay? With me?"

He licks his lip again, the bleeding already stopped. "Sure. I can stay." He walks gently across the room, his hands in his pockets, and he plops himself down on the floor with his back against my bed. "Did you want to tell me about those dreams you've been having?"

I sigh, feeling content now that he's looking at me with that gentle smile again. "Yeah, I can do that."

Alden lays his head back against my mattress, tossing a handful of chocolate-covered pretzels into his mouth. After I found my phone an hour ago and saw the text from Fay that she's hanging out in Sebastian's room, and to "not wait up", Alden and I raided her snack drawer. We found all sorts of goodies that we have been munching on while we talk about anything and everything.

My phone pings and I raise it up to read the new text.

FAY: "Is Alden still there? OMG, is he in your bed with you?"

I giggle and roll my eyes at my beautiful friend. I guess Alden called her after bringing my drunk ass back here, and he promised to take care of me until she returned. After congratulating Fay for getting some alone time with Sebastian, I mentioned that Alden was here with me. She clearly has a wandering mind on that subject.

ME: "He's sitting on the floor. We're just talking. That's it."

Alden smiles at me as I drop my phone back on the nightstand. "Is it Fay? Is she alright with Sebastian?"

I nod, trying to hide how cute I think it is that he cares. "She's over the moon, trust me."

I'm lying on my side on top of my bed, a small blanket thrown over my legs, and Alden has remained on the floor while we've talked. I told him about my crazy Sage dreams, where he remained unnervingly quiet and told me he'd look into it. I decided to move on from that topic because it made me feel queasy.

Alden told me all about Silis as a little boy. Apparently, he hasn't changed much, aside from his obsession with the opposite sex. He has always been a quick-witted kid with way too much energy and a huge heart. The way Alden talks about him, I can see why they consider one another brothers.

Alden turns a little as he drops his bag of pretzels and his blue eyes meet mine. "Can you tell me about your parents? All I know is that they passed away, but I'd like to know what they were like."

My cheeks flush from the intensity of his gaze. "Um, yeah. I don't talk about them a lot. They took this little airplane out on their anniversary when I was fourteen. There was some freak accident with the engine and it went down." I chew on the inside of my cheek. "They were the best, though. My dad was a goofball, always cracking jokes and making everyone around him smile."

Alden smiles at that, his eyes crinkling at the edges. "So, not the over-bearing type."

I shake my head. "He had his sterner side, but my mom was the bigger worrier. She was our rock, always making sure that chores were done, homework was finished and we always had a full belly. I swear she could cook just about anything without even reading the recipes."

"Do you look like them?" Alden's fingers play with a loose piece of thread on my blanket.

I remember the image of my parents in the woods from my nightmare. They were exactly how I see them every time I close my eyes. "I look like my mom, actually. People always called me her mini-me." I chuckle. "My sister, Lorelei, looks just like my dad, though. Same blonde hair and blue eyes."

Alden smiles again and I'm beginning to crave that look on his face. "She's coming to visitation day, right?"

It's my turn to grin. "I'm seriously so excited to see her, but I'm also terrified."

"Why terrified?"

I raise a single eyebrow at him. "Come on. We go to a school of supernaturals. I don't see this working out when Lor shows up. She's smart, and she doesn't miss a thing."

Alden shrugs, his lips pressing together in the most kissable way. *Cool it, Ivy.* "You could always just tell her the truth. I mean, I know you hated being lied to, not to mention how much I hated doing the lying." His eyes look away from me.

I reach out and touch Alden's cheek, but his soft gasp and the way his eyes flick back to mine, pupils dilating, makes me rip my hand back. I clear my throat. "I'm not upset about that anymore, Alden. You don't need to feel bad." He smiles softer than before, and I want to change the subject. "What about your family? Who's visiting for you?"

Alden's face falls, and I immediately want to kick myself for asking that question. I knew he was estranged from his dad. It's the whole reason he lives here year-round. *Jeez, I'm an idiot.*

"It's getting late," Alden says quickly, standing up.

"Wait, Alden. I'm sorry," I stutter, moving to follow him.

He looks back at me with a shake of his head. "No, don't be sorry." He sighs. "I've got my family here already. Stella and Si." He smiles sadly before running a hand through his hair.

I climb out of my bed and reach out to touch him, but he steps out of my reach. My heart breaks a little, but I try not to let him see it. "Hey, thanks again, for healing me." I touch the back of my head where the bump has disappeared.

Alden nods with a gentle nudge to my arm. "No problem. What are friends for?" He steps toward the bedroom door and pulls it open, glancing back with those blue eyes boring into me. "Goodnight, Ivy."

As soon as the door shuts, I fall back onto my bed with a groan. I throw my pillow over my face and mumble to myself against the fabric. *"What are friends for?* Oh, lord, I need help."

CHAPTER 28

I tighten the ponytail on my head as I walk across the lawn and take a seat on the grass beside Alden. He looks over at me with a smile before turning back to wait for our instructor, Mr. Greyson, to finish talking with a student.

This is my first physical training class, and I haven't been able to stop fidgeting all morning. Especially since I only found out in Creative Writing that Alden would be in this class with me.

It has been four days since the party, and Alden has spent every night outside my door, looking after me. It's a good thing too because the nightmares are only getting worse. It's always the same voice calling out to me, or rather, calling out to Sage. Alden has stopped me in the hall twice to wake me from sleepwalking, and the other times, I end up waking in my bed, drenched in sweat.

I can feel the weakness in my muscles from lack of sleep and I know starting training will only make me wish I were dead. I glance over at Alden again, studying his features from the side. He has dark circles under his eyes and his stubble is becoming more of a short beard. I can't imagine the strain it puts on him to sit outside my door, worrying.

But, hey, that's what friends are for, right? At least, that's what he keeps saying. He flicks his gaze back to me and I quickly look away, my face flushing red. I don't think I'll ever get used to his eyes on me.

Mr. Greyson finally turns to the small group of students gathered on the lawn and his dark brown eyes land on me. He doesn't look pleased to see me as he clears his throat. "Ah, right. Welcome to class Miss Hart. You'll be paired up with Mr. Astor until further notice."

I look around for whoever that could be in the group of nine students, but nobody raises their hand. Alden nudges my arm gently and leans in to whisper. "Astor is Sebastian's last name. He's always late since this class is right after lunch."

I perk up, grateful that I won't have to get to know another person, just as Sebastian's loud voice interrupts whatever Mr. Greyson had been saying. "I'm here! Sorry, Mr. G!"

Sebastian grins when he spots me and plops down on my right. "Hey, Ivy."

"Hey, partner. I guess we're a team now." I raise my fist and he bumps it with his own.

Sebastian's eyes go wide. "Oh, cool. I'm psyched to kick your butt."

My eyes fall to Sebastian's neck and I have to bite my tongue to keep from laughing. "Uh, Sebastian. You've got a little something on your neck," I whisper.

He touches the small purple bruise and he chuckles. "Hey, you tell your roommate to control herself and we won't be in these situations." He doesn't even blush about the hickey as he grins down at me. "I'm totally kidding. Please don't tell her to ever stop."

"Ew," I say, shoving his arm. "You guys are so gross now that you're together."

Sebastian laughs again, drawing Mr. Greyson's attention. He turns our way with a glare. "If you two are done interrupting, I'd like to get class started."

My cheeks flush and I nod as I mumble an apology. Mr. Greyson proceeds to have us all separate into groups of two with our assigned partners. As far as I understand, Sebastian and I will need to spar with one another, practicing defense. I've never learned how to fight, though I've been in enough of them to know how to block a hit.

I watch Alden as he and a guy smaller than him circle one another. The smaller guy lunges and Alden easily evades the hit. Alden is so light on his feet, stepping around his opponent like a ghost. My eyes are glued to the way his arm muscles flex against his gray t-shirt when he throws a punch, and the way his tongue swipes across his bottom lip when he focuses.

"So, are we just gonna drool over Alden all class? I mean, he is pretty damn dreamy." Sebastian's voice makes me nearly jump out of my skin.

I spin around to find him smiling with a teasing eyebrow raised as he watches me ogle Alden. "Shut up!" I whisper-shout, hoping Alden can't hear us.

Sebastian laughs. "And you tell me I'm gross with Fay. Hello Pot, my name is Kettle." He sticks a hand out for me to shake, but I slap it away.

"Whatever, let's just fight." I hold up my hands in a stance that I hope makes me look like I know what I'm doing.

Sebastian lightly kicks the inside of my leg, making me stand wider. "You ever been in a fight, Ivy?"

I shrug. "Sure. I've always had a temper, so I've thrown a few punches in the past."

He shakes his head. "Getting in cat fights with human girls is a little different than what we do here, killer. I want you to come at me with all you got. Fists, feet, teeth. Whatever it takes, okay?"

I nod and lunge without a second thought. I step forward as I throw my fist toward Sebastian's face. His dark hands come up and he grabs my fist with ease. I swing my leg up to kick him in the knee, but he dodges that and drops me on my ass with one shove.

"Ow," I groan, looking up at him. "How pathetic was that?"

He crosses his thick arms. "Pretty pathetic. You're fast, though. That's a great start." I take his offered hand and he lifts me back to my feet. "Now it's your turn to try and dodge me. I won't aim to injure you."

I nod, holding my hands up again. Sebastian punches at me at a normal speed and I dodge to the right, missing the hit. He throws his knee up toward my stomach, but I jump back so he barely grazes me. Before I realize it, he's already throwing another fist toward my cheek and I almost don't throw my arm up fast enough to block him.

"That's not a bad defense, Ivy. Now, what if I go full speed at you? Dragons aren't as quick as wolves, but you haven't met your wolf yet, right?"

I shake my head. "I don't think so. I've felt stronger at times, but I don't know how to tap into that." I wave him toward me. "Just have at it. I might as well see what I'm up against. Don't be afraid to hurt me, or I'll never learn."

I'm not afraid of getting hit, even though Sebastian is huge and supernaturally strong. I crouch, holding my arms up in front of me. Sebastian nods just before his brown eyes darken and he clenches his meaty fists. He circles me like a predator and I keep my eyes locked onto him, ready for the worst.

His eyes flick down so quickly that I barely notice it right before he strikes out and his fist connects with my stomach. I move back just enough to lessen the impact of the hit, but he's already kicking a large leg out toward my thigh. His foot slams into me and I'm knocked off balance. I fall to the grass, landing hard on my side with a thud, getting the wind knocked out of me.

I look up at Sebastian's cocky grin and I'm about to challenge him to round three when Alden slams into his chest. He pushes Sebastian to the ground so fast that I gasp from the shock.

I rise to my feet and grab Alden's arm, pulling his attention to me. "What are you doing?" His eyes are black and his chest rises and falls with heavy breaths.

I leave him there to turn my attention to Sebastian where he's sitting on the ground with his hands up. "I'm fine," he says quickly. "Soothe the guy before he tries to kill me."

"What are you talking abo–" A low growl cuts me off and I whip back around to see Alden moving closer to Sebastian. His eyes are glued to my friend, holding so much fury that I shiver.

"Touch him, Ivy. Let him see that you're okay," Sebastian says behind me. "And do it fast, if you don't mind."

I have no idea what's going on, but I trust Sebastian. I step in front of Alden, blocking his view of my friend. "Hey," I say gently, laying a hand on his chest. His heart is pounding beneath my touch, but he's still not looking at me. "Alden, look at me. I'm right here."

I reach up to touch his cheek with my other hand. His eyes flick to mine and he growls again, like a wild animal in a trance. "Good," I say, smiling for him. "I'm okay. He didn't hurt me at all, see." I spin around for him to examine my body. Sure, I'm a little sore from the hit, but he doesn't need to know that.

Alden sighs, loud and long as he continues to stare into my eyes. His hands touch my face gently, and then he's pulling me into a warm hug. He squeezes me tightly against him, his face falling to my neck as he holds me. He breathes in my scent and I can feel his heartbeat slowing down.

I wrap my arms around his waist, feeling like I need this hug as much as he does. I lift my head to look around and I gulp as I realize the entire class, and Mr. Greyson, are all watching Alden and I with wide eyes.

I don't know what the hell just happened, but I feel like something has changed inside of me. Whatever connects me and Alden has tightened just a little, and I have no idea what to think about any of it.

"He seriously lost it, Fay. It was like he was sucked into some sort of trance and completely unaware of the world around him." I shake my head, clearing the memory from my mind. I turn to Fay, but she's quiet, not at all like herself. "What's up with you? I figured you'd go all squeaky and giddy when I told you about Alden going caveman."

Fay smiles from where she sits across from me at the small table at the edge of the cafeteria. It has become our usual spot. "I'm sorry. You're right, and I swear the moment you told me he grabbed onto you, my heart fluttered for you. It's just…"

"What? Do you know why he acted that way? Is there something I'm missing?" I search her face, but she looks anywhere else. "Fay!"

She groans and sticks a French fry in her mouth. "Okay, yes. I know why Alden acted that way when he thought you were hurt. It's a natural reaction for some of us supernaturals in certain situations. That's all I can say though, because it really isn't my place, Ivy." She frowns. "All I can say is to go talk to Alden about it."

I sigh, feeling defeated. Alden didn't say anything to me when he finally let me go after a ten-minute hug. The class ended and he just walked into the school without looking back. The idea of confronting him now is terrifying.

"I'll go find him now. I can't stand the suspense." I take a long drink of my soda before smiling back at my friend. "Are you going to go find your dragon boy and suck on his neck some more?"

Fay actually blushes as she throws a French fry at me. "I didn't mean to leave a mark! He's just so...*yummy*." Her violet eyes sparkle and I giggle at her happiness. She grins at me. "I'll tell you what. If someone hurt Sebastian, I'd straight up kill them. Remember that when you talk to the caveman."

I nod and toss her fry back as I move away from the table, hurrying out of the cafeteria as fast as possible. I'm ready for some answers.

I fire off a quick text to Lorelei as I pass by the massive library doors.

ME: "Remind me to show you the library while you're here! You'll want to live in it."

LOR: "Are you in a legit fairytale over there? I seriously can't wait!"

ME: "Just two more weeks! Prepare to be amazed."

I tuck my phone away into the back pocket of my jeans as I approach Alden's bedroom door. Last time I was here, he had me on his lap, touching me and making my pain go away. I sigh at the memory, even though it can barely compare to the way it felt to kiss him this weekend. If only he did those things because he wanted to, and not just because I was hurt.

I wipe my sweaty hands on my top and knock twice on the wooden door. It's only seconds before Alden swings the door open and his eyes widen at the sight of me.

"Ivy, what are you doing here?" He licks his lips in that entrancing way, and I already want to jump into his arms.

I step back as Alden leaves his room and shuts the door behind him. "I uh…was hoping we could talk."

Alden searches my eyes with his and he nods. "Yeah, I guess I scared you earlier, huh?" He bites on his bottom lip. "Listen, I'm really sorry about that."

I shake my head. "No, I didn't come for an apology. It's really okay." I turn my head as students pass by us lost in their own conversations. "Can we talk in your room? Or, somewhere quiet?"

"Of course, but I have some news first." His eyes seem to light up as he says it.

"What news?"

He steps closer, lowering his voice. "I know what has been messing with your dreams. I have been trying to figure it out all week, but I think I finally did."

My eyebrows shoot up. "What is it? Can we stop it?"

"It's something called a *Dreamwalker*. There are so few left in the world nowadays that the thought didn't cross my mind until a few minutes ago. It has to be what's messing with you, Ivy."

Alden sighs and I get a whiff of spearmint in the air. I have to hold back my shiver and tell myself to chill the hell out before I respond. Alden's talking about some creature infiltrating my dreams and I'm imagining what it would be like to kiss that spot on the side of his neck where three small freckles sit together. *Holy hell.*

"So, if it *is* a Dreamwalker, how do we get rid of it?"

Alden rubs a hand along the back of his neck. "It's going to take work, and an ambush." He reaches out to grab my hand in his rough one, stopping my breath. "Come on. We need to gather everyone in Stella's office to get a plan together."

"Everyone, who?" I ask as he tugs me behind him through the school.

He glances back at me, determination on his perfect face. "*Your* people, Ivy. The ones who want to help you."

My heart swells as the realization dawns on me. I have *people* that care about me here. *Thank you, Wolfe Asylum.*

CHAPTER 29

Come on, Ivy. Suck it up and stop the damn shaking! You're a badass, remember? Did some time in juvie for heaven's sake. Sure, it was just one day, but it was still time spent. I clasp my shaking hands together under my pillow, knowing that I need to go to sleep already, but my mind is running wild.

I took two sleeping pills to knock me out, but they haven't kicked in yet. I imagine Alden sitting outside my bedroom door like he has for so many nights now. I don't want him getting hurt. I don't want any of them getting hurt, especially to save me.

A steadiness washes over my limbs, calming me. I sigh at the feeling, grateful that the pills are finally doing their work. *Just rest now, Ivy,* I tell myself. I have people now, and nothing can hurt us when we work together.

I gasp as I lurch up in bed. My vision is fuzzy around the edges and the air is too cold against my skin. *Am I asleep?* I look around my room. Fay isn't in her bed where I left her. It's just me.

"Sage, I'm waiting for you." The sing-song voice calls to me from the hallway. I know that voice. It's the Dreamwalker.

I step out of my bed, trying to focus on the reality that I am within my own dream. Fay told me to control what I could, and that means making my feet move forward. I walk shakily across my room and out into the long hallway. I glance down to find Alden, but just like my past dreams, he isn't there.

I can do this. They're trusting in me. I continue forward, every few steps wanting to fall down and lay still. Controlling my movements in a dream is like exercising heavily. I can feel sweat on the back of my neck as I carefully take the stairs one at a time.

"Where are you, Sage?" The voice asks, floating everywhere and nowhere at once.

I reach the bottom floor and whisper to the Dreamwalker. "I'm coming to find you."

This is all a part of the plan, and I know I can make it out onto the lawn. *Just keep moving forward. They're out there, waiting for me. Ready to help me.*

I shuffle my feet forward, down the front steps of the asylum. *Almost there. So close.*

"Sage," the voice rumbles, too close to my ear.

I spin around, falling backwards onto the cold lawn. Moisture from the grass soaks into my pajama pants, making me shiver. "Where are you?" I call out, hoping I can keep the creature focused on me. "Come here!"

Shadows move around the dark lawn, circling me. I want to scream from the fear rising in my throat, but I try to control my rapid breathing instead. "I'm here. Sage is here, now let's talk!"

Dark laughter makes goosebumps rise along my skin. "You aren't Sage, little girl. She is inside of you."

I open my mouth to ask what that means, but the creature starts to scream. My shoulders shake from an outside force and I can hear Stella's voice speaking beside me. "Wake up, Ivy. You did it."

I open my eyes, my heart pounding and my entire body shaking from exhaustion. I'm sitting on the grass out in front of Wolfe Asylum, and the sound of something screeching pulls my attention toward the circular driveway.

Fay is bent over on the ground, a large circle of stones laid out in front of her. She is breathing hard as she touches the stone circle with one hand and holds the other hand in the air. Inside the circle, a creature like nothing I've ever seen writhes in pain. It's a nightmare in front of my eyes.

It's the Dreamwalker. His entire body is hairless, made of thick, pale skin and his long arms reach the ground where three large claws extend from his skinny hands. He doesn't have any eyes on his face, just a big mouth with jagged teeth lining the opening where he screams at the top of his lungs.

Alden stands beside Fay, his eyes glued to the Dreamwalker. He's waiting on Fay to make her next move. Across the circle, Silis and Sebastian stand a few feet apart, waiting for their signal along with Alden.

Terror fills me, but not for myself. I know that this creature is unpredictable, and the three guys that have become dear to me are about to risk their lives to stop it from piercing my subconscious.

Stella leans into my side, gripping onto my shoulders. "Let me take you inside, Ivy. You don't need to watch."

I shake my head. No way in hell am I leaving my friends out here with that thing. "I'm staying," I say sternly, and Stella doesn't argue. Those are her boys out there. I can't imagine she's okay leaving them either.

Fay mumbles something and the three boys look at one another with a nod. Alden's body shakes as a low growl leaves his lips. He looks back at me for just a moment as his eyes turn black and his wolf takes over. Light brown hair sprouts along Alden's body and his clothes rip off of him as he drops onto four legs and shifts into a huge wolf. I shudder at the sight of him, but this time I'm not afraid. I know this wolf won't hurt me.

Sebastian claps his large, dark hands together and cranks his neck to the side as he begins to shift. I watch in awe as black scales spread across his thick arms and he grows long claws instead of fingers. Wide, scaled wings sprout from his muscular back and in the next second he grows to five times his size as a massive black dragon.

"Holy shit," I mutter, not meaning to swear in front of my headmistress. I mean, he's a freaking *dragon*.

Silis looks from the wolf to the dragon and shrugs as his eyes find me. "Sorry, Ivy. I'm not as impressive as these guys, but I've got a few skills."

Silis's own, much smaller wings sprout from his back, like dragonfly wings that flutter at a constant pace. His green eyes glow and he grows long, thin claws that I know from experience are quite poisonous.

My mouth hangs open as I watch these creatures in front of me. The Dreamwalker has calmed down some but he still breathes hard from exertion. This is something we went over last night as a group. Stella informed us that a Dreamwalker could be ripped from the dream world but it can't stay out for long. Fay called her grandmother and learned of a spell to bring the Dreamwalker to the waking world and keep it here for a few minutes where we can kill him.

They can only die in this form. If we let him return to the dream world, who knows if we could get him back.

Fay stands and steps back as she releases whatever hold she has on the monster. Now it's time for the guys to do their thing. The Dreamwalker immediately charges Fay, but Sebastian jumps into action. He breathes out a stream of fire that scorches the monster's back and makes him spin around to attack the dragon.

Alden runs in from the Dreamwalker's side and latches his meaty jaws onto the monster's side. Alden shakes his wolf head back and forth, tearing into the thing's flesh. While Alden holds strong, Silis blinks completely out of sight, making me gasp from shock.

"Where did he go?" I ask, freaking out.

Stella runs a hand along my back. "Faeries can become invisible. He's just sneaking."

I jump as Silis appears right in front of the Dreamwalker, and he lashes out with his poison nails, running them down the thing's long torso. Silis blinks out of sight again and then he's behind the creature, where he scratches along its back in the same way.

The Dreamwalker is screaming again, blood dripping from his side where Alden still holds onto him. Silis moves out of the way now, his part done. The monster swings a long arm around to dig his claws into Alden's back. Alden yelps as he drops the creature and backs away. In a flash, the Dreamwalker spins around, and if it had eyes, I swear they'd be looking right at me.

I whimper, crawling backward into Stella's arms as the monster hisses. "You can't keep my queen down. She *will* come out."

Before it can take a step toward me, Sebastian's dragon drops onto the monster's back and lifts into the air with the Dreamwalker in his talons. Sebastian flies up so high that I can barely see the outline of his wings against the shining stars. In a loud whoosh of air, he plummets back to the ground, crunching the monster under his weight and the impact of falling from such a long height.

Silis bends over to take in the mangled body of the thing that has been haunting my dreams, and then his glowing eyes turn to me. "He's dead, Ivy. You're safe now."

CHAPTER 30

I skipped school today, thanks to Stella's recommendation for me to rest as much as possible. How can I sleep after the events of last night, though? My mind won't stop racing. I've texted Lorelei throughout the day, talking about her progress in nursing school. I've eaten all of the snacks in my room and watched half a season of Fay's favorite show, *Buffy the Vampire Slayer*.

As a vampire herself, Fay finds the entire show hilarious. I used to think it was kind of creepy, but after seeing what I've seen, TV makeup doesn't faze me. Seeing my friends like that, as what I once imagined monsters to be, it has changed my world.

They are incredible, every single one of them. Fay has magic that is indescribable, and I can't even imagine what else she's capable of. Silis is a literal faerie that can freakin' disappear, and he flirts with every girl he meets instead of showing off the beauty of his wings twenty-four-seven.

Sebastian is a beast, huge and absolutely magical in his dragon form. His black scales are hauntingly beautiful and I wasn't even afraid when he towered over me. And Alden. He's...*everything*. Something about watching him in his most wild form has stirred something within me. Maybe it's my own wolf itching to be set free. Either way, how could I possibly sleep today?

Fay is out with Sebastian tonight, and I can't possibly sit in this dorm room for another minute. I have too many questions about the world I live in now. And I need to know more about those final words from that Dreamwalker.

"You can't keep my queen down. She will come out."

Stella told me that when the infamous Sage was still alive, she had a following of dark creatures that she bent to her will. Dreamwalkers were among this army. That thing was looking for Sage, and he came to me to do it. It means something, and I aim to get to the bottom of it.

The halls are quiet tonight as I make my way to the library. It's open to the students all hours of the day and night, so I slip inside the large door and begin searching for whatever I can find on this Sage woman.

I'm three books deep, reading about possession, when Alden slides into a chair beside me. "Ivy, what are you doing in here?"

I turn to find anger in his blue eyes, but I ignore that. "I'm reading, Alden. Isn't that what libraries are for?"

He leans in so that I'm forced to look at him. "You're supposed to be resting. You've lost enough sleep this week, and you must be worn down after controlling your dream like you did."

I shrug. "It's fine, Alden. This is my body and I know what I can handle." I'm a little angry now. He tries to control me out of some friendly worrying, but I'm tired of the hot and cold of him. "Worry about yourself for once. You haven't slept all week either."

I look back down at the book in my hands, but Alden pushes it away so that I remain focused on him. "Ivy, seriously. Just go to bed. I'm worried about you."

I groan and drop my book on the table with a thud. I push out of my chair and walk back to the bookcases, ignoring Alden altogether.

He follows me, his heat surrounding me. "What? Are you mad at me for some reason?"

I spin around to face him, feeling pent up anger that I can't control. "Yeah, I'm mad!" I yell, feeling irrational. "I think, I mean. I don't really know how to feel, but I know you drive me nuts sometimes, Alden!"

He throws his hands in the air, his eyes blazing as he stares down at me. "All I've done is try to protect you. You have no right to yell at me for being a good friend."

I scoff, shoving a defiant finger into his chest. "Oh really? That's what you are? A good friend?"

"Yeah, of course I am."

I roll my eyes, attitude rolling off of me. "Well, I have a few good friends for the first time in my entire life, and none of them act like cavemen when they worry about me. They don't lose their minds when I dance with someone, and they don't go all catatonic when I get hurt!" He goes silent, so I continue a little calmer. "So, tell me, Alden. Why exactly do you do these things?"

He sighs loudly, his blue eyes shifting everywhere but at me. "You're new to this world, Ivy. I've been trying like hell not to freak you out."

I shrug. "Okay, well it's a little late for that, don't you think?" He looks defeated so I lay my hand on his chest. "Just tell me the truth, Alden. That's all I want."

He nods, licking his bottom lip before sucking it into his mouth. "Okay. The reason I act like an idiot when it comes to you, is because you're...I mean, *we* are fated mates."

I try to figure out if that's something I should already know about. "I don't know what that means."

Alden takes my hand in his and lays it against his chest again. "Humans have something called soulmates. It's not something they can really recognize because they don't see past reality, but they can feel it when they find the person they're meant to...love." He pauses, searching my gaze. "Us supernaturals have what we call *fated mates*. Each creature is created to connect fully with another creature, the other half of themselves. Fate designed it this way so that each one of us can find true love."

I blink, slowly understanding. "So, me and you? We're like, meant to be together?"

Alden nods. "At least, that was fate's choice. You for me, and me for you. As wolf shifters, when our mate gets hurt, we become unhinged in a way. We are very protective creatures, and since you are my other half, I lose all sense when you're hurt. My wolf will not allow it."

I pull my hand away from his. "Does this mean we have to be together? Do we have a choice?"

Alden's face falls a little at my question. "No, we don't have to be together, Ivy. Everyone can choose their own destiny."

I chew on the inside of my lip, trying to grasp the heaviness of what this all means. It makes sense why I feel so drawn to Alden, and why he is the first thing on my mind at the start of each day. He was made for me, primed to be the object of my desires. I can't deny that I really like the idea of being that one person for Alden. I can't possibly *not* want him.

Alden takes a step back from me, his eyes hooded. "Anyways, that's the truth. That's why I want to be a good friend to you, Ivy. I can't imagine losing you."

A good friend? How many times has he said that to me this week? Clearly Alden wants to be the master of his own destiny, and that means having me as a friend. He couldn't imagine losing me, just like I can't imagine losing Fay, or Silis, or Sebastian. We're fated friends, and now I need my heart to get on board before I let this break me.

Continue on the next page to read Alden & Ivy's first kiss from Alden's point of view!

CHAPTER 31

ALDEN

Come on, Ivy. Please wake up. I hoist her higher in my arms as I climb the stairs back to her room. When I woke up to Ivy sleeping with her silky black hair sprawled across my lap, I thought I had died and gone to heaven. Heaven wouldn't want me, though. I couldn't even stop her from throwing herself down the stairs. I should have done something.

"Alden?" Ivy's voice re-starts my dying heart.

I look down at her and sigh. "Christ, Ivy! I'm so glad you're finally awake."

She shakes her head before I can warn her not to and her gray eyes unfocus from me as she gets dizzy. "I've been awake since you left me in the hall. I was looking for you."

I search her pale face, worried that she may have hit her head too hard. "I never left you in the hall. I woke up to you stirring in your sleep. You were laying your head in my lap and I tried to wake you, but you just got up and started walking away." I kick Ivy's bedroom door open. She didn't close it all the way when she came out to me. Good thing Fay isn't back yet, because she would freak out.

I drop Ivy onto her bed as softly as I can and I kneel down in front of her. "I followed you, and you went downstairs to the second floor. I called for you to stop, but you were sleepwalking, I think. You ignored me, and then you threw yourself down the damn stairs. You just started falling and hit your head at the bottom." I try to find any visible injury as I scan her body. "I picked you up and that's when you finally woke up and looked at me."

Ivy feels the back of her head. "Shoot, that hurts."

I touch my hand to the same spot and wince at the size of the bump I can feel. "I should've tried harder to wake you, but people say to never wake someone who is sleepwalking. I'm so sorry, Ivy. I stayed outside your door to make sure you were safe, and I failed."

I flinch as Ivy's soft hands rest against my cheeks. "You didn't fail, Alden. I've been having crazy dreams. I guess they've evolved into sleepwalking." She giggles, but her eyebrows pull together in confusion as she does.

I have the urge to lean into her, to taste what I'm sure is rum on her parted lips. "You might have a concussion, Ivy, and you're probably still drunk. I need to get you some ice. Some water too."

I need to stand, to get myself away from her, but her hands fall to my shirt and grip onto the fabric, tugging me closer. "I'm not drunk," she slurs. "I don't want you to go."

"Ivy," I whisper. *Why does she have to be so gorgeous?* "I can't be here like this. You're not yourself." I lay my hands on top of hers, knowing I should pull them away. "I don't know what you drank, but Gabe shouldn't have given you what he did. The liquor is stronger at these parties, for the shifters and vampires. It takes a lot more alcohol to affect us, but you haven't shifted yet. You should have had the human stuff, and Gabe is a moron who needs his ass kicked." *And I'll kill him for putting his lips on you.* I don't say the last part.

Ivy's grin is wide as her eyes begin to sparkle. "You're jealous." *Shit.* "You don't want that guy touching me, because *you* want to touch me." Her fingers walk up my chest, so slowly as she keeps those gray eyes glued to mine. She gently touches my lips and I have to fight the urge to lick her. "Did you know that you lick your lips a lot?" She strokes my bottom lip and I swear I'm about to lose it. "It drives me *crazy*."

I let out a long breath. If only she knew how crazy I was about her. "Ivy, *please*." I don't mean to sound so weak, but every inch of me is on high alert. "You need to be taken care of. You could be really hurt."

She shrugs. "I don't care. You can just heal me, remember? You have *sexy* magic."

Oh, Lord. I accidentally groan. If I use my Incubus magic on Ivy now, I might not be able to control it. "You're too drunk to consent to me using my magic on you. It's not right."

She nods, but it instantly makes her eyes cross as she becomes dizzy again, nearly falling over. "Ow, that's not fun," she says, whimpering from the pain.

I growl as I reach out to catch her by the back of the neck. I hold onto her, my heart aching from the pain I see on her face. This is my fated mate, the one that I would do anything for. I can't just let her struggle when I know I can fix it.

"Screw it," I snap as I crush my lips to hers.

She doesn't close her eyes right away, and I hold back my Incubus magic for a moment. Just the softness of her lips is enough to make me crave more and turn my blood to fire. Ivy's shock fades away and her eyes flutter closed as she kisses me back. *This*. This is what I've been dreaming of.

I keep one hand behind her neck, holding her right where I want her, and I let my other arm slip behind her back. I can't help but tug her closer, that dark magic pouring into her with every stroke of our lips and every touch of her skin.

The kiss is slow at first, our mouths finding a perfect rhythm, until a spark of electricity from my magic healing that spot on her head makes Ivy gasp into my mouth. Her breath is so hot as I drag it into myself, and when her arms wrap around me as her chest crashes to mine, I groan, letting the magic slip away and my desire take control.

I slide my tongue along her lip, tasting the sweetness that is Ivy, and her mouth opens to me, an invitation for more. I feel like I could drown in the heat of her tongue colliding with mine, taking all that I have to give. And then she drops from her bed and lands against my lap. Her legs straddle me, causing my stomach to clench with need.

"Ivy," I whisper, needing to stop before I physically can't anymore.

She doesn't let me back away, though. What started out as my need to help Ivy has become a need to claim her and be claimed by her. She slips her delicate fingers into my hair and she tugs my mouth hard against hers. I slip my

216

hands beneath her shirt as I cling to her back. My mouth feels hot and wild, out of control as it explores hers.

Ivy and I breathe one another in, fast and warm like we've run a marathon together. Every time I exhale, she inhales, and I drag her scent into me again and again. How could I have survived without this feeling?

I'm ready to drop Ivy to her bed and climb on top of her when she growls and bites down on my lip so hard that blood trickles into my mouth. It's an attack, and I immediately retreat from her, feeling like I just took advantage of the person I care most about. And now she has punished me.

I place Ivy back on her bed and turn away, unable to look at her while I try to reign in the aching desire inside of me.

"Alden, I'm sor—"

I turn around with my hands up to cut off her apology. She never needs to say sorry to me. "No, it's okay. I got carried away. I shouldn't have…"

Her face seems to fall as she looks up at me. "Either way, I *am* sorry. I didn't mean to hurt you. I wasn't myself."

It's not the first time she has pushed me away. I'm not surprised that she stopped me before I could take things too far. *Maybe I already went too far.* I look down at her beautiful mess of black hair that hangs over her shoulders. Her legs are bare all the way up to those tiny shorts that leave little to the imagination. I can't be here, looking at her like this.

"Get some sleep, Ivy," I say as I reach for the door handle.

"Wait," she calls after me. I turn to meet her nervous gaze. "I don't want to be alone tonight. Can you…stay? With me?"

I rub my tongue along the healing wound on my lip, and look deep into Ivy's gray eyes. She looks scared. Maybe she doesn't want to be alone with the things happening in her dreams. I give in, knowing I couldn't leave her like this.

"Sure. I can stay." I focus on keeping my eyes to the floor as I sit beside her bed and lay my head back. "Did you want to tell me about those dreams you've been having?"

She smiles at me with a soft sigh. "Yeah, I can do that."

My heart may ache for Ivy, and the possibility of her choosing me, but I need to keep my distance. Ivy doesn't know what being a demon can mean, and I won't subject her to that life. She's my mate, and that means I will always protect her, even from myself.

PART

4

CHAPTER 32

"Does this mean we have to be together? Do we have a choice?"

"No, we don't have to be together, Ivy. Everyone can choose their own destiny. That's why I want to be a good friend to you. I can't imagine losing you."

I comb my fingers through my hair, needing to do something with my nervous hands. When I sat down on the front steps of Wolfe Asylum an hour ago, I hadn't planned on my mind replaying my conversation with Alden from two weeks ago. All I wanted was to sit here and imagine all of the things I want to show Lorelei when she gets here.

It's family visitation day, and Lor is in a car headed toward me right now. Still, every day I manage to drag myself back to that night in the library, looking into

Alden's gorgeous blue eyes and hearing him tell me we are fated to be together, but he wants me to be his friend.

He hasn't spoken to me about our fated mate bond since then, and I refuse to bring it up. All I dream about is him, and I constantly crave his touch, or even just his attention. Fay and I have talked about what the fate bond means, and she hasn't heard of anyone ever refusing to give into it.

It was exciting to hear that she and Sebastian are fated mates, but neither of them realized it until their first kiss. I wonder when Alden first felt our bond. I can't pinpoint a moment in time, but I know that I was drawn to him from the very beginning. *And he just wants to be friends.*

I sigh, laying my face in my hands as I stare off into the trees. I just want to see my sister. It has been a month since I got to hug her last, and I know she is the only one who can calm my breaking heart.

A small movement drags my eyes to the edge of the steps below me, where the brick meets the green grass. It's hot outside now, and nature is in full bloom. A tiny green caterpillar moves along between the blades of grass, working its way through its little jungle. A smile tugs at the corners of my lips as I watch the little creature.

A week ago, I finally completed the caterpillar fiction story that Alden and I wrote together. I stuck the printed pages under Alden's bedroom door, and he texted me that night, telling me that he knew I was lying about being a bad writer. He turned the story in for us and we both got an A plus from Mr. Hale.

Getting a good grade made me happy, but having Alden's praise was something different altogether. It made my heart soar. We've texted on and off since then, but we only see one another in classes. We don't talk hardly at all, and Alden doesn't spar near Sebastian and I in our physical training class. That's for the best, considering how he lost his mind that first time. *Am I crazy for wanting him to lose his mind a little more?*

I scoff at myself as I watch the little bug disappear into the blades of grass. A loud honk makes me jump and a grin stretches my cheeks as I notice the small Uber car pulling up into the circle driveway. It's barely stopped before the back door flies open and Lorelei leaps from the vehicle.

"Ivy!" She screams, already running toward me.

I laugh and brace for impact, letting my sister plow into my open arms. "Lor, I'm so happy you're here!"

Lorelei is slightly shorter than me, and beautiful with long blonde hair and sparkling blue eyes. Her skin is a shade lighter than mine, and she resembles our father so perfectly. She wipes a single tear from her eye as she pulls away from me. "Oh, my baby sissy. I missed you so much."

I giggle and grab her hands in mine. "I'm not a baby, Lor. You sound just like mom, and you cry like her too."

She chuckles, sniffling as she does. "I'm a mess! I don't even know how to live as a single twenty-something. I'm used to chasing your ass around."

"Excuse me?" A voice calls from behind Lorelei, and we both spin to the Uber driver. He's a middle-aged man, standing with my sister's purse in his hands as he smiles shyly up at the two of us. "I have to get going."

Lorelei laughs softly and runs back down the steps. "I'm so sorry. Here," she hands the guy a few bills and takes her bag before thanking him and running back to me.

"I totally forgot he was here. That's how much I've missed you, Little Bear!"

I wave my arms around in a grand gesture. "Are you ready for your tour of the school?"

She scoffs and her eyes trail up the massive building. "Don't you mean castle? There's no way this is a school, Ivy! You're royalty!"

I link my arm with hers and tug her up the stairs with me. "It's pretty great, huh? I think I was actually speechless when I got here."

Lorelei snorts and I've missed that sound so much. "So, if I get myself in a few fights, do I get to come live with you with a fully-paid scholarship?"

I nudge her as we step into the large entrance, coming face-to-face with the twin wolf statues in the foyer. "No, Lor. You need to finish college and be the best nurse ever, with the worst bedside manner."

She turns to gape at me. "Hey! I have great bedside manner!"

I raise a single eyebrow at her. "Remember when I got in that fight with that Leslie girl freshman year? She busted my lip and you practically busted it more with the force you used to clean me up. And you grumbled at me the whole time!"

Lorelei throws her head back in laughter, letting the sound echo off the high ceilings. "I was so pissed at you, Ivy. *You* started that fight, and you acted like a big baby when I barely touched your face. My patients will get much better treatment." She's right. That was my first real fist fight and I never imagined it could hurt that much. I watch, amused as Lorelei gapes at the Wolfe Asylum interior. "This place is unreal."

I nod, knowing that I can't tell her exactly how unreal this place is. "Wanna see the classrooms?"

She shakes her head with a huge smirk on her pink lips. "Show me this library of yours, first. I want to feel like a princess."

I laugh loudly as I tug her toward the library, and for the first time in a month, I feel complete peace.

CHAPTER 33

"Feel like a princess yet?" I ask Lorelei as I lead her through the girl's dorm hall.

Lorelei grins, her gaze still taking in every inch of the building. "It's seriously like Beauty and the Beast. I mean, there are even creatures carved into the molding. It's creepy and beautiful all at once."

I don't respond. It's increasingly difficult to lie to Lorelei about what really goes on here. There is so much I want to tell her about magic and shifters. Keeping it a secret feels wrong, but I also feel like it's necessary in keeping her on her own path. She doesn't need to worry about me anymore than she already does.

I open my bedroom door and wave Lor inside. Her jaw drops as she takes in my bedroom. "It's bigger than I thought!"

I laugh, plopping down on my bed. "I showed you in video chat, remember?"

She shakes her head, her blonde locks brushing across her back. "Video didn't do this justice, Ivy." She sighs, sitting down beside me. "I'm just so happy that you're doing well here, sis. Do you know how much I worry about you?"

I nudge her arm. "Yes, I think I do, because I worry about you too. We're all each other has, you know?"

The bedroom door swings open and Fay skips into the room, reminding me that it's not just Lorelei and I in my life anymore. An older woman with wavy black hair and olive skin like Fay follows behind my friend, soft wrinkles decorating her oval face.

"Ivy!" Fay grins at me and tugs the woman close to her. "I'm so glad you're here. I wanted you to meet my mom." She gestures to her mother like she's presenting a prized trophy, but her violet eyes land on Lorelei. "Oh, and this must be your sister, Lorelei!"

"Hi," Lor says, standing and shaking Fay's hand.

I stand with her and hold my hand out for Fay's mom to shake. "It's nice to meet you, Mrs. Clark. I'm Ivy Hart."

The woman doesn't grab my hand, but she tugs me into her small arms to hug me just like her daughter does. "Oh, Ivy, I am so happy to finally meet you." She pulls back to study my face. Her eyes are a darker purple than Fay's, but still beautiful. "And you have to call me Callista." She grins at Lor. "You too, Lorelei. I am family to you both now."

Lor giggles as Callista pulls her in for a hug too. "Oh, thank you. I never imagined Ivy could have found such a great friend so far away from home." She flicks her eyes to me and murmurs. "Or at all, for that matter."

"Hey," I say, not really offended. "I've made friends before."

"But I'm better than them all," Fay says, making us all laugh.

"You two want to walk with us to dinner?" I ask the Seer women. If only Lorelei knew the magic these two hold.

Callista grabs Lorelei's hand and smiles brightly. "Yes, and I hope to have you at my home for a meal sometime soon, Ivy. We're less than a three-hour drive from here, up in Redding."

Fay links arms with me and we follow our guardians out the door and into the hall. "Mom, Ivy has classes all week. She can't go driving through California for some of your pot roast."

I laugh and my stomach wants to growl at the thought of a homemade dinner. "Actually, that sounds incredible."

We make our way down to the cafeteria, passing tons of students and their family members. Some have one person visiting, like Fay and I, but others have a whole crew of people surrounding them. The air is thick with joy and excitement.

I'm smiling when we enter the school cafeteria, but the large room is almost like an entirely new place, stopping me in my tracks. The round tables still sit across the floor, but they are draped in white cloth, decorated with crystal place settings and blue flowers at the centers. Long streams of glittering fabric hang from the ceiling, surrounding the chandeliers in silver and blue. The bars where the food is normally served have been moved to make for more standing room and waiters move around the floor with trays full of appetizers.

"Holy crap, this is amazing." My mouth hangs open as I take it all in.

Lorelei turns to me with wide eyes. "Ivy, we have never been to a dinner this fancy before. Should we have dressed up?"

Callista giggles as she looks behind her. "We're not dressed up either. Look around. Everyone is very casual, so quit your worrying." Her eyes find Sebastian and a girl a few years older than him making their way to us. "Oh, I believe that is my daughter's handsome boyfriend."

Fay gasps and her face turns pink. "Mom, do not embarrass me in front of my ma— my boyfriend." She flicks her gaze to me with a look of apology for almost calling Sebastian her mate.

I just smile and shake my head as Sebastian stops in front of us. "Good evening, ladies." He grins cheekily at Callista. "Mrs. Clark, I haven't seen you in so long."

Callista grabs his hand and practically beams up at him. "You have grown into such a hunk, Sebastian. No wonder my baby girl has finally laid her claim on you."

Fay groans in embarrassment and I try to hide my chuckle behind my hand. Lorelei looks back at me with amused eyes as Sebastian blushes under Callista's gaze.

"Thank you. I really do love Fay, and I hope that's alright with you and your husband." He winks at Fay and I swoon for her. "Have you met my sister, Naomi? She was a senior when Fay and I were freshmen."

Sebastian steps back for us to see the tall girl beside him. She looks a lot like her brother, with dark ebony skin and chocolate-colored eyes. I wonder how her dragon form compares. "It's nice to meet you all. I apologize on behalf of my little brother."

"For what?" I ask, smiling at the teasing look on her face.

She shrugs. "He's bound to need apologizing for something. I know how he works."

We all laugh together, drawing a few eyes our way. Nobody is outright glaring at me, so that's nice for once. My heart stills, though, when a particular pair of blue eyes connect with mine.

Alden is standing alone beside the cafeteria doors, his hands stuffed in his pockets as he watches me with a small smile on his perfect face. He's dressed in all black, but looking smokin' hot in his button-up shirt and slacks.

I don't like seeing him without family, so I wave a hand for him to come join us. I'm aware that his only family is already here at the asylum all the time, but there's still a sadness about the way he holds himself tonight.

Alden walks across the room to stand beside Sebastian and he gives our group a small wave. "Hi, everyone. I hope you're all enjoying family day."

"Best day of every year, man." Sebastian slaps Alden on the back.

Alden's eyes find mine again and I clear my throat, touching Lor's arm. "Alden, this is my sister, Lorelei. Lor, this is Alden. We— Uh, we have Creative Writing together." *Oh, kill me now.*

There has to be a better introduction for Alden, but my mind blanks as I look between him and my sister. *He's my friend, the guy who kissed me senseless in my bedroom, my fated mate.*

Lor smiles up at my handsome "classmate". "It's great to meet you, Alden. Ivy has told me all about the wonderful friends she has made here. I couldn't thank you all enough for helping her settle into a new place."

Alden flashes a sexy grin at my sister and then looks back at me. His eyes don't leave mine as he speaks. "She has been a light in the darkness. Wolfe Asylum wouldn't be the same without you here, Ivy."

I blush and try to look anywhere but into his heavy gaze. *Is it suddenly really hot in here?*

"Oh, there he is," a shrill voice pierces the air, making me cringe. *Xena.*

Sebastian and his sister are stuck in conversation with Fay and her mom as Xena makes her way over to Alden's side, she grabs his arm in her manicured claws and bats her eyelashes up at him. *Take those filthy, poisonous claws off of him.*

"Alden, I am so glad we found you." She turns him around to meet her father whose face never changes from nonchalant. "Daddy, this is Alden. He's one of my best friends."

I scoff a little too loudly, drawing all of their eyes to me, but Lorelei saves me by tugging me back a few feet. "I take it you don't like that girl," she whispers in my ear.

I glare at the back of Xena's braided blonde hair and try incredibly hard not to grab ahold of it and yank her off of Alden's arm. "Not so much."

Alden must feel my distress because he pulls free of Xena's grip as he talks with her father about who-knows-what. He glances back at me for just a moment with a reassuring smile, and I feel okay again, that easily.

232

"Okay," Lor says. "I've met the guy that you clearly have a crush on, but now I want to meet the kid that flirts with everything that moves."

I laugh out loud at her description of Silis as I tug her through the noisy room, choosing to ignore the comment about my crush. "Oh, you are going to love Silis, Lor. Be ready to wish you were fifteen again."

CHAPTER 34

Lorelei stuffs a huge bite of her smothered, grilled chicken into her mouth and I bite my lip so I don't laugh at the look on her face. She's enjoying herself way too much at this amazing dinner. I can't pretend I'm not having a blast myself though.

Lor's eyes flip up to mine. "What are you grinning for?"

I shake my head. "Nothing really. I just love seeing you eat like a starved animal."

Lorelei wipes her mouth with a napkin and glares at me. "I get home late from school and work most days, and without you there, I don't have anyone to cook for me."

"You need to find a man who can cook. Preferably a rich one with great abs," I tease, but her sudden blush makes me curious. "Wait, is there a guy?"

Lorelei avoids looking at me, and Fay jumps into the conversation, taking her attention from Sebastian by her side. "Ooh, guy talk? Who is he, Lorelei?"

Callista smacks Fay's hand. "Stop it. It's her private life and she hardly knows anyone at this table." Sebastian and his sister sit silently, smiling at the drama unfolding.

Lorelei sighs. "No, it's alright. I haven't seen my baby sis in a month, and I need to vent. Bystanders may enjoy my tragic love life."

Everyone chuckles at her, and I lean forward on my elbows. "Okay, so spill. Just tell me he's not your professor, because I've read those books and you should probably keep that story to yourself."

She rolls her eyes and her blush returns. "No, he's not my professor. He's a family doctor who runs a clinic by the hospital." She looks around at the others at our table. "I'm in nursing school, and I just got a job at his clinic."

"I didn't know you got your first nursing job," I say excitedly. "That's incredible."

"How old is this doctor?" Callista asks, her eyebrows raising.

Lorelei giggles. "It's not anything crazy. He just started his own practice after graduating with his doctorate last fall. He's twenty-seven, and I just turned twenty-three."

I lean further, realizing how much happiness is on my sister's beautiful face. "Do you love him? He's not married or anything, right?"

Everyone chuckles again, and Lor shakes her head. "Of course he isn't married. It has only been a few weeks, but I am leaning toward love, I think."

Fay, Callista, and even Naomi all sigh with me at the look in Lor's eyes. Sebastian shakes his head with an amused grin. "Wow. I am *not* made for this conversation."

Fay nudges him in the ribs and he grunts, but the way he looks at her has me wanting to sigh all over again. Someone clears their throat into a microphone and we all turn toward the sound. We find Stella standing on a table across the cafeteria, looking gorgeous in long black tights and a glittery blue blouse that matches the theme of the night.

"Welcome family members! I'm so glad that you can all be here for our wonderful students tonight, and I hope you've all enjoyed touring Wolfe Asylum, also known as my home." Her eyes look around at the many faces watching her, and she smiles bigger when she spots me. "I get to be here with my own two boys year-round, and I can't imagine the difficulties of being so far from your loved ones. Thank you for trusting in me and my faculty members to make this their home away from home."

She glances down at the chairs circling her and my eyes find Silis and Alden sitting side-by-side. It's as if Alden can feel me watching him, and his blue eyes flick to mine. He smiles at me, a real smile that I don't get to see from him often. Stella's voice is drowned out as we continue to watch one another. Alden licks his kissable lips and his shoulders rise in a heavy breath.

The memory of what it feels like to be in his arms and be kissed by him makes me squirm in my seat. I've thought about that night every day for two weeks and I wish I was back there in my room with him.

The cafeteria erupts in cheers and clapping, breaking me from my Alden spell. I look at Lorelei and she's grinning back at me, as if she knows something I don't know. I'm just grateful that the supernatural secret hasn't been busted wide open all evening.

I might be a wolf shifter with a dark side, but Lorelei will never know about any of it…if I have my way.

"I wish you could stay the night." I cling onto Lor with all of my might, not wanting to let go.

She steps away from me with a sad smile. "Sorry, Little Bear. I have a hotel booked in Sacramento and a flight really early. Family day was just that, one day. Besides, I have work Monday morning."

"Where you'll see your super smart and sexy doctor boyfriend?" I waggle my eyebrows at her and she giggles like a teenager.

"I'll keep you updated on that front, okay?" Her blue eyes search my face for a long moment. "You know, I'm really proud of you, Ivy."

My heart clenches at her words. She sounds so much like our mother that I'm practically transported back in time. "What are you proud of me for? I'm just surviving over here."

She shakes her head. "You're more than surviving. Maybe *barely* surviving is what you were doing back home after Mom and Dad passed, but you're different now. You're *thriving* here. Making incredible friendships and smiling more than I've seen in a really long time. I don't know why, but you belong *here*, sis."

Lorelei blinks rapidly as her eyes fill with tears, and I instantly have to take deep breaths to stop my own waterworks. "Thank you, Lor. I'll deny saying this if ever asked, but *you're right.*" I chuckle and she joins me.

"Also, that boy, Alden?" She wipes her tears away and gives me a very knowing look. "You're crazy about him, and I know he's super good-looking, but be careful."

I blush. "It's not like that with him."

She rolls her eyes and sighs. "Oh, it is definitely like *that* with him. I saw the way he looked at you and that boy is smitten with my baby sister." I chew on my bottom lip, unsure how to respond to that, but Lorelei changes the subject. "Anyways, stay safe, okay? I'll text you in the morning."

I nod, pulling her in for one more hug. "Love you, Big Bear."

She squeezes me tight. "Love you more."

CHAPTER 35

I can't sleep. That nagging feeling in the back of my mind feels more present than ever, and no amount of studying or reading romance books can get rid of it. The more I try to understand what it is that's inside of me, the more it feels untouchable, like a separate consciousness.

I shudder at the thought as I flip a large book shut, the sound bouncing off of the library's high ceiling of windows. "Get out of my head," I groan, hoping I can command this thing somehow.

It's past midnight now, and I've flipped through three massive books already, looking for information on hearing voices and possession. I know possession might be a little off base, but I'm desperate. All I've gained from this study session is a lot of brand new nightmares and a newfound fear of churches. *Great.*

I jump at the sound of my phone pinging, but a smile stretches my face at the new messages coming in one after the other.

ALDEN: "I'm trying really hard not to be overbearing, I promise."

ALDEN: "But...I noticed you went into the library a while ago and you haven't left."

ALDEN: "Sorry, super stalker-ish, I know. But, are you okay?"

I shake my head and do a quick look around for my stalker. Alden is a demon-slash-wolf shifter, so I doubt I'd be able to find him if he *were* sneaking around. Knowing that he's keeping tabs on me is somehow both frustrating *and* incredibly exciting.

ME: "I'm okay. Just doing some supernatural research."

ALDEN: "Anything I can help with?"

ME: "Do you have any idea why an un-shifted wolf shifter might be hearing voices in his/her head?"

ME: "You know, for research purposes only, of course..."

ALDEN: "Of course...Have you looked into Soul Sharing?"

ALDEN: "Heard about it in History class last year, but don't know a lot."

ME: "I'll look into it. Thanks, Alden."

ALDEN: "Anytime, Ivy. Do you want company in there?"

I pause my fingers over the phone, unsure how to respond. Of course I want Alden's company. His silence lately has been unbearable, and my body literally craves his. It has to be the fated mate bond we have, and I don't know how Alden can take the agony of being separated. Maybe he doesn't feel it like I do. *Say yes. Tell him to come.*

ME: "I'm all good here. Thanks, though."

I groan, wanting to slap myself and run to his bedroom. Three little dots appear on the screen and then stop. He doesn't respond, which only makes my chest ache. I sigh and drop my phone onto the table while I search the library for books on "Soul Sharing".

I grin when I find a fat, worn-looking book with the title "The History of Soul Sharing" written on the wrinkled spine. *Perfect.*

I hurry back to my table and begin pouring over the contents of the book. With each page, my heart races faster.

"With the help of a necromancer, a person can die and transfer their soul into another body."

"Soul sharing is done to preserve the mind and power of a being whose body is no longer viable."

"The new body will carry the soul of the deceased inside of them, and may either cast the old soul out, or allow it to take control."

"The soul hosts have reported being able to communicate with the shared soul, or hear them speak within their mind. Some have been driven mad by the voice, unaware that they have two souls inside of their body."

"Soul sharing has become an illegal act. Anyone who performs it is punished for life."

I'm hyperventilating. My breathing is fast and shallow, making my mind feel foggy. My chest feels tight and I can't take in a deep enough breath to make my lungs expand. I check the date on the inside of the book and see that it was published nearly fifty years ago. If soul sharing is illegal, someone broke a massive law to get inside of my body.

I shake my head, closing my eyes as I try to drag in deep breaths. *It can't be true.* I'm just me. Ivy Hart, girl with a temper, possibly a wolf shifter. That's crazy enough, right? *It. Can't. Be. True.*

"Ivy, are you okay?" Fay's sweet voice makes my eyes snap open. She's kneeling in front of me where I've doubled over in my chair.

I shrug. "I don't know, Fay. I think I'm losing my mind."

She touches my arms, running her hands up and down my skin to soothe me. "Hey, take a breath, okay?" She takes a long breath through her nose to demonstrate and I copy her.

244

We do this for a few minutes, a deep breath in and a long breath out. My body starts to relax until Fay's violet eyes become less worried. "Will you tell me what's going on?"

I nod, but I pause when I realize she's in her fuzzy pajamas and her purple-streaked hair is a mess. "Why aren't you sleeping?"

She smiles softly at me. "I *was* asleep until Alden called me. He said you've been in the library for hours and he was worried about you."

My eyebrows raise. "Oh. Why didn't he just come here himself, then? His room is right outside."

She chuckles. "Aren't you the one who freaked out about his overprotectiveness? I'm sure he's trying to give you space."

She's right. "I guess that didn't stop him from protecting me in some way, huh?" I can't help but smile.

Fay grins back at me. "Nothing will stop him, Ivy. But, now that I'm here, you need to tell me why I found you having a panic attack."

My smile falls and I look back at the open book on the table beside me. "This." I raise it to show her the title. "I'm about ninety-percent sure that there's some other soul sharing my body, Fay."

Her eyes widen as she looks from the book to me. "What? No way. That's just crazy."

"Can wolf shifters have mental disabilities? Schizophrenia? Multiple personalities?" I eye her, already knowing the answer.

She shakes her head, her face paler than usual. "No, they can't. None of us here can…"

"Well, I've been hearing this female voice in my head off and on. Someone dark and dangerous. I guess I can't even be sure it's a woman." I touch the side of my head. "And if you think about the things that have happened to me since coming here. The creatures that have attacked me and told me there's a demon in me, or called me evil. Could they be seeing that *other* soul?"

Fay shrugs. "I can't say no, I guess. But, *how*? Why would someone put their soul in your body? And *who*?"

I scoff. "All good questions, Fay. Ones I would love to have answers to. I mean, I'm sort of freaking out right now."

She lays her small hands on top of mine, discarding the book. "Hey, I'm your best friend. I'll do whatever it takes to help you figure this out. Maybe there's meditation or a spell…" She gasps, her eyes widening to an unreal size. "I know what we can do!"

I wait for her to answer and squeeze her hands. "Tell me, then!"

She stands, pulling her cell phone from the pocket of her fuzzy pink pajamas. "I'm going to call my mom. She is incredible with spells, and she works as a healer. She'll have something to help us reach whatever is inside of you." Her eyes sparkle. "First thing in the morning, we'll drive out to her. I'll find us a car."

I lean back in my chair, feeling the slightest sense of relief. "Okay, let's do it. There's no way I'll be able to sleep after tonight, so the sooner the better."

Fay nods, dialing a number on her phone. "Mom? Yeah, I'm sorry for calling so late. I need your help." She wanders away while she talks to her mom, and I pick up my own phone.

246

ME: "Hey. Want to be overbearing a little bit? I think I need you."

The response comes just seconds later.

ALDEN: "I thought you'd never ask."

CHAPTER 36

The sun is barely coming up, just the golden rays splitting through the evergreen trees ahead. It's already warm outside today, summer well underway. It feels insane to be at school in the summertime, but it's nice to enjoy the heat in the woods. It's practically a vacation just being here.

I take the outside steps down to the circular gravel driveway, shielding my eyes from the bright sunshine. As soon as I reach the shade at the bottom, my eyes adjust to a sight that has me blushing from the neck up.

Sebastian's hands are on Fay's ass, lifting her to her toes as he devours her mouth like a man starved. Her small arms are wrapped tightly around his thick neck and she willingly gives every inch that he takes.

"Oh, christ," I mumble, spinning around with my eyes squeezed shut. "My innocent eyes are burning!"

Fay and Sebastian both laugh, sounding very out of breath behind me. "Sorry, Ivy," Fay says.

Sebastian's large hands tickle my waist and I yelp, spinning around to glare at him. He grins from ear to ear, his chocolate eyes glistening. "It was just kissing, newbie. Nothing to blush about."

I scoff and run my fingers through my freshly combed hair. "I've seen kissing, and there's a difference between kissing and cannibalism."

Sebastian's laugh is booming, bouncing off the outside walls of the asylum. I don't get to say more as a royal blue Jeep pulls up beside Fay. Silis leans outside the passenger window, his red, curly hair a mess atop his head.

"Road trip!" He calls out, making Alden roll his eyes from the driver's seat.

I run up to the Jeep. "I didn't know you'd be joining us, Si. Is Stella okay with this?"

He shrugs. "Mom said Alden could take the Jeep, and this will technically be my vehicle once I get my license. I go where *she* goes."

Alden steps out of the vehicle and comes around to stand beside me. "I couldn't stop him. He can literally turn invisible, so it's a little hard to get rid of him."

I shake my head. "No worries. The more the merrier." I look up into Alden's blue eyes, loving the way the morning sun shines through his sandy hair. "Thanks for helping me, Alden."

His hand reaches out to me, but he quickly pulls it back and stuffs it in his jeans pocket. "I've told you. I'll do anything for you."

My throat feels thick with emotion as his eyes stay glued to mine, but we're quickly interrupted by Fay as she

250

grabs my hand excitedly. "I think Sebastian should drive. He knows how to get to my mom's house. And I'll sit up front with him in case he needs help."

I give my bestie a hard look, knowing exactly what she's trying to do. "It's their car, Fay. Stella would probably want one of them to drive."

"It's alright," Silis adds. "I'll squeeze in the back between my bro and Ivy. My two favorite people." He hops out of the car.

Fay shakes her head as she lays a hand on Silis's shoulder. "It's customary for the men to sit the woman in the middle. To protect her from side impact in a wreck. Same with walking beside a road. The guy takes the outside."

"That's not a thin–" Silis starts, but Fay gives him a look that shuts him right up.

"It's fine," I sigh, knowing Fay will never stop until she gets what she wants. "I'll take the middle seat. I'm smaller anyway."

I try not to look up at Alden as I climb into the backseat of the Jeep. Sebastian and Fay hop in the front, holding hands instantly as I'm squished between Alden and Silis. Alden's arm goes across the back of the seat, behind my shoulders, and his scent floods me in an instant. I try not to audibly smell him as I wiggle just a tad closer into his side.

I look up at Alden, immediately regretting the action when I find him staring down at me, his blue eyes dark and stormy. He licks his lips, and I find myself leaning just a little more against him, taking in his warmth. His body is rigid against mine and he sucks in a quiet breath.

"Are you comfortable?" I ask him, worried I might be hurting him.

He nods, the tips of his fingers playing with a strand of my dark hair from behind me. "More comfortable than I've ever been," he says so quietly that I barely hear him.

I blush, feeling like I'm floating, but Sebastian's loud voice brings me back to earth. "Here we go!" He takes off down the long driveway, winking into the rearview mirror at me. "Passengers, keep your arms and legs inside the vehicle at all times."

"Home sweet home," Fay says, a big smile on her face.

I reluctantly lean away from Alden to get a better look through the windshield. Fay's home is gorgeous. I've been living in a mansion for a month, and I'm still impressed. The entire home is styled like a Mexican villa on the beach, only beside a quiet pond instead. The walls are a light tan stucco, and it's two-stories high with tall windows and a dark ceramic-tiled roof.

Trees surround the home, shielding it from the California sun. It's a paradise.

"Wow, Fay. You grew up here?" I ask, my voice a little shaky from the three-hour drive pressed against Alden's side.

She turns in her seat, unbuckling her seatbelt. "Yeah. This is my favorite place in the world. Come on."

We follow Fay and Sebastian out of the Jeep, each of us stretching our legs and taking in the warm summer air.

My legs wobble a little and my entire body feels like it has been super-charged from the ride. I glance up at Alden who is smiling from ear-to-ear as he watches me shake out my tingling limbs.

"What?" I ask, suddenly feeling self conscious. "Do I have something on my face?"

He shakes his head, but that amazing smile doesn't disappear. He doesn't say anything, but I can tell he feels just as good as I do after practically cuddling for hours together. It has to be a part of this mate bond thing, and it's even more frustrating that he wants to be my friend. *Oh, the things we could do together...*

I sigh, shaking my head to get rid of that line of thought. Silis speaks up, heading along the stone pathway that leads to the large, wooden front door. "Last one in is a rotten egg!" he calls, running toward the house.

In the blink of an eye, Fay goes from standing beside the Jeep to leaning against the front door of her home. "What was that, Si?"

Silis throws his head back with a groan. "No fair! Vampire speed is just cheating, Fay!"

Sebastian, Alden, and I all laugh as we follow Fay into the house. I catch up to Fay, ogling the Mexican-style interior. "I've never seen you run that fast. Can all vampires do that?"

She smiles at me, moving through the house with ease. "Yeah, but it's not really running. It's called *fading*, technically. It's like our body charges up and we can move through air and space in moments. I can't do it very far, but my dad can go like three miles in a minute."

My eyes widen and I'm pretty sure my jaw drops clear to my chest. "I will never get used to this world, I swear."

"You have time to learn," she says, calling for her mom as we exit through the back of the house and into an open patio decorated for outdoor dining.

Time to learn? "Hopefully," I mumble to myself, feeling like my body is becoming less and less my own.

"Yay, you guys made it!" Fay's mom comes running from where she had been tending to a long row of fruit trees. This place is practically an orchard in their own backyard. Callista runs to us, tearing off her wide sun hat and running fingers through her black hair. "How was the drive?"

Fay embraces her mom. "It was good, even though my mate is a crazy driver." She rolls her eyes and lets them land on Sebastian.

He throws his hands in the air. "Hey, you can choose not to love me."

"No, I have zero choice," she says, grinning up at him.

I can't help but glance over at Alden, drawn to him like Fay is to Sebastian. He flicks his eyes to me, letting a lingering gaze trail from my toes to my face, and I have to pry my eyes back to the people in front of me. Even though my whole body feels like it's on fire.

"So," Callista says, grabbing my hands. "I understand we have a problem."

I nod, being pulled back to the reason we're here. "I need your help, Callista. I'll do whatever it takes to fix this thing in my head."

She nods, her dark purple eyes softening for me. "First, let's feed you kids. Then, we'll get to work."

CHAPTER 37

Silis is practically hopping in his patio chair as he finishes off his third chicken salad sandwich. "Callista, I might be in love with you."

Fay's mom laughs loudly as she grins back at the boy. "My husband is a very powerful vampire, young man. He also gets extremely jealous."

Silis's freckled face pales and he looks around the table for help. It only makes each of us laugh, and causes Fay to do her adorable laugh-snort. "My dad's not going to kill you, Si. He's too much of a softy for that."

Callista nods. "It's true. He got over his mean streak when Fay was born. I wish he was here to see all of you together. We've missed our baby girl being home for lunch on the patio. Speaking of which," she says, pointing to Fay. "Drink up."

Fay takes a long drink of her mug of blood, and I watch in fascination. Being out here in the sunshine will give her headaches if she doesn't keep up her blood intake, and even though I should be disgusted, I'm just incredibly intrigued.

"Where is Mr. Clark this weekend?" Alden asks, leaning on his elbows against the white table.

"London," Callista says with a sad sigh. "His parents are living in the city, so he's visiting. I would have gone with, but I couldn't miss family visitation day!"

"I'm glad you stayed, Mom." Fay clears her throat and looks over at me. "Go ahead and tell Mom what's been going on, Ivy."

I twist my fingers together. "Uh, how much did Fay already tell you, Callista?"

She leans on her elbows in the same way as Alden. "When I got the call last night, Fay mentioned that you've been worried about a voice in your head, and she said you believe it to be a separate soul. So, I offered to do some digging around in your mind. That's as much as I know." Callista opens up a box of incense from the center of the table, plucking one long stick out of it. With a single thought, she lights the tip of it. "Go ahead and explain what this voice feels like. What it says to you."

I can feel sweat on my brow as I watch the white swirls of smoke dance in front of Callista. I glance around the table at the many pairs of eyes watching me. "You all don't need to be here for this. It's kind of…embarrassing."

Fay and Silis both look at me like I must be joking. Sebastian just leans back in his chair, settling in and shoving a Dorito in his mouth. Alden continues watching me, no sign of leaving anytime soon.

"Okay, then," I say, fighting my smile that wants to come. I turn back to Callista. "While I was growing up, I had this explosive temper. Kids would pick on me or push me around, and I just lost it. I'd feel fine and calm one minute, and like I could start a war the next. It's more than what Stella said about my wolf side coming to the surface. This is a part of myself that wants *chaos*, that revels in destruction."

"Feeling your wolf isn't like that. That sounds like a demon trait," Alden says, his eyes sobering.

I nod. "And, as far as I know, I shouldn't have any demon blood in me."

Callista shakes her head, waving the incense back and forth, her eyes narrowing tightly. "No. You don't have a drop of demon in you, dear. At least, not in your blood." She looks deep into my eyes. "I can see *something* through the smoke, though."

"What does incense do for you?" I ask, watching her swirl the stick around between us.

She smiles, her dark eyes focusing on mine again. "The smoke from the incense is like an X-ray screen. I can see through it to you, and use my magic to peek inside of you." I blanch, wanting to cover myself, but that makes her giggle. "Not the physical parts of you, Ivy. The spiritual parts."

I nod as she starts to focus again. "Well, it wasn't until recently that this voice started coming to me. It is sometimes just a feeling without any words. Other times, it's as if a darkness in my mind is coercing me, threatening things and wanting me to…hurt people." I gulp, avoiding Alden's eyes, even though I can feel him watching me. "And then there are the strange encounters. A girl at school told me I had evil inside of me. And a uh…kar, krast–" I pause.

"A krantus demon," Silis says, saving me. "It targeted Ivy for some reason, and they only target evil souls. I think we can all agree that Ivy isn't evil."

I smile at him. "Well, I hope not." I look back at Callista. "And then there is the dreamwalker thing. It seemed to find something in me too. Something, or someone not myself." I shudder at the memory of the creature.

Callista nods. She focuses on something in the smoke that causes her lips to tighten as her shoulders seem to droop in sadness. "I'm so sorry, Ivy."

Alden stands, his hands turning white as he grips the table edge. "What is it? What do you see?" I blink up at him, fear shooting through me at the fear in his own eyes.

Callista clears her throat before setting the incense in a polished holder. "Ivy, your studying brought you to the topic of soul sharing, correct?" I nod. "Well, I believe you're right. I can see two souls in your body." I clutch my chest as I lean back in my chair. "Your soul is bright, a wolf shifter's soul with strength, determination, and incredible power. It's a good soul, Ivy."

I nod, tears threatening to fill in my eyes. "What about the other soul?"

Her eyes seem to darken as she leans further onto the table. "The second soul is like a backpack on yours, clinging onto the edges of your mind. It's entirely dark, acting as a plague against your healthy soul."

Alden growls. He moves around the table while everyone else seems to freeze in their seats. I can feel

Alden's presence behind me, but I can't look at him. His heat is behind my chair, and his anger is palpable.

His voice is gravel when he speaks. "This dark soul. Can it hurt her? Can it be removed?"

Callista looks up at him with a sigh. "Ivy hasn't yet shifted, and I believe if she had grown up in this world, training and harnessing her power, she would be stronger than a lot of wolf shifters." She drops her eyes to me. "But, since you only just learned about who you are, I worry that it will take you a long time to gain that strength. This will give the darker soul an advantage."

"What does that mean?" I ask, my voice barely a whisper.

"It means that the dark soul in you is stronger than you are. I think, if it wanted to, it could take over your body and discard your pure soul completely." I gasp, and Alden's hands drop to my shoulders. "But, I believe, if this hitchhiker knew it was being deposited into a wolf shifter body, it had planned to wait until you shift for the first time, and then take your body at its strongest, making whatever this other being is even stronger."

"Can it be removed?" Alden asks again, even more growling in his voice as he gently squeezes my shoulders.

Callista shrugs. "If you want my opinion, I think this other soul planned everything perfectly. I think they knew Ivy was a shifter, they knew she would be raised in the human world, thus making her weaker. And, I think they planned to take her body after she shifts. They had a necromancer transfer their soul in the event of their death, and pick someone just like Ivy to manipulate." She shakes her head in defeat. "I can't remove the soul. Only Ivy can fight against it with her own strength."

I sag in my chair, my face falling in my hands as I start to have a panic attack. I can't suck in a deep enough breath. I'm shaking, and my chest hurts. I can feel soothing hands along my back, trying to comfort me, but I'm on the verge of passing out.

"Breathe, Ivy. You need to try to catch your breath." It's Alden, leaning beside me with dark eyes. "Please, just *breathe*."

I try to focus on his face as I drag in all of the air I can. He nods to me, continually rubbing his hand up and down my back. I watch as he turns his eyes back to Callista. "Who is the soul, Callista? Can you tell us that?"

I don't look at her, trying to focus on every detail of Alden's face. His clenched jaw, the pulsing of a vein in his neck. The stubble of light brown hair across his tan skin. The way his long eyelashes flutter just a little.

Still, I hear Callista's response. "I don't know yet, but I can find out if you five stick around for the night. You can all stay here, and I'll call Stella to excuse you from classes tomorrow."

Alden turns back to me, his nose just inches from mine. "We're going to fix this, Ivy. Okay? I promise."

CHAPTER 38

"Tests?" I ask, looking back at Callista where she lays heavy stones in a circle around me. "What kind of tests, exactly? Because, the last time Fay laid out rocks in a circle, it captured a dreamwalker and tortured him."

Callista chuckles, and Fay helps her perfect the circle of stones. "No, dear. This is not that kind of circle. Us Seers use stone circles for many different things. Stone is earth, and the earth steadies our magic. The circle harnesses our power to one space, and it's really helpful during our spells to have that spot narrowed down."

I nod, turning in circles as my friends watch the preparation. It's officially night time, and the moon is supposed to help enhance Callista's magic as well. We've spent the entire day here at her home, though I've done nothing but internally freak out over the news from this afternoon. I have a dark soul inside of me, clinging onto me and threatening to take over my body. It's incredibly unnerving.

The more I think about it, the more I can convince myself that I can feel that soul, and then I just want to throw up. Basically, I skipped dinner and am now exhausted. Alden has been hovering around me all day, but I can't face him again. I feel ashamed of this sickness in me, and I'm afraid that he'll look at me differently, as...*ruined*.

Fay and Sebastian have tried comforting me, but I have a hard time listening to either of them. They're happy, so amazingly happy together, and I don't want to sour their moods with my own. As for Silis, he seems to be joking even more than usual. He's stoked to spend the night away from home for once, but he's also doing everything in his power to lighten the mood in the house. Bless his perfect soul.

"Done," Callista says, stepping back and smiling softly at me. "Now, we do the tests." She looks around at the others in the large living room. "Who wants to provoke Ivy? We need to draw that dark soul to the surface, to take control of Ivy's body."

I gasp. "Wait, what?"

"I'll do it!" Sebastian volunteers, way too eager. "What do I gotta do?"

"Bast!" Fay yells, throwing her hands in the air. "Be nice."

Callista turns to me. "What has made the soul speak out in the past, Ivy?"

I shrug. "I don't know. I mean, anger, I guess. Moments when I've been mad have spurred it on."

Sebastian turns to Alden. "If I pick on your girl, are you going to kill me?"

Alden glares back at him, but he shakes his head. "I'm going to convince myself that it's in order to help her, so no." He looks at me. "As long as you're okay with this, Ivy."

I scoff. "I don't have much choice, do I?" I look up at Sebastian and wave him over. "Just do it."

Sebastian grins cockily as he saunters closer to me. "Hey little shrimp. I hope we'll get to fight again." He looks me up and down with a sneer on his lips. "I know I'm supposed to like you because I'm dating your roommate, but you make it damn near impossible."

My jaw drops open and Fay covers her ears. "I can't listen or I'll get pissed too."

Sebastian steps even closer, his toes touching the stones around me. "You know that girl, Xena? She's all over Alden, isn't she?" I grind my teeth together, imagining Xena touching Alden like she does. Sebastian doesn't stop there. "Wanna know a secret, newbie? Wanna know what Xena and Alden used to do together before you were dropped at our doorstep like junk mail?"

Alden growls, and I watch as he turns away with his fists clenched hard at his sides. I turn to Sebastian, my veins heating with his words. It can't be true. It's just him trying to make me mad. "Tell me, Sebastian."

He smiles, but the look is sinister as he leans in to whisper in my ear. "Ask Alden about that little tattoo that's hidden in a very special spot on Xena. Word is, he's the only one to ever find that little prize, and he *loved* it." My jaw clenches, but he's not done. "There's a reason he doesn't want you, ya know? Why would you want bronze when you've had gold?"

My body shakes from anger and I shove Sebastian away from my personal space. "Shut up, Sebastian," I growl, every inch of me ready to let my wolf take control, wishing I had that power so I could rip him to pieces.

Callista's voice interrupts my fuming. "I can see that you're incredibly angry, Ivy, but it's not working. This is *your* anger, not the dark soul's." She sighs. "We have to try something different."

Sebastian sighs and his whole body sags as he charges me. I flinch, but he lifts me up into his arms and holds me gently. "I'm so sorry, Ivy. It was all a lie, every word."

He sets me down, but I'm still pissed. "Why do I feel like you were telling the truth, then? You can't be *that* good of an actor."

"He is," Alden, Fay, and Silis say at the same time.

Alden's jaw is tight but he's looking at me again. "He was lying, Ivy. I've never touched Xena as more than a friend. *Ever.*" His face is sincere, but he still looks like he's as mad as I am.

Fay grabs Sebastian's hand, but her eyes are on me. "And, Sebastian adores you, Ivy. He has told me many times how glad he is that we've become best friends."

I look up at Sebastian, finding sadness in his usual sparkling eyes. My anger softens a bit. "You really are too good at that, Sebastian. I wanted to throttle you."

"I wanted to be an actor when I was a kid. I got pretty good at it." He smiles. "Do you forgive me? I swear, there were no rumors about Alden and Xena. She's been pining after him since Freshman year, but he's a major loner."

264

"Hey!" Alden shouts, but the anger has drifted off of him too.

We all laugh and everything feels okay again, until I look at Callista and remember why we're here. "What do we do now?"

She smiles at me. "Can you remember any specific moments where that voice took over? Maybe we can recreate one."

"I–" My face flushes with heat as I think over the past month. Most of the times that I lost control of my body were the times where I was getting close to Alden. I look his way, and then at my friends. "Can everyone step outside for this?" I clear my throat. "Except for Alden."

"We want to help," Silis starts, but Fay grabs his arm.

"Come on Si. She wants us out, we go out." She turns to me with a subtle wink as she drags Silis and Sebastian out of the room.

I look down at where Callista sits, watching me. "You have to be here for this, right?"

She nods. "I do, but don't be nervous about me, hon. I've seen a lot in this world, and I don't judge."

I slowly turn towards Alden. He's watching me intently, but he hasn't said a word. "So, I know we talked about being friends," I start. "But the times that voice has interrupted me the most, or taken over my body…are the times where you and I got a little too close."

I can see his Adam's apple rise and fall as he nods. "I'm here to help you, Ivy. Any way you need me to."

I wave him over to me, and he closes the distance between us. He steps into the stone circle with me, and his fingers brush a strand of hair off of my cheek. His blue eyes are so dark as he waits for me to give him instructions.

"Um, I guess just kiss me, maybe? If you're okay with that." I laugh uncomfortably, my body shaking. "Gosh, this is incredibly awkward."

"Just forget about everything else for a minute, okay?" Alden says, letting his fingers slip into my hair. He presses his palm to the back of my neck, forcing my head to tilt back so that I'm looking into his eyes.

Everywhere he touches me tingles, making me truly forget everything but this feeling. I press up onto my toes, connecting our chests and showing Alden that I'm ready for this. The first time he kissed me, he was healing me. This time, he's helping me again, but I'm going to take what I can get.

Alden's lips drop to mine, instantly heating up my body with a gentle kiss. One of his large hands slips around my waist, holding me as his other tugs lightly on my hair. I press my palms to Alden's chest, feeling the fast pace of his heartbeat through his t-shirt.

The roughness of his stubble scrapes against my chin, and I have to stop myself from sighing at the amazing contrast between that and the softness of his mouth. I move my lips against his, testing all of the angles that we fit together, and his fingers flex against me as he lets out a hot breath of air against my mouth.

Something squirms in the back of my mind, a feeling of needing to stop, but I fight that presence. *I want this.* I may never get to taste Alden again. I throw my arms around his neck and pull him so tight against me that our kisses turn heavy and fast.

The only thing that breaks into the moment between us is Callista's sharp gasp. I break away from Alden, out of breath as my eyes land on the woman's wide, purple eyes that look like they've seen a ghost. "Callista?" I ask, dropping to my knees in front of her.

Alden follows me, waiting to hear what Callista has to say. She blinks a few times and then clutches her chest with true fear in her eyes. "It's *her*. I'm so sorry, Ivy. I'm so sorry."

I take her shaking hands in mine and she finally meets my gaze. "Do you know whose soul it is, Callista? Did you get a name?"

She nods, and her eyes flick to Alden. "It's Sage Whitaker." Alden stands abruptly, and Callista looks back at me. "It's *her* soul in your body, Ivy, and there's nothing I can do to help you. Do you know who that is?"

I nod, my blood turning cold as my fears are realized. I know who Sage is. The woman that killed shifters. The demon that was so heartless that she amassed an army to murder children, women, entire families.

I turn toward Alden, watching his face go from shock, to fear, to fury. He runs his hands through his hair and then bolts for the door without even looking my way, disappearing into the night.

CHAPTER 39

I can't stop shaking. Fay tosses a blanket over my shoulders and sits beside me on their family sofa. She places her arm around my shoulders and tugs me in close. "It'll be alright, Ivy. We'll find a way to get her soul out of you."

Silis and Sebastian sit across from us on the matching loveseat, both of them eyeing me like I might break any second, or suddenly become a raging, psycho demon chick hell-bent on killing them. I don't know which is more likely anymore.

"Should we go after him?" I ask, worrying about Alden.

He ran off half an hour ago without a word. It's dark outside, but I have to remind myself that he's literally a werewolf and can handle running around in the night. If anything, he probably prefers it to being indoors.

Callista comes into the room with a steaming mug in her hands. "Don't worry about him until you drink this, hon. I can sense where he is, and he hasn't gone far." She places the pink, flowery mug into my hands and I sigh at the comforting warmth.

I take a tentative sip of the tea, and I'm grateful for the taste of honey. "This is actually really good. So, I just drink this and Sage's voice disappears?" Callista nods. "For how long?" I add.

She twists her lips in thought. "I'd say a few days, possibly a week. It's hard to know for sure." She watches me slowly drink her magical concoction. "It won't take her away for good. Her soul is still in there, waiting for its chance. But she'll shut up for a few days and give you a break."

I sigh, drinking a little faster and ignoring the burn of the hot tea in my throat. All I want is to get rid of this demon in my body, but I don't even know where to begin. Not long ago, if someone told me that I was a wolf shifter with the soul of a dead murderer hitchhiking in my body, I probably would've just laughed and run the other way from the crazy person making crap up. Now, I accept it as the truth, and that's the most terrifying thing of all.

"My birthday is in less than two months. What do I do, guys?" I take a long drink of my tea as I search their eyes.

Silis shakes his head. "We'll get a plan together, Ivy. We all love you, and Callista said you're meant to be strong. We'll do whatever it takes to help you kick that chick out of you."

Fay scoffs. "That sounds crazy, but you know I'm on board."

"Me too, newbie." Sebastian reaches a large hand out to rest on my bouncing knee. "You've got us, alright?"

I nod, finishing off my tea and trying not to cry at the love in this room. I've found my people somehow, even though I never imagined I could have people like this. "What about Alden? He doesn't seem too ready for battle."

Silis opens his mouth to say something, but Callista holds a hand up to stop him. "It's not our place to dive into Alden's history, but his absence isn't because of you, Ivy. Hearing Sage's name like that did something to him."

I scrunch my face up in confusion, but like Callista said, it's not our place to discuss. Callista stands and waves us all to follow. "Okay, time for bed. We could all use a good rest after today's events." She eyes Sebastian and Fay. "Boys upstairs, girls downstairs."

"We got it, Mom," Fay says with a roll of her eyes.

Sebastian and Silis follow Callista up the carpeted stairs, leaving Fay and I alone in the living room. My friend turns to me with wetness in her eyes. "Are you coming to bed with me, or are you going after him?"

I pull her into a warm embrace, needing the comfort as much as I believe she does. "How'd you know I was going to go find him?"

She smiles. "I know how it feels to have a fated mate, remember? I bet it kills him to not be comforting you right now too."

I shrug, not so certain. "I'll come back as soon as I talk to Alden."

Fay nods and gives me one more soft smile before heading toward the guest bedroom attached to the living room. She shuts the door and I shrug off my blanket as I make my way out to the backyard. Fairy lights light up the porch, but beyond that, the night is dark. The only other light comes from the stars above.

I close my eyes and focus on the feeling that Alden gives me. The heat of his presence, and that invisible string that's always pulling us together. I step off the patio and walk in the direction that I hope Alden will be.

I end up in the large grove of peach trees behind Fay's home, drawing in the deliciously sweet scent from all around me, but another scent reaches me. That of spearmint and pine. I spin around toward Alden's signature smell, and my eyes land on him. He's sitting on a metal bench between the trees, his elbows on his knees and his face in his hands.

I slowly make my way over to Alden and sit beside him on the bench. "Alden, are you alright?"

A harsh laugh comes from him, surprising me. "You're the one who isn't alright, Ivy. Don't worry about me."

I hold my breath as I reach a hand out and touch his arched back. Alden flinches, but he lets out a long sigh shortly after. He rises in his seat to turn and look at me. My heart breaks at the puffiness around his eyes like he has been crying.

"Please tell me what you're thinking," I beg, letting myself touch his cheek for just a moment.

Alden raises his hand to take mine off of his face. He laces our fingers together and places our entwined hands on his lap. "Did you know that my parents knew Sage Whitaker? When she was alive?"

I nod. "They went to school together, right?"

"They did." He pauses. "As far as I know, Sage had a thing for my dad, and figured since they were both of demon blood that they'd end up together." He scoffs. "My

272

dad and mom realized they were mates their Senior year of high school. After that, Sage didn't have a chance."

I nod again, but I have no words for him. He continues, "My father's rejection was the start of Sage's rebellion. He chose a shifter over his own kind, and to Sage, that was the worst thing he could have done. She lost her mind then, if she ever had it to begin with." His eyes flick to me for only a moment before falling to our hands again. "Sage set her sights on all the shifters at that moment. She decided that they were the enemy, and they needed to die...including my mom...and me"

I gasp quietly, trying to hide my reaction to his story, but failing. "Did she, I mean, did Sage kill your mom?"

Alden swallows hard and then looks into my eyes again. "She tried to kill me first, her revenge on both of my parents. She came into our home when I was just a baby, and she took me from my bed. My mom and I were home alone that night, and Sage had planned to kill me and then my mom, leaving us for my dad to find."

I squeeze his hand, my emotions threatening to pour overboard. He was just a baby, and this demon woman was going to kill him. *And now she's inside of me.*

Before I can be sick, Alden strokes his fingers along the back of my hand as he continues his story. "My father told me that he arrived home that night, having taken an early flight back to us. He found Sage and two of her minions in the house, one of them with a knife to my throat while Sage was tying my mom to a chair. He lost it at that moment, and he killed all three of them before they could so much as hurt us." Alden's eyes are dark when they reach mine. "My dad killed Sage that night, not knowing that the very second she passed, her soul latched itself onto a newborn baby."

"Alden," I whisper, my voice uncertain. *What do I say to him?*

He releases my hand and stands up, looking up at the wide sky. "Five years later, my mom ran into one of Sage's people who had hidden himself from the supernatural world. He found out who my mom was, and he killed her on the spot."

CHAPTER 40

Every part of my racing heart is broken as I stare at Alden's back. The woman who owns the soul inside of me ruined Alden's family. Sage took his mother from him, and now he has to look into my eyes and face that monster all over again. How could he care about me after tonight?

No matter how much I wish I could run from him right now, I find myself standing at his back and reaching out to him. "Alden, I'm so sorry." I step around him so that he's looking down at me. "I know it fixes nothing, but I am so damn sorry."

He searches my face for something, but I don't know what he finds there. "You didn't do anything, Ivy. You don't have any reason to apologize to me."

"Didn't I, though? It was me who Sage latched onto. If I didn't exist, you wouldn't need to face that woman ever again." My eyes fill with tears and I want to scream at myself to stop.

Alden's eyebrows press together. "If it wasn't you, it would have been another child, another body. You didn't cause anything, Ivy, so don't ever think I would rather you not exist."

I wipe at the tear that tickles its way down my cheek. "Then why can't you look at me like you did an hour ago, before you knew about Sage? I understand if you hate me, or at least hate a part of me."

He gapes at me like he can't believe what I'm saying. "Hate you? That's what I made you think by running out of there?" He groans and his hands cup my face, forcing me to stare back at him. "I *hate* that Sage attached herself to you, and I *hate* that she is the reason my mom is gone. I *hate* that my mom's death caused my father to lose his belief in happiness, and to lose his humanity." His voice cracks. "The moment she died, my father stopped being a parent to me. He beat me, screamed at me, called me things that no child should ever hear. He tortured me for years before Stella decided to take me away from him. All of this because of *that* woman."

My tears are flowing freely now, for Alden, for the boy he was and the life he had to live. I even cry for his father, even though I want to kill him for what he did to Alden, he lost his mate, and that broke him.

Alden doesn't release me, but his thumbs swipe my tears away. "But do you want to know what my first thought was when Callista said Sage's name back there? I thought, it's *my* turn to be broken. Even so many years after her death, Sage has finally found me, and she is going to break me by taking the one thing in my life that I can't live without." His black eyes bore into mine with so much intensity that I fear I'll stop breathing. "You," he breathes.

I reach for Alden, desperate to hold him, but he pulls away. He steps away from me and growls loudly at the sky. "Alden, stop doing that," I shout, needing him to hear me. "Stop running away from me before I have my chance to talk."

He spins around to face me, but he stays a few feet away. "I already know what you'll say. You will want to comfort me, just like I want to do for you. You have a kind heart, and you will tell me everything good to make me believe that I'm something worthy of you, but I'm not."

I scoff, wanting to rip my hair out. "Weren't we just talking about how *I'm* the one not worthy? *I'm* the one with a blood-thirsty demon woman attached to my soul."

"But the only reason you're here, cursed like this, is because demons are evil. All of them. We're dark, abusive, heartless. Sage was, my dad is." He points to himself. "I'm one of them, Ivy. Your fated mate is a damned demon, just like that leech inside of you."

I blink, sure that I'm not understanding him correctly. "You're not like them, Alden. Do you really not see that?" I step closer to him, praying that he doesn't retreat. "Sure, half of your bloodline comes from demons. But, you saying they're all evil is wrong. Your dad was heartbroken after losing your mom. He had no reason to turn on you, but that was his doing, not his blood. As for Sage, she was just a jealous bitch." I laugh humorlessly. "There are evil humans out there too, all over the world, but they don't define the rest of the population."

I step closer, landing just a foot from him now. Alden's shoulders slump, and his eyes hold so much pain.

"I'm my father's son, Ivy. The child of a man-turned-monster."

"You're also your mother's son. The child of a woman who comes from people like Stella." I take a steadying breath. "Remember our caterpillar story, Alden?"

"Of course," he mutters.

"I know I was supposed to be the main character. The caterpillar, pushing through life, surviving, to one day change into that beautiful butterfly. But I think you and I are both caterpillars, and I think we were meant to find one another in order to change for the better." I touch his cheek and sigh at the contact that I needed. "You're not a monster, Alden, and you *never* will be. Do you need proof that you are good for me?"

He stares down at me, his breathing shallow, and I don't give him a chance to respond. I push off of my toes and press my lips to his. I worry that he'll pull away, but he gives in with a growl and lifts me into his thick arms. I kiss him with all of the emotion that has been threatening to burst out of me, and it's the most amazing thing I have ever felt.

Alden holds me against him, not pressing any further than this one kiss. Our tears blend together as he explores my mouth with his, and for a moment, everything feels right with the world. There are no demons, no past pains, and no future fears. Just this. Just us.

Continue on the next page to read Alden's point of view! What was he thinking on family day?

CHAPTER 41

ALDEN

"It's just more people," I tell myself. "I can handle people, even happy families."

I shake my head as I look at myself in my bathroom mirror. My collared shirt is ironed, buttoned all the way up to the neck just like Stella wanted. I refuse to put that nasty gel in my hair, though, and hopefully she doesn't notice.

I scoff. Who am I kidding? I've lived with Stella as my guardian for years. I already know she'll give me hell for not using the gel. I also know that Silis will *accidentally* forget the gel too, and that thought brings a smile to my lips.

I watch myself smile into the mirror, and my mind travels back to Ivy. Everything reminds me of that girl, and letting myself kiss her two weeks ago only made this need a thousand times stronger. Everything about that night changed the way I see her. I know her taste now. I know the soft noise she makes when our lips touch.

I growl, running my hands over my face and through my hair. *Great, now my hair is even more of a mess.*

I shrug, not caring enough to fix the problem, and I reluctantly leave my bedroom for the big family day dinner. This day happens every year, and each time, I want to spend the whole evening in my room. I don't have a traditional family. I have my aunt, and her adopted son.

I can't even just place them in that box, though, because they're way more than that. Stella has been a mother to me in every way she can, and I couldn't have asked for a better little brother. Still, why do I feel so lost everytime I walk into these dinners and see the students laughing with their families?

I step through the open doors to the cafeteria, and I'm impressed with what Stella has accomplished. The ceilings are even decorated, for heaven's sake. That woman puts everything she has into this school.

Laughter and voices fill the room, but one laugh in particular has my body vibrating with excitement. I'm immediately drawn to Ivy across the room, her gray eyes looking out at the other students, until they find me. The smile on my face is unintentional, but she's damn good at bringing it out just for her.

Her small hand raises as she watches me and she wiggles her fingers for me to come over. The gesture is like a magnet, and I can't fight against it. I barely register the people surrounding Ivy as I walk toward her, but I try to focus on each of them. "Hi, everyone. I hope you're all enjoying family day."

"Best day of every year, man." Sebastian slaps me on the back in a friendly gesture.

I look down at Ivy, knowing that it has to be her sister standing beside her. Ivy blushes as she grabs onto the girl's arm. "Alden, this is my sister, Lorelei. Lor, this is Alden. We— Uh, we have Creative Writing together."

Creative writing? Is that what defines us? I want to laugh at the idea that being classmates is all that connects Ivy and I.

Ivy's sister smiles at me, and it's a nice look. It's immediately clear that she has a heart as good as Ivy's. "It's great to meet you, Alden. Ivy has told me all about the wonderful friends she has made here. I couldn't thank you all enough for helping her settle into a new place."

I smile down at Ivy, hoping to make her lips lift along with mine. "She has been a light in the darkness. Wolfe Asylum wouldn't be the same without you here, Ivy." *Shit, I sound like a schmuck.*

Ivy's pink cheeks are worth sounding like an idiot, though. I want to say more stupid things, but Xena's voice pierces through the room. "Oh, there he is!"

Before I can excuse myself, Xena's hands grip onto my arm and she spins me around to face a tall, thin man with a bored look on his face. "Alden, I am so glad we found you. Daddy, this is Alden. He's one of my best friends." *I look down at her like she has lost her mind.*

Ivy's scoff behind me makes my eyes shoot up, and I try to give a nice introduction to Xena's dad, but I don't hear my own words since my attention is all on Ivy and Lorelei.

"I take it you don't like that girl," Lorelei whispers to Ivy. *Thank you, wolf ears.*

Even from this distance, I can feel the tension floating off of Ivy as she whispers back to her sister. "Not so much."

I pry my arm out of Xena's grip as her dad praises his perfect daughter for her school work, and talks about the architecture of the building. I nod and agree where needed, but I can't help it as I glance back over my shoulder at my beautiful Ivy. *My? No, she isn't mine.*

"Okay," Lorelei says to Ivy, unaware that I can hear every word. "I've met the guy that you clearly have a crush on, but now I want to meet the kid that flirts with everything that moves."

Ivy's laugh is loud and incredible, and I want to laugh with her at her sister's description of Silis. I don't know if Ivy has a crush on me, but it feels amazing to imagine that people see a certain look in her eyes. I know I have that same look in my own, and that will *never* change.

PART

5

CHAPTER 42

I never imagined that air could literally feel thick. I've heard the saying about cutting the tension in a room with a knife, but I swear I'm choking on the heaviness surrounding me. It's both frustrating, and *incredible*. I glance out of the corner of my eye, struggling to keep my gaze on Mr. Hale in front of the class.

How could I, though? How could I focus on Mr. Hale rambling on about famous novels and authors when I know what Alden's lips feel like? When he's sitting beside me with his mesmerizing scent floating between us.

It has been three days since I kissed him outside of Callista's house. Alden and I were both a little broken that night. My body has been in the process of being hijacked by a crazy, murderous demon soul. Alden had just informed me of his terrible childhood that caused his heart to be left in pieces for so long. We needed one another that night.

On Monday, Fay, Sebastian, Silis, Alden, and I all drove back to Wolfe Asylum in complete silence. Nobody knew what to say about our latest predicament. I don't blame any of my friends, though. Right now, the future looks bleak, and it's going to take time to deal with.

Yesterday, I barely saw anyone as I spent the day catching up on school work and trying to switch my nervous mind off. Callista's magical tea concoction shut the evil Sage up for the week, which has lifted a huge weight off of me already, but I wasn't sure what to do with this lightness inside of me...Until I saw Alden this morning.

The way his eyes were heavy on me as I walked toward our shared desk had my heart pounding. The way his seat slid just a little closer to mine, and when he leaned into my ear to whisper good morning. I could've fallen into him right then, had Mr. Hale not come into the room and started teaching.

Now, every inch of my body tingles with some crazy reaction to the proximity between Alden and I. We've sat side-by-side in Creative Writing every other day for a month, but something has shifted between us after that kiss.

I glance over at Alden and my gaze clings to his. He's watching me with an intensity that I can feel in my veins. His blue eyes are hooded as a slow smile tugs at the corners of his kissable lips. "Pay attention, Ivy," he whispers.

"You first," I say back, raising a single eyebrow.

Alden doesn't move, though. He's focused on me every bit as much as I am on him. I squirm a little in my seat, scooting just a tad closer toward him. He licks his lips as he pulls his chair in my direction until our thighs touch.

My breathing picks up at the heat between our bodies. Alden's arm is thrown over the back of his chair, and his hand hangs over, so close to me. His finger twitches until it's against my bare shoulder. He strokes the skin there, causing goosebumps to spread across my arm.

Dear lord, this class has lasted a year!

I swallow hard, forcing my gaze forward so I can try to catch up with what Mr. Hale has been lecturing about. It's only a few seconds before my eyes are drawn back to Alden though. He continues to touch me with feather-light caresses, and I shiver in my chair.

Alden's eyes widen briefly as he watches my reaction, and then he smiles cockily back at me. *Oh, so it's going to be like that, then?* I accept his challenge, even though I in no way know how to be alluring.

I press my leg tighter against his, and my hand falls to my thigh, resting just an inch from where his connects to mine. Alden's gaze falls to my hand, and I let him watch as I reach my fingers out and trail a line from his knee to the bottom of his jean pocket. I watch Alden's Adam's apple bob up and down with a heavy swallow as he continues to stare at my traveling fingers.

I slip my hand further over his thigh, applying pressure as I feel to the inside of his muscular leg and slide my hand back to his knee. I stop there, though. It's a tease, just a sample of my touch, but when Alden's eyes flick back up to mine, I know immediately that it worked. His eyes are nearly black, the color of the wild wolf's irises that lives inside of him.

Alden stretches his legs out and runs a hand through his hair. He looks up just as Mr. Hale dismisses the class, and then I'm pulled to my feet by Alden's hand in mine. "Finally," he growls, tossing his backpack over his shoulder.

I grab my bag too, just in time to be tugged through the shuffling class members by Alden. I apologize to a few of the students that we bump into on our way out the door, and in seconds, Alden yanks me into an empty hallway, and through a door that leads to an even emptier stairwell.

"Alden, what are you–"

My question is cut off by his lips as they crash into mine. He drops his bag to the ground and his hands press against my waist until I'm shoved gently against the wall behind me. I gasp, letting our lips break apart for just a moment before my mind catches up and I give in.

I let my own backpack fall from my arm and I grip onto Alden's biceps. My fingers trail up his arms and over his shoulders, feeling the flex of his muscles under my touch. I slip my hands into his hair and cling onto him as his kisses become frantic.

Alden takes his mouth from me and he presses his body roughly against mine as he peppers kisses across my cheek, to the sensitive spot just below my ear. "That class was torture, Ivy." He whispers to me between kisses. "Your touch is *everything*."

His lips continue down my neck and to my collarbone. I suck in a sharp breath, overwhelmed by the feel of his lips on places they've never been before, the way his body is hot against my front and the wall is cold against my back.

"Alden," I whisper, needing to speak even though I have no idea what I want to say. I remember the time he kissed me in my bedroom and the way my need for him brought Sage to the front of my mind. Fear fills me in an instant. "Wait, Alden," I say louder.

He immediately stops kissing my neck and he raises his head to peer into my eyes. His breathing is heavy as he watches me. "What's wrong? Is it too much? Too fast?"

He starts to pull away from me, but I slip my hands around his waist and tug him back against me. "No, it's not that at all. I'm just...I'm afraid Sage is going to wake up." I blush and look down at his chest. "She's not a fan of you kissing me..."

Alden's fingers gently grip my chin. He raises my face so that our eyes meet again. "Is she still suppressed?" I nod. "Okay, then. If she comes back, we'll deal with it." His thumbs slip along my jaw as his hand dips into my hair. "Nothing feels as right as when I'm touching you, Ivy." He places a soft kiss against the corner of my mouth. "Or when I'm kissing you."

I slide my hands up his long back, pressing us closer together. "I feel the same way."

His smile is wide as he drops his forehead to mine. "Then let's just enjoy this while we can, okay?"

He's right. The tea only lasts so long, and Sage will be back eventually. It's time to take advantage of this situation. I don't hesitate for another moment as I rise up to press my lips against his again. Alden groans and I slip my tongue in between his lips as they part slightly. The world becomes foggy as I get lost in the taste of Alden.

Every inch I give, he takes greedily, and it's true. *Nothing* has ever felt this right.

CHAPTER 43

I sit at the usual table in the back of the cafeteria, trying desperately to avoid Fay's watchful eyes. "Hey, roomie," I say as I take a huge bite of the red apple in my hand. The loud crunch fills the silence between us.

Fay's voice is irritated when she speaks. "Stop that right now, Ivy, or I will kick you in the shin under this table."

I sigh and finally let my eyes meet her violet ones. "Stop what? I'm just sitting down for lunch." I take another loud bite of the sweet apple.

Fay grins as she studies my face. "Rosy, red cheeks. Messy hair." She narrows her eyes as she leans in. "And is that a hickey on your neck?"

I gasp and throw my hand over my neck. "*He didn't!*"

Fay laughs loudly, her eyes wide now. "No, there isn't actually a hickey, but you certainly answered my suspicions about you and Alden."

My jaw drops and I throw a wadded-up napkin at my friend. "You tricked me!" I groan and roll my eyes before giving in. "Fine, I'm late to lunch because Alden and I were…" I roll my tongue around in my mouth, still able to taste Alden.

"Canoodling," Fay finishes for me. "Fooling around? Hooking up? Getting lucky?"

I can't stop my stupid laugh as I raise my hands for her to shut up. "Quit it! We were just *kissing*. Don't get too excited."

Fay studies my face again and she shakes her head in disbelief. "You are seriously giddy right now, Ivy. Aww, I love that you're in love."

My eyes widen momentarily. "I don't know about *love*, Fay." She doesn't look convinced and I am so ready to change this subject. "Anyways, how are your classes?"

She scoffs at me and shoves a few potato chips into her mouth. "Fine, I won't push you. Still, I'm happy for you and Alden. Especially considering your current situation…" she trails off.

I nod. "We can talk about it, you know? I'd like to figure out how to get this soul out of me. We can't do that if we pretend she doesn't exist."

Fay slumps forward, looking defeated. Thankfully, we're interrupted by Sebastian plopping himself down next to his mate. "Hey, girls." He looks between Fay and I. "You alright?"

I sit up straight in my seat. "We're great. Just talking about the joys of high school."

Fay smiles up at Sebastian and he plants a sweet kiss on her lips. "Glad you could join us for lunch, Bast."

He grins back at her and steals some of her chips before looking excitedly back and forth. "Okay, we need to go over our plans tonight. Who's all going to the full moon bonfire?"

"Oh," Fay says, her spirits lifting. "I forgot that was tonight!"

I grimace, remembering the last party I went to with them. "Is this another kegger? Cause, I'm not sure I've recovered since the last one."

Sebastian laughs as he pulls Fay close to his side. "Nah, this isn't like that. It used to be a wolf event back in the day, but everyone goes now. There's a big bonfire, dancing, and some night games. It's a blast."

"Is there a crazy secret door?"

He shakes his head. "The staff knows about this party, but they leave the students alone as long as we agree not to drink." He glances across the cafeteria toward Xena and her group of friends. "*Some* people still bring alcohol, but that can't be helped."

I shake my head. "Well, I'm never drinking again. I made a fool of myself last time." I blush, remembering how I danced with Gabe and said awkward things to Alden. I haven't talked to Gabe since, and I'm more than okay with that.

Sebastian and Fay get lost in a discussion about the bonfire last year and when they're going to meet up tonight, but I pull my phone out and shoot off a text.

ME: "So…apparently there is some sort of party tonight."

Subtle, Ivy. It's only a minute before Alden responds.

ALDEN: "That's what I've heard. I planned on asking you to go with me, but I got a little sidetracked this morning…"

I blush and try to hide my goofy smile as my fingers fly over my phone screen.

ME: "What a shame. I would've liked to go to a party with you. The last one ended on a great note."

ALDEN: "I think I vaguely remember that…"
ALDEN: "Do you want to go with me tonight, Ivy? I believe I owe you a dance."

Now I'm grinning from ear to ear, and I don't care who sees.

ME: "I'd love to. Meet me out front at nine?"

ALDEN: "I'll be there. Bye, Ivy."

ME: "See you tonight, Alden."

Twinkling fairy lights shine along the path through the trees. Sebastian and Fay lead the way, holding onto one another as they whisper sweet things back and forth. I feel like I could float away in the serenity of the evening and drift off into the full moon above. The only thing keeping me grounded is Alden's warm hand in mine.

I sneak a glance at him, catching the hint of a smile on his handsome face. His hand squeezes mine gently as his eyes turn to meet mine. The blue of his irises sparkles against the glow of the lights surrounding us.

Alden raises one eyebrow. "Something on your mind?"

My cheeks blush with heat. "Nothing really, just...*you.*" My eyes widen as I realize what I just said out loud.

Alden's grin is incredible and he chuckles softly back at me. "What a coincidence. You're on my mind too."

I swear my heart flutters from his words. Aside from the day I found out that my parents passed, I got the worst news of my life just three days ago. Still, being with Alden this week has been the best time I've ever had. I want to live in this feeling for as long as I'm able, but I know reality will come crashing down sooner or later. *Likely sooner.*

"Here we are." Fay's sing-song voice brings me back to the moment.

The path ahead of us opens up to a large break in the evergreen trees. A roaring bonfire lights up the night, flickering in the center of a noisy crowd of students. The scent of campfire floods my senses, bringing with it feelings of nostalgia from camping trips with Lorelei and our parents. A lifetime ago.

I scan the throng of students and recognize some of my classmates, and there are a lot of unfamiliar faces as well. A small lake sits off to the side that's almost unnoticeable in the dark, sitting perfectly calm and still behind the ruckus. Bluetooth speakers blast a new DNCE song that makes everyone cheer.

"It's gorgeous out here," I say, breathless.

Alden tugs me closer to him and places his large hand on the small of my back. I look up at him and wonder if he realizes the crazy things he does to me with such a simple touch. He's grinning at something across the bonfire, and I follow his gaze to Silis.

"I should be embarrassed to be related to that kid." Alden laughs softly with a shake of his head. "I'm honestly just impressed, though."

Silis is surrounded by a group of girls that are giggling and gasping at some wild story he tells with unbridled enthusiasm. His arms raise wildly as his green eyes widen and then narrow while he talks. All of the freshman girls are enthralled by whatever he tells them, and I laugh right along with Alden.

"He's going to break so many hearts, and he won't even realize it." I sigh, feeling that place in my heart where Silis takes up his own little spot.

Alden spins me toward him so that my chest is pressed against his. "As long as your heart is safe, I'm good."

I nod. "My heart is better than it has ever been."

Alden's eyes hood as he stares down at me, and the slightest look of fear crosses his face before it's changed to a look I've come to love from him. The look that he gives me right before he kisses me.

I lick my lips in anticipation, but Sebastian's booming voice interrupts the thumping of my heart. He's too good at that. "We're going to dance. See ya guys later."

Fay grins at me as her mate drags her into the dancing crowd, leaving Alden and I alone. I spin back to find him still watching me. "Should we dance too?" I ask.

He shrugs. "That depends. Can you dance while not intoxicated?"

I blush and roll my eyes with a soft groan. "That was a one time thing." I hold up one finger for emphasis. "Now, you wanna dance or not?"

He chuckles and tugs me closer to him so that every breath I take is his. "I would love to dance with you, Ivy Hart."

CHAPTER 44

The moon is so bright above Alden and I while we dance as if we've done this together a million times. Our bodies fit together like they were made for the other, and I guess they sort of were. I wonder if this fated mate situation is as crazy to Alden as it is to me. Probably not.

I let my fingers dip into the hair at the base of Alden's neck as his hands on my hips sway me from side to side. His eyes never leave my face, and I'd kill to know what he's thinking about. Before I can ask him, he opens his mouth.

"I'm glad you still want to dance with me even though you're not wasted." He raises a single eyebrow as he leans in closer. "Though, you are significantly less handsy this time."

I roll my eyes and try to hide my smile. "Stop it. I'm still really embarrassed by how I acted that night."

Alden chuckles, the sound building like a steady fire. "You shouldn't be embarrassed. Even though I was halfway to losing my mind over you dancing with Gabe, I really enjoyed the rest of the evening." He pulls me tight against him and takes a deep breath as if he's breathing me in. "And, look at us now."

The melody in the air is sweet and slow, perfect for this moment. I don't have a response for him. All I can do is grin from ear to ear like a lunatic as he places a gentle kiss on my forehead.

Alden leans in close to my ear with a whisper that sends goosebumps to my toes. "What are you thinking about, Ivy?"

I stare up at him as he pulls his head back. "Actually, I was just wondering the same thing about you. Seems like our minds are in sync."

He gives my hips a little squeeze. "That's all thanks to our wolves. I guess yours is getting pretty active."

I shake my head. "What do you mean?"

Alden licks his bottom lip. "Well, our wolves are mates, and when we're together, they can feel that connection as strongly as we can. Even though your wolf isn't fully ready to shift, she is already wanting to reap the benefits of being mated."

"Are we *mated* now that we're…um, together?" *Yikes, that's a stupid question.* We haven't had the talk about our relationship yet, and now I'm pressing him to define it. I look away from him, trying to find a way to backtrack this conversation. "Nevermind. Don't answer that."

Alden's fingers slip below my chin and tug my attention back to him. "It's okay. I get that you have questions." He smiles, though it doesn't reach his eyes. "We aren't technically mated, no. We are mates, and we are tightening our bond by being close to one another, but the only way to officially mate is…"

I swallow hard. "Is to have…"

He nods. "Sex. Yes, it's the act of giving your body fully to your mate that seals the deal. It's how we claim one another, and give in to the bond completely."

I chew on my bottom lip, suddenly feeling really warm. "Okay, so…" *Move past it, Ivy. You can freak out later!* "You mentioned that my wolf wants the benefits of being mated. What benefits are you referring to?"

Alden smiles again, but I can't help this churning in my gut that tells me something is off with him. "So, you know how we want to be able to read one another's thoughts? Fated mates who complete their bond can communicate telepathically. That way, they are constantly in tune with the other's emotions, and they can communicate while shifted." My eyes widen as I try to imagine that. Alden continues. "Since we're feeling this now, our wolves are likely hoping for that connection. They're impatient for something that may or may not come."

I freeze in Alden's arms, my eyebrows scrunching together. "May or may not? Are you not sure that we'll get there?"

Alden blinks and looks away from me, his body slightly separating from mine. "We'll see. The future is never set in stone."

I pull back, not sure I'm reading the situation correctly. Does Alden not know if he wants to mate with me? Or is he saying that he doesn't believe I'll survive long enough to see that day? Either way, my heart breaks a little at his words. I want to press him for more answers, but people start to move around us excitedly, gathering into groups.

"What's going on?" I step away from Alden, but he grabs hold of my hand before I can lose him in the crowd.

"Are you guys ready for a treasure hunt?" A voice shouts over the music still floating around us. Students cheer loudly, some jumping up and down as they hoot and holler in excitement. "We go in sixty seconds!"

I look up at Alden, confusion clearly written across my face. A real smile lifts his plump lips as he leans into me to talk over the sound of the students. "It's called *Treasure in the Dark*. The students play it at the bonfire every year." He looks around us. "It can get a little wild."

Adrenaline courses through me as the air becomes thick with anticipation. "Are we going to play?"

Alden smiles down at me with his eyebrows raised high. "Do you want to play, Ivy?"

Someone yells the word "go" above the crowd, and all hell breaks loose as students rush off into the dark woods. I nod, my palms turning sweaty and my legs bouncing, ready to go. "Yeah, let's do it," I say, my eyes meeting Alden's.

He smiles a toothy grin as he grips tightly to my hand. "Okay, then. Let's run!"

CHAPTER 45

My heart is pounding, my palms and neck slick with sweat. Adrenaline pushes me forward through the dark shadows of the towering trees. Alden is the only thing keeping me from freaking out and running back to the bonfire that flickers in the distance now.

Alden tugs me behind a wide tree trunk, and I take a moment to catch my rapid breath. "Okay, so explain to me the purpose of this game."

Alden looks down at me, and I can barely see the blue in his eyes in the darkness. "*Treasure in the Dark* is like hide and seek, but with a few twists." He looks around and quickly drags me a few feet to the right to duck behind a bigger tree. "Everyone separates into teams, or some choose to go alone. The goal is to find this old wooden treasure box that's hidden each year." He pauses to listen for a moment before continuing. "The box is some antique that my grandfather kept in the school basement for years. It was empty until one day, probably forty or so years ago, a group of students decided to fill it with money and drop it in the woods as a game."

"This game," I add.

Alden nods and starts to walk through the trees again with me tucked in his side. "Yeah. It became a tradition. Each year, some seniors will fill the box with something of their choosing, and hide it on the night of the full moon bonfire. Whoever finds the box wins."

I look around for any sign of some old wooden box. "Sounds easy enough. Just a good old treasure hunt."

Alden stops in his tracks at the sound of twigs cracking behind us. He slips an arm around my waist and spins the two of us behind a mass of overgrown bushes. We crouch low in the shadows, our breaths mingling together between us.

Alden touches my cheek and shakes his head as he whispers. "It's not exactly that simple. I haven't told you about the sentries yet."

I gulp. "What the hell is a sentry?"

"The sentries guard the treasure box. This is where hide and seek gets interesting. If the sentires find us on our search for the treasure, they can capture us and take us back to the bonfire for execution."

I gasp as bile rises in my throat. "*What?*"

Alden places a finger against my lips to quiet me down. "It's all role playing, Ivy. It's cops and robbers. The sentries have to just touch someone, and that person forfeits their rights to the treasure. They have to go back to the bonfire and wait out the game."

A long breath leaves my body as I steady my racing heart. "Christ, I thought I was in the real life Hunger Games."

Alden laughs as he watches me under the light of the moon. "No worries there. I'm by your side, remember? The overprotective mate?"

My silly grin stretches my cheeks. "So, overprotective mate, you got a plan?"

He nods, raising back to his feet and dragging me with him. "I'm going to sniff out the treasure. That box is basically made of rotting wood. It's not too hard for my wolf to pick up the scent."

I watch Alden raise his nose in the air and take a long whiff. He turns his head from side to side before nodding toward my right. "That way. You ready?"

I squeeze his hand and take a steady breath. "Yup, lead the way, wolf boy."

Alden smiles as he starts to move quietly through the woods again. I try my hardest to be as stealthy as him, but it's amazing how light he is on his feet for such a large person. He has the grace of a wolf on the hunt, and it's incredibly sexy.

Every few yards, Alden pauses and pulls me behind a tree or some deadfall. I can still see the bonfire off in the distance, and I catch the occasional yell or scream of students getting caught by the sentries. Laughter floats through the night off and on, but suddenly the woods become eerily quiet.

I freeze, pressed against Alden's back where he has stopped moving and sniffs the air. He clenches my fingers in his and opens his mouth to tell me something just as two people dressed in black masks jump out from behind a small group of Aspen trees.

"Shit," Alden shouts, shoving me back a few feet as the sentries charge him.

I squeal in fear and excitement as I stumble backwards, away from the students in black. Alden dodges to the left, but another sentry about my size leaps onto his back with a less-than-scary growl.

"Alden," I yell, ready to save him from what I know isn't a real threat.

He turns to me with amusement on his face as he shrugs off the small person. "Run, Ivy! It's not too late!" It's incredibly dramatic, and I laugh at how ridiculous he sounds.

One of the larger sentries starts toward me, but I eke out a little scream as I glance once more at Alden's happy face, and then I dodge into the cover of darkness. I run along the moonlit woods, half giggling, half gasping for breath. Without Alden's wolf senses, it's hard to know which direction to go, but I don't want to just give up. I've never won a game before, and I think it would feel really great.

Once I realize the sentry hasn't followed me, I slow my pace and focus on searching for the treasure box with my eyes. I know what a treasure box should look like, but I've never seen this particular one. The night is incredibly quiet now that I'm all alone, and that small tendril of fear starts to wiggle around beneath my skin. *It's alright. I can still see the fire.*

I take a few deep breaths, trying to push that fear to the back of my mind. *I have a demon soul in my head, so this little game is the least of my worries.* I try not to laugh at the insanity of that particular thought process.

Something glinting in the moonlight catches my eye from the left. I whip my head in that direction and squint as I move my head around to find that little glow again. I take a few steps forward and my eyes widen at the sight of a literal treasure box sitting in the crook of a broken tree.

I gasp, my body filling with a newfound excitement. *Yes, yes, yes! I win!* I do a silent victory dance as I sneak toward the box, way more ecstatic than necessary. I step into the light of the moon that shines directly on the wooden box with straps of metal across the top.

I don't even have a second to gasp as a large hand covers my mouth, and I'm tugged against a hard body. I try to scream past the gloved hand, and I wiggle my body around to fight the grip of whoever has grabbed me. I throw my head back far enough to catch a glimpse of the black mask of a sentry.

I want to relax and go with the flow of the game, but this doesn't feel like a game. He's holding me too tight, and he's dragging me backwards with him. I can see the glow of the bonfire far ahead of me, but I'm being pulled in the opposite direction. Definitely not a part of the game.

Panic officially settles into me and I thrash around, kicking my feet and swinging my fists at any point of contact I can find. My elbow connects with the guy's ribs and his hand falls from my mouth.

I don't waste a second to scream at the top of my lungs. "Alden!"

The hand smacks against my mouth once more, but everything freezes as a low growl pierces the night behind me. It's not my captor. It's something else, something inhuman that's deep in the trees behind us.

I'm whipped around in the sentry's arms as his breath becomes ragged in my ear. Another rumbling growl comes from where I'm facing now, but the shadows ahead are too dark to see into. A new fear, having nothing to do with the sentry behind me, has taken hold of my heart.

"Ivy!" Alden's voice sparks a new hope inside of me, coming from the direction of the bonfire. I'm whirled in another circle. In a single breath, Alden bursts through the trees and his hands grab onto the person still holding me.

The sentry is dragged away from my body, and Alden rips his black mask off with a sharp growl from deep in his throat. I gasp at the face of my captor, my hands moving to my throat in shock.

"Gabe?" I squeak out his name. "Are you freaking kidding me? What the hell?"

Alden doesn't wait for Gabe to answer me. He throws a fist right into the pretty-boy's face with a loud crack. Gabe falls back onto the ground, gripping his nose in pain.

"It was just a prank," Gabe shouts, holding a hand up to stop Alden from continuing.

Alden growls again, his eyes black as he steps closer to Gabe. "What is wrong with you? You scared the shit out of Ivy, Gabe! This isn't funny!" He holds his fist high again. "Give me a reason not to kill you right now!"

Gabe stumbles to his feet, his nose dripping with blood. "I didn't hurt her, man! It was a joke, seriously!"

Alden turns to me with wild eyes. "Are you hurt, Ivy? I swear, if he hurt you at all, he's dead."

I blink a few times, swallowing my fear from moments ago, and I shake my head from side to side. "No, he didn't hurt me. I'm okay."

Alden lowers his fists and moves toward me. Only when his arms encircle my shoulders in warmth do I realize a crowd has formed around us. Students snicker and whisper to one another as they take in the scene before them.

I groan, digging my face into Alden's chest to hide my mortification. *Great. And I thought I could just play a little game.*

CHAPTER 46

"Are you going to be okay, Ivy?" Alden kneels beside my bed, his hands rubbing up and down my shaking arms. "You're sure you weren't hurt at all?"

I breathe in through my nose and out through my mouth, trying to rid myself of the shivers. "Yeah, I really am okay. I think it's adrenaline or something. I just can't stop shaking."

Alden's hands continue their soft caresses, but I can still see the fire in his eyes. The hidden fury. He clenches and unclenches his jaw, blowing out hot breaths. It has been like this since he dragged me out of the woods with him and walked me to my bedroom twenty minutes ago.

I raise my shaking hands and touch Alden's taut jaw. "Hey, stop worrying."

He closes his blue eyes tight and leans forward until his head is resting against my shoulder. It's a completely vulnerable move and I don't know how to react.

Alden takes a deep breath and his hands slip around my back. "Gabe is such an ass. I can't believe he could do that to you. I swear if he so much as looks at you again, I'll—"

"Alden," I say, cutting him off before he starts talking murder again. "Gabe's prank was idiotic, yes. But it's not the only reason I was so scared out there."

He leans his head back to look up at me with confusion. "What else were you afraid of? Did something else happen?"

I sigh, remembering that growl that stopped Gabe in his tracks. "There was an animal, I think. After Gabe grabbed me, he was taking me away when something started growling at us. I think it scared Gabe too."

Alden's eyebrows raise. "Did you see it?" I shake my head. "You've heard my wolf growl. Did it sound like that?"

I shrug. "I guess it was similar, but more menacing if that's possible, deeper. Maybe it was just my own fear that made it seem that way."

Alden stands from the ground and pulls me to my feet in front of him. "Maybe I'll run out there and listen for it. My wolf could use a run right now to relieve this anger inside of me."

I lay my hands on his chest, the shaking in my body significantly less than it was. "I don't want you getting hurt, Alden. What if it's something more dangerous than even you."

He smiles a little at that, his ego surely pumped up. "I'm glad you think I'm so *dangerous*, but I have to do something. I feel like I'm about to burst."

I bite down on my bottom lip, leaning into his chest as an idea fills my mind. "You know, a certain soul in my body is still suppressed. I think we could come up with another way to relieve your stress that doesn't involve you leaving me."

My heart pounds heavily in my chest as Alden's eyes darken and his eyelids flutter. He licks his lips much too slowly, and his fingers lace together at the small of my back. "Ivy, you're killing me here."

"I'd much rather be *kissing* you," I say, rising onto my toes so we're eye-to-eye. I don't know where this daring, honest part of me came from, but I'm glad for it.

Especially when he looks at me like that.

A deep groan leaves Alden's throat as he clings onto my waist and his head falls until his lips are just a fraction of an inch from mine. He doesn't kiss me just yet, only teases my lips with the tickle of his hot breath, and then just the brush of his bottom lip against mine. My eyes flick up to latch onto his as he watches me so close, taking in my reactions to him.

In just one more breath, my eager mouth is on his. My eyes flutter closed in sync with Alden's, and my body feels like it lights on fire as I melt into his chest. How can every kiss with him feel like the first? Like I've never been kissed before this moment.

With the supernatural speed of his wolf, Alden lifts me off my feet and lowers me back onto my bed. His body follows mine, barely breaking away from me for half a second. His weight stays off of me, but his heat is a heavy force all its own, both suffocating and life-giving.

Alden pulls his head back for just a moment to watch me pant like a dehydrated animal beneath him. If only he knew that I crave him more than I crave water.

His fingers leave my hip to brush a lock of hair from my cheek and then stroke a tingling trail down my neck. "You're so beautiful, Ivy." His voice is just a rough whisper, and it lights a new fuse inside of me.

I slip my hands behind his head and pull his lips back to mine, wasting no time to allow my tongue space to explore. Alden's hot tongue crashes with mine as he digs deeper, taking complete control over my mouth.

His hands are on my waist again, the pads of his thumbs stroking that bare skin that became exposed when he pressed me against my bed. He keeps his body off of mine, but I can't handle the distance. I throw my legs around his hips and lock my ankles together behind him.

"Ivy," Alden gasps my name out before falling against me finally.

His weight is intoxicating, and I've lost all sense of control, needing all I can get from this man. I've never been this close to someone, never even kissed a boy more than a peck on the lips. Yet, here I am, clinging to Alden with everything in me and ready for him to be mine.

Mine, my mind whispers to me. This time, though, I know it's my wolf. She wants this as much as I do.

"Take your shirt off," I whisper, breaking the kiss to reach for the hem of Alden's shirt.

I tug on the fabric, my fingers brushing against Alden's hard stomach, but his hand clamps over mine and stops me with black eyes focused on my gray ones. "Ivy, no."

I can feel my eyebrows press together. "What do you mean *no*?"

"I mean, we can't." His hands grab my thighs and he gently urges my legs off of him. I let them fall to the mattress, immediately feeling cold air separating us.

My heart still races from the last few minutes, but it slowly begins to ache as I watch the look in Alden's eyes. It's a look of being unsure, and a look of regret. Does he regret this?

I blink quickly, not wanting to get all emotional. "Do you not want to...to be mated to me?"

Alden's face scrunches up and he sits back on my bed. I suddenly feel all too vulnerable lying here in front of him, so I sit up too. He's so quiet as his eyes look everywhere in my room but at me. I draw my knees to my chest and wait for him to say something. Anything would do at this point.

Alden stands from my bed and finally looks down at me. "It's not that I don't want to be mated to you, okay? I just..."

"You just *what*?" *Tell me!*

He sighs and runs his fingers through his sandy-brown hair. "You should get to sleep, Ivy. It's been a long night and Fay will probably be here soon."

That's not an answer. "Okay," I say, trying not to let my throat close up.

His eyes land on me once more and he quickly leans in to plant a kiss on my forehead before he leaves my room without another word. I fall back onto my bed, my chest aching and an irritating tickle behind my eyes from the tears that want to come. I don't understand what just happened, but I felt on top of the world in one moment, and buried beneath it in the next. *Is this what love does?*

As if she knows I'm feeling alone, a text pops up on my phone from Fay.

FAY: "On my way back to the room. Bast and I found the treasure, and then we heard what happened to you. Want to watch a movie and eat junk food?"

I smile at my phone, but I don't respond to her. She'll be here in a minute, and I'll pretend to be asleep. I may not want to be alone right now, but I also don't want to talk about it. If this is love, maybe I don't want it.

CHAPTER 47

Fay shakes her head, her arms flailing around as she leads the way to our dorm room. "Who does that? The treasure should have been *big* money! Do you even know how rich some of these kids are?"

I pull my backpack higher on my shoulder and laugh as I trail behind my animated friend. School is out for the day, and we're heading back to our room. Fay has been talking the entire time about the treasure hunt last night, and despite my less-than-fun experience, her story is entertaining.

"So, it was just pennies?" I ask. "Did you count them?"

She scoffs. "Yeah, Sebastian counted them after he got back to his room. He said there were a thousand of them."

Her violet eyes are round as she turns to me. "Who in the world has a thousand pennies sitting around?"

I laugh as we start down the third floor hall. "Well, you and Sebastian now have a thousand pennies sitting around."

Her glare isn't the least bit intimidating as she fires an angry huff back at me. "Whatever. At least I got to dance."

We approach our dorm room and I smile at the visitor sitting outside our door. "Hey, Silis. What are you doing here?"

He stands with his signature grin. "I didn't get to dance with my girls last night. I wanted to come make you both feel bad for not asking me to dance."

I shake my head and raise an eyebrow at him. "How could we even reach you through the throng of freshmen girls drooling at your feet? I think you had plenty of female attention last night, Si."

"Seriously, player," Fay adds with a shove to Silis's arm.

Silis smiles wider and his cheeks turn a little pink. "You both know I'll never love those girls the way I love you." He winks, making Fay and I both laugh. "Anyways, I really wanted to come talk to Ivy." He turns his green gaze on me. "Wanna go for a walk?"

Before I can answer, Fay tugs my bag off my arm and nudges me toward Silis. "Yes, please get her to talk. She's been all moody today and won't tell me why."

My jaw drops as I turn to Fay. "Hey! I'm not moody!"

She gives me a knowing look. "You pretended you were asleep last night when I got back, and you've been dragging your feet with that sad look on your face. Remember, I'm part Seer. I know how to read you, girl."

Right, I always forget that.

"So, walk with me?" Silis asks again.

I roll my eyes but nod. "Yes, let's walk." I look back at Fay. "Thank you, bestie."

She gives me the sweetest smile before disappearing into our room. I spin back to Silis and start walking as he leads the way.

"So, I heard what happened last night. You okay?"

I shrug. "Yeah, mostly. I'm just embarrassed."

Silis nudges my arm with his elbow. "Why would you be embarrassed? Gabe should be the one embarrassed for acting like a tool in front of everyone."

We take the grand staircase, our feet falling together on the polished wood. I get what Silis means about Gabe, but he'll always be the golden boy, the prince of the dragons. I'm just a messed up girl, and the students here know it.

I shake my head as we land on the main lobby floor of the school. "Gabe acted like an idiot, and I get that. I just wish I was…tougher, maybe. He wasn't even trying to hurt me, and I flailed around like a weak little girl. Anyone else here could have fought him off."

"Come here, Ivy." Silis sits down on a black metal bench. He pats the bench seat to his side, and I slide in beside him. "Even Fay's mom told us you were meant to be strong. It's not your fault that you haven't had the time to explore that part of you. You'll get there."

I tilt my head toward Silis and press my lips into a thin line. "Si, I think we both know that I don't have time on my side." Saying it out loud makes my fate feel heavy on my chest. "I can't fight her, Silis. I'm going to lose." My voice cracks on the last words.

Silis's usual perky face falls as he slips a long arm around my shoulders and pulls me into his side. I don't need to tell him who "*her*" is. He already knows that I'm talking about Sage. She's going to kick me out of my own body as soon as I shift, and that thought terrifies me. I only have a month to go until my death.

"Ivy, don't give up." Silis squeezes my shoulders. "You have people that love you, and we can't let you lose." His arms are comforting, but his words don't land like they should. I feel...defeated.

I lean back and try to change the subject. I won't pretend that I have faith in my future, but I also can't stand to see Silis worry over me. "So, you love me, huh? I don't know how your brother will feel about that."

Silis rolls his green eyes and his lips curl up just a little at the corners. "I may have been into you for like five minutes, Ivy, but I am not about to go head-to-head with Alden over you. You're like my family now. Practically my sis-in-law." He winks.

I scoff. "I don't know about that. Alden can be incredibly jealous, but I have a feeling that he doesn't want me around forever."

Silis's laugh is sharp, like a loud clap in the air. "You're his fated mate, Ivy. Trust me, he wants you."

I shake my head, not so sure after last night. "I think he's going to eventually reject me. I can't get him to open up to me, and it's like he carries around this impenetrable shield to keep me at a distance."

"Is this why Fay said you're moody today?" Silis eyes me. "Did something happen with you and Alden?"

I shrug, not knowing how else to show my utter confusion over my mate. "It's embarrassing, Si. I can't talk to you about this."

He jabs me in the ribs with one of his long fingers. "Knock that off. What in all the time you've known me has given you the idea that I'm shy about talking? Lay it on me, sis."

I laugh, but it's not full. "Okay, well, Alden and I have been…" I swallow and look around the empty room before lowering my voice. "We've been getting close, uh…physically." *Oh, gosh.*

"And?" Silis asks, completely unphased.

I squirm in my seat. "Don't look at me while I say this." I stare at my hands on my lap. "I wanted to officially mate with him. I'm ready, but Alden isn't. If he really felt the way about me that I do about him, he wouldn't wait another minute."

I can hear Silis's long sigh beside me, and I barely peek at his thoughtful face out of the corner of my eye as he leans back against the metal bench. He seems to be mulling over my admission, but his silence is torture.

"Are you going to say anything?" I practically snap at him.

He chuckles and leans forward again. "I'm just trying to figure out a way to tell you that you're an idiot without sounding so harsh."

My jaw drops open at my normally sweet friend. "Excuse me?"

He laughs for real this time, not at all caring that I'm offended. "I'm sorry, okay? It's just…" He sighs again. "You are overthinking this like a girl." He holds up a hand to halt my lashing out. "Do you remember how Alden acted when you first got to Wolfe Asylum?"

"Yeah."

"Well, he was quiet, brooding all the time. I almost never saw a smile on his face, and as his brother, that killed me." Silis's green eyes meet mine. "He hasn't had a happy life, Ivy. He barely knew Grandpa Wolfe, his mom's dad. Hell, he barely knew his own mom. The only role model he had in his early years was his father, and that man was..."

I nod, understanding. "Alden told me how he abused him after his mom passed."

Silis shakes his head. "I don't know what all Alden told you, but the details would make you sick, Ivy. I know I'm this happy, goofy kid all the time, but when I think of the pain Alden's dad inflicted on him daily, his constant flinching and waking up screaming in the night after Stella brought him here...I want to go find that guy and rip his black heart right out."

I blink rapidly at Silis. I've never heard him speak like this, and it's heartbreaking.

He continues. "My point is that, while you're worried Alden doesn't want to mate with you, Alden is probably doing everything in his power to distance his demon side from your good heart. If I were to guess, he's not pushing you away, he's holding himself back."

Everything in my body sags at those words. *He's holding himself back.* Alden would never hurt me, but he feels like he could because of his damn father. How do I convince him that he's not that person?

Silis shifts in his seat, his knee knocking into mine to bring me out of my sad thoughts. "Did you know that

Alden is in line to take over Wolfe Asylum after my mom?"

I sit up with wide eyes. "No, I had no idea. That's great, though."

"Yeah, except that he has refused. Mom told me that it was because he told her he's not worthy to run this place." Silis shakes his head. "Can you believe that?"

My heart breaks a little more. "You know what, I can believe he said that now."

A tingling tickles up my spine and I would know that feeling anywhere. I whip my head to the side and see Alden standing beside the grand staircase, his hands in his pockets and an angry look on his handsome face.

I jump to my feet. "Alden, hey."

He shakes his head. "Sorry, I didn't mean to interrupt your private conversation about my shortcomings." His lips are in a thin line as he speaks with thick sarcasm in his rough voice. He looks from Silis to me. "I'll just go." With that, he turns and walks away.

Silis nudges me forward. "Go talk to him."

Well, crap.

CHAPTER 48

"Alden!" I call after him, running through the school to catch up to his retreating back. *Why does he have to move so damn fast?* "Stop walking and talk to me."

He doesn't stop. I follow behind him, getting a long view of the black t-shirt he wears that's tight on his broad back. His muscles flex beneath the fabric as he stalks away from me. His hands are clenched into fists at his sides, and every step he takes is practically a stomp across the brick floors.

Alden passes the library and pauses when he reaches his bedroom door. He whips around to stare down at me, halting me in my tracks, and the hurt written across his strong features is enough to make me lose my train of thought.

"You wanted to talk. Then, talk, Ivy." His voice is rough and laced with anger as his tight jaw ticks against his skin.

I play with the hem of my shirt, suddenly feeling anxious. "You don't need to be angry with me or Silis, okay? We weren't saying anything bad about you."

Alden huffs out a harsh breath. "So, talking about how I'm not worthy to run the school isn't bad?"

I take a step toward him. "Neither of us said you weren't worthy to be the headmaster some day. That's what *you* said to Stella."

"And, I said that to my aunt in private. I told her how I was feeling, and not so that it can be gossiped about in the school lobby!" He throws his hands in the air.

My own temper begins to flare now. "Silis and I weren't gossiping, Alden! How could you even say that?" I take another step, just a foot from his pulsing heat. "We care about you, and as much as you choose to overlook that, it's the truth."

His dark blue eyes narrow on me. "Why couldn't you just come and talk to me instead of going behind my back to get information from *my* family?"

"Going behind your back? Really?" *Okay, I'm pissed.* "Silis isn't just your family. He's my friend, and I trust him. And, he will actually open up to me instead of clamming up and running away when he starts to feel something!" I flinch at my own harsh tone, but I hold my ground.

Alden's eyes widen slightly and he takes a step back. He's watching me with so much hurt in his blue eyes. I want to slap him and hug him at the same time, my head warring with my heart.

326

Alden straightens out his shoulders and crosses his strong arms over his chest. "You'll never understand," he says, barely above a whisper.

I cross my own arms, suddenly feeling too exposed. I shrug. "You're right. I'll never understand you... until you let me." I close my eyes for a moment and then turn on my heel and leave Alden standing there. It's my turn to run away.

ME: "Why are boys so complicated and dumb?"

LOR: "Too bad they don't teach Understanding Boys 101, huh?"
LOR: "Wanna talk about it, Little Bear?"

ME: "No. I just wanted to see if you had the answers to the questions of the universe. Particularly the one about stupid, good-looking boys."

LOR: "Hey, good-looking is a positive! But sadly I don't have the answers. If I did, I wouldn't have dated Johnny in high school. *vomit emoji*

ME: "Ew. Yeah, that guy was the worst. Why am I even asking you for advice?"

LOR: "Hey! I'm just letting you know that everyone experiences heartbreak. You sure you don't want me to call you and hash it out?"

ME: "No, thanks though. Love ya."

LOR: "Love you too, sis."

I stick my phone in the back pocket of my jeans and take a deep breath of the warm summer air. I do want Lorelei to call me, but I can't give her all of the details. I can't tell her that I'm fighting with my fated mate, or that I'm terrified about the extra soul inside of me. *I wonder what they'll tell her when I'm gone.*

I groan loudly, stomping my feet across the soft grass beside the Asylum. The sun is setting, and all I wanted was to be able to breathe fresh air for a minute before I head upstairs. Fighting with Alden the other night has left me with a pain in my chest.

I've avoided him to the best of my ability, not that it has been hard. He seems to be making an effort to stay out of my way too. Training class was the hardest yesterday when Alden didn't show up. Sebastian is great at picking at me until I want to scream at him. I couldn't talk to my friend, though. Seeing the hurt in Alden's eyes after talking with Silis has killed my talking mood.

Now, I'm just alone.

There's a cool breeze tonight that has a way of calming me just enough to keep me upright. I close my eyes to bask in the feel of the fading sun on my cheeks and the crisp breath in my lungs. I watch the trees of the forest sway and a few birds lift off to find their loved ones. I love it here.

The soft pad of footsteps has me turning toward the school. The physical training teacher, Mr. Greyson is walking beside the building with his hands in his pockets and his head hung low. He looks up and freezes when he spots me.

"Hey, Mr. Greyson," I say, giving him a small wave. He's an alright teacher, but I've always felt this coldness from him toward me. Just as expected, he doesn't smile back at me.

"Miss Hart," he says simply, his brown eyes narrowing a little. He doesn't continue walking away like I expect. Instead, he takes a few steps in my direction. "What are you up to out here this evening?"

Small talk? Really? I shrug. "I just needed some fresh air, I guess. I've had a lot on my mind."

Mr. Greyson nods, his frown deepening. "I'm aware of your affliction. That can't be easy to live with."

I'm taken aback. "Uh…what do you mean?"

He tilts his head and looks at me as if I'm stupid. "Your body isn't your own, is it?" I don't know how to respond, but he takes another step my way. "You know, Sage Whitaker hurt a lot of us shifters." He says her name with a growl to his tone.

I swallow, suddenly feeling uncomfortable. "I do know that, Mr. Greyson. I'm sorry."

"You're sorry?" He snaps out the words. "You're a kid. You don't know anything about that time. About the loved ones that woman murdered. The lives she ended!"

I take a step back, fear building in my bones at the anger in his voice. "Mr. Greyson, I understand that Sage was evil. I'm going to do whatever I can to make sure she goes away for good."

He snarls at me, his brown eyes darkening. "I saw that boy grab you that night, Miss Hart. You crumbled like a human, weak and scared in his arms." He steps closer once more. "You don't have the strength to stop her, and we both know that."

I try to wrap my head around his words, and realization hits me like a runaway truck. "Were you out there the night of the bonfire? Was that you that I heard? The growl…"

Mr. Greyson doesn't acknowledge my questions. His eyes shift completely to black as he cracks his neck to the side. "I can't let Sage come back. *I won't.* May the gods forgive me."

Someone help me.

CHAPTER 49

I spin away from Mr. Greyson as a low growl rumbles from his chest, and I run for my life. He's not going to let me live while Sage lives inside of me. I wish I could blame him for this, but how can I? There's a monster in my mind, and she can never come back.

Still, I run. I'm not ready to give up. I don't want Lorelei to lose the only family she has left. I don't want to die without telling Alden that I love him, because I really do.

The cracking of bones and the crash of a body against the dirt come from behind me. I know that sound. The sound a body makes as it shifts into an animal. Fear has gripped me and I can't turn back to see the beast that's about to tear me to pieces.

Fight him! Kill him before he kills us! I gasp, all of the air leaving my lungs as that familiar voice floods my mind. It's Sage.

"Get out of my head!" I scream, hoping she can hear me as I hit the steps to the side door of the school.

Instead of listening to me, I can feel Sage's soul writhe inside of me, tugging and clawing at my insides. She's trying to take control, and I'm not prepared for it at all. She spins my body around to face the incoming threat, and if I could, I would scream at the huge brown wolf that's barreling toward me.

The large, furry body lunges for me, and Sage makes me jump to the side, avoiding the impact of fangs against flesh. With the skills of a warrior, my body spins around, and I leap over the wolf's back, causing the animal to trip over his own legs trying to turn after me.

Sage is helping me fight back, but I know she's not doing this for me. She's doing this to preserve this body for the day she'll need it. All I can do is allow her to fight for me.

I watch my hands clamp onto a metal rod in the ground beside a newly planted tree. The rod is supposed to support the growth of the tree, but I rip it out of the ground instead, using strength that I never knew I had.

My arms raise with the rod held like a baseball bat in front of me. Mr. Greyson snarls at me, his wolf teeth dripping with saliva as he stalks closer. If I were in control, I would run inside and scream for help, but Sage is down for a fight.

Come and get me, mutt. She snarls right back at him from within my mind.

As if the wolf can hear her, he charges forward, only to get hit from the side by a mass of sandy-brown fur. I recognize Alden's wolf immediately as it tumbles with Mr. Greyson in the grass. Both of the wolves snap their jaws at one another, the sound like swords clashing.

I can only watch as Sage keeps us put with the rod in hand. Mr. Greyson bites into Alden's neck, but he's shoved off quickly. Alden whirls around to growl and latch his teeth onto the teacher's back. Mr. Greyson howls in pain, his large brown head thrown back.

He shakes Alden off, though, and then he gets his teeth into Alden once again. My mate is the one to howl in pain this time, his hind leg going limp from the force of Mr. Greyson's fangs digging into it.

"Alden!" I cry out, but I still can't move. *Help him!* I yell to the demon inside of me, but she doesn't even try to help.

Mr. Greyson whips back to me, his black nose scrunching up as he bares his blood-stained teeth, his ears pointed to the sky. Alden is too hurt to follow him as the teacher barrels toward me once again.

My body hops from foot to foot without my assistance, and as the wolf gets closer, I lunge to the side, faster than I have ever been. I twist on my toes in an expert move and plunge the metal rod right into the side of the huge wolf.

He whines, his chocolate-brown body falling to the earth in a bloody heap. He raises his head, trying with all of his might to get to me, but Alden's wolf stumbles forward and latches onto the teacher's neck. With one snap, it's over.

In the next instance, the solid force of Sage in my body dissipates, and I can feel her retreat back to the shadows of my mind. Just like that, I drop to the floor.

ALDEN

I watch as Ivy's body shivers in front of me, and then she suddenly drops to the grass, her knees giving out beneath her. I call my wolf back, forcing the shift as fast as I can while trying to use the magic to keep my lower half covered. I don't even care as long as I can get to her.

I want to roar in pain at the slice in my thigh thanks to Mr. Greyson's bite. *Dammit, Mr. Greyson.* I never imagined he could be capable of something like this. *And now I've killed him.*

Sweat coats my body and I fall to my knees as the shift completes. I crawl around the dead body in front of me, and throw my arms around Ivy's waist. I hoist her off the ground and brush the damp hair from her face.

"Hey, Ivy. Come on, baby. Wake up." There's so much I want to say to her. I can't let her leave me.

Ivy's eyelids flutter as she comes to, and I sigh in relief. I'm worried about rushing her, but I need to know if it's really still Ivy inside of there. I know it wasn't her that fought Mr. Greyson, and that knowledge scares the shit out of me.

Ivy's shaking hands lift to grab my bare shoulders and she slowly raises her head like it weighs a ton. Her beautiful gray eyes open up and she tries to smile up at me. "Alden," she whispers.

"Hey, beautiful," I whisper back, wanting to cry like a big baby knowing that my Ivy is still in there.

I hoist her higher in my arms, turning her away from Mr. Greyson's shifted body. He's back to his human form now that he's dead, and she doesn't need to see that. Hell, I wish I never saw it.

"Alden, are you okay? You got hurt..." She trails off, her eyes scanning my body. She spots the blood that still drips from my thigh, and she gasps with a hand over her throat.

I take her hand in mine and lay my forehead against hers. "I'm okay, I promise. I heal fast, remember?" She nods, but a tear drips from her eye. "Don't cry."

She looks into my eyes, her lip quivering. "Mr. Greyson wanted to kill me. Sage, she..." New tears fill her round eyes.

I shush her, tugging her trembling body closer to mine. "I know what Sage did. I could tell it wasn't you, baby."

Ivy shakes her head. "Gosh, I love the sound of you calling me baby, but how can you even give me a cute little pet name, knowing that *that* woman took control of me? It was so easy for her."

I touch her cheek, trying to get her to focus on me. "Stop. You are *mine*, do you hear me? I don't care what Sage tries. She *cannot* take you away from me, and nothing she does can make me look at you differently."

Ivy sniffles, but she nods her head. "Is Mr. Greyson dead?"

I clench my teeth together, but I nod. "I killed him, Ivy. I didn't know what else to do." I close my eyes tightly. "He wasn't a bad person."

I can feel her small hands against my cheeks. Her soft lips gently kiss the corner of my mouth, causing my eyes to open again. "Alden, you're right. He was just a man with vengeance in his heart. I can't even blame him for wanting me dead if it stopped Sage, but *you* saved me." She sighs, her eyes searching mine. "Did you hear that? You saved my life, and you cannot be mad at yourself for that."

I nod, but I can't get rid of that guilt inside of me. I'd do it all over again to save Ivy, but killing never gets easier. Maybe there's hope for me after all.

Ivy sits up in my lap, her shoulders straightening out like they do when she's mad. "Sage violated my body, Alden. Every move she made, every time she drew strength and speed out of me to fight, she took those things from *my* wolf." She wipes the wetness from her cheeks. "I will never let her control me like that, but she gave me a gift today."

I can feel my eyebrows scrunch together. "What do you mean by that?"

"I mean, Sage showed me what *I'm* capable of. Sure, she was trying to save herself, but she may not realize that she gave me the push I needed. Now I know I'm strong enough and fast enough to fight. My wolf is inside of me, and I'm not going to let some demon with an evil soul end my life before it has even begun." Her face shows true resolve. "I'm going to need your help training, and when my birthday comes, I'm going to kick her ass out of my body for good."

Pride fills my chest as I look into this girl's eyes. She's ready to fight, and I am more than ready to help her.

Nobody is going to take my mate from me, and if I have to kill again, I'll do it for her. For the girl that I love.

PART

6

CHAPTER 50

"Ahh!" I shout, twisting my body to the left, barely dodging a stream of fire to the face. I catch myself on my knees, skidding against the soft earth, and then whip my head around in anger. "That was too close, Sebastian!"

The massive, black-scaled dragon huffs at me, steam billowing out of his large nostrils. He stomps his meaty feet against the ground and then throws his head back. If I were betting, I'd bet he was laughing at me right now.

Fay steps up to Sebastian's side, her head reaching the top of one of his legs. "Honestly, Ivy. Even though that was a jerk move on Bast's end…" She punches him in the leg, and I doubt he even felt it. "That twist you did was wicked fast, and I'm impressed."

"Seriously, babe," Silis adds, immediately flinching when Alden's ferocious wolf growls beside him. "I mean, *Ivy*. I've never seen you move that fast!"

My friends all grin at me, except for Alden who flashes his white fangs in what I'm guessing is a grin, but looks more terrifying than anything. I chuckle at him and shake my head. "Don't ever make that face again, Alden. You look like you have rabies."

His mouth closes and he trots up to me to rub his warm body against my shoulder. I run my hand along his back, having to reach to tangle my fingers in his soft fur. He curls himself around me and brings his nose to mine where he licks me from chin to forehead.

"Ugh," I laugh, whipping my wet face.

Fay giggles and wraps her arms around Sebastian's thick leg. "We better get inside. It's going to rain any minute and *wet dog* is not my favorite smell."

Alden snorts in anger, making us all laugh. My laughter falls short though, and my heart aches as I think about going inside Wolfe Asylum when I still have so much work to do.

I wave at my friends. "You guys go. I'm going to practice a little more before I come in."

Fay nods in understanding as she and the guys turn toward the trail that leads back to the school. "You sure?" She asks over her shoulder.

I smile and nod back at her. "Yes, I'm positive."

The three of them take off, disappearing beyond the trees, leaving just me and Alden. I turn toward the light brown wolf and give him a little pet on his neck. "You can go too, you know? We've been at this all day and I know you must be tired."

He lowers his head, pressing his massive, wolfy forehead into my chest. I kiss the top of his head, and then he backs away as his body starts to shift in front of me. I don't know if I'll ever get used to this sight.

It has been a month since the day I decided to start getting my butt into gear. The day that Alden had to save my life yet again, and I chose to start making an effort to save *myself*. Alden has been out here in these woods beside Wolfe Asylum with me almost every single afternoon, training, fighting, running. Doing everything possible to build up my strength and turn me into a fighter.

Most of the time, Fay, Sebastian, and Silis join us, like tonight. Bast and Alden will shift and teach me how to fight against their massive sizes and speed. Even Stella has been out here, her gorgeous wolf wrestling with Alden, showing me some moves in the form I'll one day take.

Fay and Silis have been incredible with hand-to-hand combat and strength training. I've come a long way in four weeks, but I don't think I'll ever feel ready to face Sage.

I close my eyes as Alden shifts, and I turn away from him, knowing the look he'll have in his beautiful eyes. The look of a man that worries about his mate. He'll want me to go inside and take a break. To sleep. But how can I go inside now when I turn eighteen in four days…

Thick, warm arms encircle me from behind. Alden pulls me against his bare chest and his chin rests on my shoulder, our faces side-by-side. "Ivy, look at me."

I sigh into his hold, feeling like I'm coming home every time he puts his arms around me. I shake my head, though. I love looking at this man, but I can't. Not now.

I lay my head back against his chest. "I'll look at you if you promise not to make me go inside."

He growls, a little of his wolf still sticking around. "Ivy, you need—"

"No, Alden!" I cut him off. "I don't need rest. I don't need fun or to study textbooks and practice tests when my life could be ending in four damn days."

I shove away from him, taking a few steps forward as the slow trickle of raindrops starts to fall against my face and arms. It feels so good on my strained muscles.

Alden steps in front of me, fresh rain dripping down his perfect torso. I take in his body, just a pair of black shorts resting on his hips. His sandy-brown hair a mess from shifting and now getting doused in rain. Gosh, why does he have to look so good covered in sweat and rain?

His blue eyes pierce me, and he licks his rain-covered lips. "I won't tell you to go inside, but will you do one thing for me?"

I shrug. "That depends. Are we going to keep training?"

He takes a step toward me, one of his large hands cupping my face. "I'll train with you if you want." His lips curl up in a teasing smile. "But, training in the rain calls for a different kind of fighting."

The drops have become a full-on shower now, drenching everything around us. "What kind of fighting can we do in the rain?"

Alden is grinning now, and I love that look so much that I want to pounce on him. His hands fall to my waist and he steps forward until our bodies are flush together, making me gasp from the contrast of his heat in the cool rain.

He presses a tiny kiss to my nose before suddenly lifting me into the air and shouting, "mud wrestling!"

Then, Alden's arms wrap around me and I squeal as he drops me into a puddle of mud. His body crashes on top of mine, and he uses his large hands to scoop mud and spread it all over my body.

"Oh my gosh, Alden! Stop it!" I'm twisting and turning under him, trying to free myself, but I can't help the burst of laughter that trickles past my lips.

He laughs with me, finally stopping his incredible torture, and he drags me onto his lap, covered head-to-toe in brown goop while rain continues to shower us from above.

I straddle his hips and wrap my arms around his neck, a real smile stretching my muddy face. "I needed this, Alden. Thank you."

He smiles back at me, his firm hands holding tightly to my hips. "You're welcome. I'll do anything to make you smile like that, Baby. Anything."

My heart melts, even with the cold rain pelting my skin. He knows I love when he calls me Baby. I lean forward and press my lips gently against his wet ones. Rain drips down our faces, slipping between our mouths as they part just enough for me to run my tongue along Alden's lips.

He groans against me, his hands moving to my back, pressing me hard against his chest as his tongue tangles with mine. The mixture of Alden's signature scent, the heat of his breath, and the taste of cold rain on his lips has me feeling all kinds of crazy things.

But I owe him some payback.

I slip one hand into his messy hair, and with my other one, I scoop up a handful of mud and lean back to slap the mud against the side of his stunned face.

His dark, hungry eyes fly open and a wide grin stretches his freshly kissed lips. "Oh, you did *not* just do that."

I giggle and crawl backwards off of his lap. "Hey, you started it, wolf boy."

Alden's eyes become wild as they narrow on me and he growls low and dangerous. If it wasn't for the smirk on his handsome face, I'd be terrified, but I know this man. I know his heart.

"You better run, Ivy Hart." His voice is growly and deep as he climbs to his knees.

Okay, I'm a little terrified, but in an exhilarating way. "Catch me if you can, big bad wolf."

With that, I jump to my feet and take off at a sprint toward the school. At least I'm running now. I *did* say I needed to train tonight, and I can't imagine a better way to do it than this.

CHAPTER 51

I slowly twist the door handle to my dorm room, trying my best not to wake Fay. Water drips from the ends of my black hair, and I carry my muddy shoes in one hand while walking barefoot across the hardwood floor. I'm a mess from wrestling with Alden out in the summer storm, running through the woods and being hunted down by the sexy wolf of my dreams. I'm faster than I was when I started my training, but Alden had no trouble keeping up with me.

Just moments ago, he left me dripping wet at my doorstep with a searing kiss against my lips before he trudged off looking like a muscly mud monster. Thankfully, it's well past dark and the other students are all fast asleep, including my snoring roommate. I never knew vampires slept so hard, but Fay has proved all of the stories wrong.

I tip-toe past her bed and slip into our shared bathroom, hoping that a quick shower won't be too loud. There's no way I'm climbing into bed with how disgusting I am right now.

After a good twenty minutes of scrubbing and trying to heat up my frozen limbs, I dress in my fuzziest pajamas and drop silently into my bed with a long sigh.

This is the part of the day that I hate the most. The part where the world is quiet and my mind begins to think too much. It's also the time when I am all too focused on *her*. Sage.

When my body is spent and I find the slightest bit of comfort, that second soul inside of me stirs. She knows what I've been doing this past month, and the idea that nothing is secret from her chills me to the bone.

My first shift comes in just four days, on my eighteenth birthday. Ever since the day that the school's physical training teacher attacked me, I've spent every day training for the day my wolf finally appears.

Just thinking of that day has images flashing across my mind. Mr. Greyson's large wolf chasing me, his threats to end my life so that Sage doesn't get the chance to take over my body and wreak havoc on the supernatural world again. Mr. Greyson had no faith in my ability to fight off Sage's possession, and he was right. Sage easily took control of me to fight him, and I was utterly helpless to stop her.

Some students saw the fight that day. Word spread fast about how Alden came to my rescue and killed a teacher. Stella put rumors to rest after that, alerting the students and faculty about what's been happening to me. She urged the others to understand and to trust that the situation is under control. People gawk at me more than ever now, though. Constant fear rests in their wide eyes when I pass them in the halls. I'm the girl with the boogeyman inside of me. I'm a ticking time bomb.

Even though Mr. Greyson lost his life that day, I learned a valuable lesson. I'm more powerful than I thought possible. I *can* fight Sage, and *win*. Every day I learn more about the strength I have within me, and each time I harness that strength, the easier it is. Sage may know that I'm training for our upcoming battle, but she has no idea what she's up against.

I won't let you cast me out of my body, Sage. I speak inside of my mind, hoping the demon witch is listening. As I've gotten stronger, I have also been able to communicate with the voice inside of me easier. It's not a fun development, but at least Sage mostly hides away when I get close to Alden.

A high-pitched cackle of laughter pierces the back of my mind. *You will have no choice in the matter, child. You can't kill me.*

I roll on my bed, staring up at the ceiling. *I'll win our fight. This is my body, and I was made for it. You're just a hitchhiker who will be thrown to the side of the road.*

Hmmm. Her voice hums inside me. *I suppose you could reject me, by some miracle. It's a good thing there are other willing bodies that will welcome me with more open minds.*

I startle at those words. There's no way she can just jump from body to body...can she? She will try to overtake me with her strength, and it will take a strong will to fight her off. This is what I've been preparing for. What I've been hoping for.

When I reject you from me, your soul will die. That's the end of it. I say the words firmly, but I really want to ask them as a question. Of course, she likely won't answer.

I close my eyes after a long break of silence, hoping for just a little bit of sleep. The haze of sleep starts to fill me when Sage's voice speaks softly as if from far away.

There is a difference between being cast out and being killed. Be sure you know that difference before you come head-to-head with me, child.

Sage's final words from last night keep replaying in my head. I haven't been the best student at Wolfe Asylum lately, but all day it has felt like I'm not even in the same realm as my classmates. I'm trapped in my head where it feels like I have no hope.

I make my way through the cafeteria, smiling softly as I spot my group of friends at our usual table. The routine has been the same for a few weeks now. We meet for an early dinner and then head out to our training spot in the woods where they all beat the crap out of me until sundown.

I laugh at myself, surprised that I look forward to these training sessions anymore. As painful as Sebastian's dragon fire is, each session brings me closer to reaching my potential. And Alden's healing touch after each injury isn't so bad either.

"There's our girl," Silis chimes, his green eyes sparkling as he scoots his chair over to give me room between him and Alden.

"*My* girl." Alden punches Silis in the arm and then drags over an empty chair from the table behind him. "Here," he says, taking my hand and pulling me down beside him.

I place a quick kiss on his cheek. "Thank you."

Fay and Sebastian sit side-by-side across from us, their bodies always entwined in one way or another. I open up my foil-wrapped burrito and take a steamy bite, practically starving lately. I guess it's a side effect of my wolf coming to the surface.

Alden's warm hand lands on my thigh, causing my entire body to tingle as I almost purr. *Another fun side effect of the coming change.* "So, what are we leading with today?" He asks the group. "Ivy and I did some sprinting last night, so I suggest weight training." He turns to me with a quick wink and I melt right here and now.

"Oh," Fay says sadly. "I guess I forgot to text you guys. Bast and I have to study for finals tonight."

I blink up at them as Silis speaks beside me. "I do too, actually. I haven't exactly been focused on school work these days…" he shifts his gaze to me, apology in his eyes. "Not that I'd change a thing, Ivy. Helping you has been more than worth my time, but I need one night to catch up."

I touch his arm. "I get it. You don't need to feel bad." I speak to the entire group. "We've been working hard together lately, and I'm truly grateful. If I survive this, we'll still need to move on with our lives. School is important."

"*When*, Ivy," Fay says, her beautiful, violet eyes connecting with mine. "*When* you survive this, we will graduate and do incredible things in our lives."

Alden's fingers lace with mine, and I turn to find him looking at me in that miraculous way he does. Where he truly sees *me*. "Just you and me tonight, okay? It'll be nice to not have to hold myself back from strangling Sebastian for one night."

"Hey!" Sebastian shouts, making us all laugh. "You've told me not to go easy, so I don't go easy!"

Fay snuggles deeper into Sebastian's side, kissing his bicep. "You dragons are so sensitive."

Silis stands from his seat, shaking his head back and forth. "Alright, I'm out. All of you couples make me sick." He turns to wink at me in the same way his brother does before taking off.

"He's lucky I don't smack that little wink right off his face." Alden growls beside me, ever the jealous wolf.

I shove him with a big smile on my face. I can't lie and pretend I don't like the alpha-male in him. *Sue me, it's hot.* "Well, let's hit the woods then. You up for another night of pushing me to my limits?"

He grins back at me, his eyes darkening. "Always."

CHAPTER 52

ALDEN

Christ, she's so beautiful.

Ivy tangles her delicate fingers into her long, sweaty hair, tugging the locks into a messy bun at the top of her head. She ties the hair into place and fans her face with her hands. Sweat coats her forehead and the skin of her neck, shining in the light of the moon. Her chest rises and falls rapidly as she welcomes the breeze that floats through the forest, cooling her off.

I'm lost in the way her body moves, the way her tank top clings to her flat stomach, wet with her sweat from the long climb she just completed.

"Alden," Ivy's voice breaks into my perusal and my eyes snap to her gray ones. She's smiling. "What are you looking at over there?"

I shrug, not sure if I should tell the truth or come up with some cool lie. "I was looking at my gorgeous monkey-girl who just climbed to the top of that tree like a champ." *Truth it is.*

Her cheeks are already red from heat, but I can still see the blush creeping in. "A champ, huh? I felt like I was going to fall the entire time."

I move closer to her, unable to keep my distance. "But you didn't fall, did you?" I touch her soft cheek and swipe my thumb along her bottom lip. "You're ready, Ivy. I'm so damn proud of you."

Ivy has worked so hard this past month, pushing her body and mind to the limit day after day, never giving up even when I beg her to take a break. I've always been enamored by this beautiful creature in front of me, but now I am completely taken. I'm nothing without her.

Ivy's eyes blink back at me as she tries to keep her tears at bay. She sniffles and looks down at the ground between us. "Do you really think I'm ready?"

I close the distance between us, my heart breaking at the way she can't see herself the way I do. I take her chin in my fingers and make her look up at me. "I really do, Baby. Without a single doubt in my mind." I lower my mouth to hers, placing a small kiss against her pink lips.

I want so much more than these little kisses with my girl, but not just the physical moments. I want all-night conversations about things that don't matter. I want days of freedom where we have nothing but time and one another's company. Maybe even little Ivy babies running up to me with their mother's gray eyes and pink cheeks. I want a damn future with her, something I never saw for myself until now.

"Hey," I whisper against her lips. "The sun is down. Will you stargaze with me?" Ivy has told me about the times she used to stargaze with her parents, and she needs those memories right now.

She smiles back at me with a nod, so I take her hand in mine and lead her away from the canopy of evergreens. We find an opening in the trees where we've trained before, having needed the space to accommodate Sebastian's dragon a time or two.

I tug Ivy to the ground with me, thankful for the layer of grass in this little glade. We lay side-by-side, the stars twinkling above us, creating our own little light show.

"What are you thinking about?" I ask her, scooting closer until our shoulders touch.

She sighs, her thumb rubbing along my knuckles where our hands connect. "The same thing I always think about lately. How can I become stronger? What more can I do to be ready to stand against Sage?"

I turn onto my side so that I can look into Ivy's eyes. She turns too, and my arms circle her. "You've done everything you can, pushed your body to every limit. Now you just need to trust in yourself."

She nods, but I can still see the hesitation on her face. "Will you do something for me, Alden?"

I don't hesitate. "Anything."

Her fingers stroke the stubble along my jaw and her gray eyes become hungry. "Will you kiss me until I forget about everything else in the world?"

A new fire immediately lights in my belly and my wolf stirs at her words. How on earth can she do this to me with just one sentence?

I tighten my hold on her waist and push her onto her back, using my elbows to raise me above her. "That's a dangerous question, Ivy. Are you sure you want to give me such control?"

Her lips lift into a wide grin. "Oh, most definitely."

A low groan leaves my throat as I drop my lips to hers. The first time I kissed Ivy, I thought all of my dreams had come true, but here and now, after knowing her the way I do. Nothing could compare to this feeling.

I kiss her softly at first, her scent flooding my senses. No matter how sweaty and dirty we get training, our fated mate bond always makes us crave one another. Ivy always tastes like sweet honey, and she smells like vanilla. Two flavors that are officially my favorite of all time.

Ivy's leg rises and her thigh rubs against mine. I move my body over hers, resting one knee between her legs and the other in the grass beside her. I snake one of my arms around her waist, tugging our bodies together as I keep myself up on one elbow. I want to lower myself down, rest against her, but we're not there just yet.

Her mouth opens to me and I don't hesitate to slip my tongue against hers. Just that one movement makes the air around us heat up. Ivy's hands are on my back, exploring my muscles. I didn't shift tonight or else I'd be shirtless and lose control from those gentle caresses of her skin against mine. But when she slips her hands beneath my shirt and scrapes her nails up my back, I can't stop the primal growl that crawls out of me.

"Dammit, Ivy," I whisper against her lips. She only smiles, and I know she's torturing me on purpose. Two can play at that game. She did want a distraction after all.

I lower my body, but not enough to crush her. Just enough to feel every curve against the front of me. I leave her parted lips and trail kisses along her cheek, to the hollow spot just below her ear. I lick that spot, causing Ivy to gasp beneath me. I continue my exploration across the racing pulse in her neck and down to her collarbone, where I nip at her.

"Alden!" Ivy gasps again, and I pull back to look her in the eyes.

"Do you want me to stop, Baby?" It's a sincere question, one that I hope she answers "no" to.

Ivy squirms a little beneath me and I can see the war going on behind her gray eyes. "*I* don't want you to stop, but Sage is *not* happy right now."

My smile falls at the mention of the demon soul. I hate Sage more than anything in this world, and she has her claws in my mate. Just that thought is enough to make me want to rip her soul from Ivy myself. If only I could.

I close my eyes and drop my forehead gently against Ivy's. "I'm so ready for her to go to hell. Just three days." Ivy's body stills, and it's like I can feel her fear. My eyes fly open. "What's going on?"

She blinks rapidly, avoiding my eyes. "I uh…I sort of had a conversation with Sage last night. She said something that made me worry."

I try to wrap my head around the fact that Ivy can have conversations with the demon soul inside of her, but that's not necessarily news to me. "What did she say?" I don't mean to growl the question, but it comes out that way.

Ivy bites on her bottom lip and finally makes eye contact with me. "She said that there are other willing bodies that will welcome her into their minds when I cast her out."

I draw my chin back, a sudden chill rolling through me. "She's saying she can jump into another body? How is that possible?"

Ivy shrugs, her fingers absentmindedly stroking my back. "I don't think she's all about the details and the how-tos. She's very cryptic." Ivy pauses for just a moment. "She said '*there is a difference between being cast out, and being killed.*' And that I should know the difference before taking her on."

I let those words tangle through my mind for a moment. What if Sage is telling the truth and she will just bounce right into another person the moment Ivy defeats her? There has to be a way to prepare for that likelihood, and we have such little time.

"What are you thinking?" Ivy asks me, her wide eyes looking up at me as if I have the answers to the universe.

I want to tell her about my fears and worries for her birthday, but she doesn't need that. She needs my positivity and my love. I shake my head. "I'm thinking about how strong you are. Sage is just afraid, and there's no reason to believe any of her lies. She's trying to psych you out, but she doesn't know what I know."

Ivy's eyes widen slightly. "What exactly do you know?"

I grin down at her, placing a kiss on her nose, and then both of her cheeks. "I know that I love you, Ivy Hart." I peer into her eyes, letting her see how sure I am. "I love you with everything in me, and nobody will ever take away what I love, *never again*."

Ivy's gray eyes pool with tears, and her chest rises and falls rapidly beneath me. "Are you sure, Alden? You really love me?"

My eyebrows press together, confusion filling me at such a question. "Are you really asking me that? You know, I always thought you were smarter than me, but I'm doubting your genius right about now." Ivy pinches me in the side and I laugh, taking her hand in mine. "Of course I really love you, Baby. You mean everything to me."

Ivy raises her head, a silly smile on her lips as she kisses me, tugging my head down to turn the kiss heavy and frantic. She leans back just enough to look into my eyes once more. "I love you too, Alden. I love *all* of you. So much that it's painful to not have you next to me all day, every day. I'm yours."

My heart, that I once thought was black and dead, swells with happiness. I know I'm part demon, and it's a part that I thought I'd hate until the day I die, but if Ivy can love all of me, I can't possibly hate any of it. I don't care what I have to do to keep this girl, but I'll do it. I'll sacrifice everything to make sure her light shines for another hundred years.

CHAPTER 53

IVY

"Yeeessss, kiss him!" Fay shouts at the television, her mouth full of buttery popcorn.

I laugh at her enthusiasm, leaning back against the mountain of pillows we stacked against the wall beside my bed. "Are you really cheering for her? She's totally cheating!"

Fay spins to me with a wild look in her eyes. "But, it's Jacob! Do not tell me you're team Edward when you have your very own muscly wolf boy just two floor below us!"

I snort, throwing my head back. "Okay, I'm *very* much team Jacob, but it's still cheating!" Fay rolls her violet eyes, and I poke her in the side. "You'd think a real-life vampire would be leaning toward team vamp."

Fay grins at me from the side. "If you really want to know, I'd be all over Emmett Cullen. The guy is all muscle!"

"You've already got yourself one of those in the tall, dark, and handsome category. I think Sebastian beats Emmett Cullen."

"Damn right, he does," she says, her eyes practically glowing as she thinks about her mate. "I'm going to text him." She pulls out her phone and starts typing.

"Hey!" I throw a handful of popcorn at my friend. "I thought it was girls' night!"

Fay ignores me, giggling at something Sebastian texts back to her. I really don't mind. We're three movies into the Twilight Saga, and I've been dying to pick up my phone and call Alden all night. This is the first evening I've gone without being near him, and I can already feel the stirring in my bones that draws me toward my mate, especially after hearing him tell me he loves me last night.

I sigh, a smile tugging at my lips as I think about stargazing with Alden. The way his eyes focused on me when he professed his love for me. I knew without a doubt that he meant what he said, and the complete elation I saw in him the moment I told him I loved him too was icing on the cake.

Alden has been distant since then, but he has made sure to text me today to tell me he still loves me. I don't know where his mind has been, but every time I have a minute to talk, he's running off with "things to do". Maybe he's worried about my birthday the day after tomorrow.

Gosh, is it really that soon?

This morning, Fay begged me to spend the night with her tonight. She knows we won't get to celebrate my

362

birthday in the normal way, so she wanted a junk food movie night, just the two of us. I know she's worried about how my first shift will go, but she's amazing at keeping our conversation light and silly. It's something I really needed, and I'm so grateful to have her in my life.

I look over at Fay to find her watching me instead of her phone. "What are you looking at?"

She smiles sadly, but she quickly changes the subject. "How's Lorelei? Have you talked to her lately?"

I smile back, letting the moment pass. "Yeah. She's crazy about her doctor boyfriend, and they are going to move in together. I'm so happy for her."

"Aw, that's so exciting!" Fay snuggles into a pile of pillows, turning in my direction as the vampire-wolf battle ensues on the television. "Are you going to tell her about yourself? You know, after you shift?"

I let out a long breath. "I've thought about it a little. I think I will tell her about the supernatural world. I already hate being so far away from her, and keeping this secret just makes it feel like another thousand miles sits between us. If I survive the fight with Sage, I'll open up to Lor."

Fay reaches her hand out and lays it on my leg. "Hey, stop saying "if". You will survive, Ivy."

I nod, but I'm honestly not so sure. "It doesn't matter now. I've done all I can do to be ready, and what happens happens. I'm just glad I'll have you there with me."

Fay shoves a whole cookie into her mouth just as someone knocks on our door. I jump up my bed, expecting to see Sebastian coming to steal my roommate from me. That boy cannot stay away. I pull the door open and my eyes widen at the sight of Alden leaning against the doorframe with a sweet smile on his face.

"Oh, hey," I say, my body tingling at his nearness. "What are you doing here?"

He almost looks shy as he grabs one of my hands in his. "Do you think we can talk for a minute?"

I look back at Fay who is already slipping on her shoes. She steps up to my side. "I'm going downstairs to say goodnight to Bast. The room is all yours." She gives Alden a look that I don't understand before she runs off without another word.

I tilt my head at Alden as he steps into my room. "What was that all about?"

Alden rubs a hand on the back of his neck, looking stressed as he stares down at the ground. "I uh...texted Fay a bit ago and told her I have a plan to help you become stronger." His eyes find mine again. "I knew she wanted to be alone with you tonight, but when I told her my plan, she thought I should run it by you immediately."

My heart flutters with new purpose. "What is it? I'll do anything to make sure I can be ready to face Sage."

He steps closer to me and licks his bottom lip in that nervous way that he does. "Maybe you should sit down."

I take a step toward my bed and sit down slowly. "Okay, I'm freaking out a little here, Alden. What's the plan?"

He kneels in front of me, and from this spot, our faces are level with one another. He takes my hands in his and rests them on my pajama-clad lap. "So, do you remember when we talked about what it means to be officially mated?"

Oh, this is a sex talk. Great.

A blush fills my cheeks as I think back to our conversation at the full moon bonfire. "Yes, I remember."

Alden licks his lips again. "Well, what I didn't tell you is that once a couple is mated, they become stronger. The bond enhances their strength, speed, and power. For shifters, it means that they can shift faster and easier. As well as being able to communicate telepathically with their mate, like we talked about."

I swallow hard, trying to remain unfazed by this conversation. "So, are you telling me that we should sleep together so that I become stronger?"

Alden's eyes widen slightly and he drops his head against our hands with a groan. "I am so not doing this right." He looks up at me again, and the vulnerability in his gaze makes me melt on the spot. "I'm going to try to open up and speak my mind. I'm no good at this, so just bear with me, okay?"

I nod. "I'm listening."

"I love you, Ivy. I told you this last night, and I meant it." One of his hands rises to stroke my cheek gently. "Yes, I want to mate with you. I've wanted this since the moment I realized you were my fated mate, but I sure as hell never imagined we would get to that point. I've had my insecurities, and I have acted like a complete idiot time and time again." His eyes search mine, and I let him see the love I have in me for him. "I don't want to *just* sleep with you. Not to make you stronger, or to fight a battle. I want to complete our bond together because I cannot live my life without you. I want to make love to you, to show you that every part of me is yours, and I will give you anything in this world to make sure you are mine." He strokes my cheek again, and my heart beats out of control in my chest as he continues. "So, I'm here to ask you if you will give yourself to me, as my mate and as the love of my life. I am

365

part demon, so you would be taking on that part of me just as much as the shifter part. This would change you in more ways than one, but it will only bring us closer together. So, Ivy Hart, will you have all of me? Insecurities, broken pieces and all?"

I blink, silently willing my tears to stay back. Alden's hand in mine is solid, a lifeline that I could hold onto forever. My heart already belongs to him, and here he is asking me to take his heart for myself. How could I be this lucky?

He waits patiently for me to answer his question, but another thought slips into my mind. "Wait, did you text Fay all of that? No wonder she ran out of here so fast."

Alden's grin is intoxicating as he drops his head in my lap again, a short laugh falling past his lips. "Ivy, you are killing me, I swear."

I giggle and grip the sides of his face, lifting him up so he has to look into my eyes again. "My answer is yes, Alden. I will take all of your broken pieces and love every single one of them for as long as you'll let me. I love you so much, and I'm ready to mate with you. I told you last night that I'm yours, and I meant it."

He doesn't respond with words, but his lips crash into mine. His hands slip into my hair at the back of my head and he pulls me against him, claiming my mouth in a powerful way. I let him kiss me like that for a few minutes before pulling away and laying my forehead against his.

"What will we do about Sage, Alden? She won't let us go through with this."

He leans back with a nod, his blue eyes darker than before. "That's what I asked Fay, actually. She said she can make her mom's tea for us, but it won't be as strong since you drank it once already. It should be enough to give us tomorrow night though. One night for just you and me, no distractions."

I can't stop the stupid smile on my face. Even though my birthday is looming, and my future is unsure, I get to mate with Alden. How could I not smile at that?

Alden's thumb brushes across my smiling lips, and he stands, pulling me to my feet with him. "Once we're mated, there's nothing that will stop you from winning this fight, Ivy. I believe in you, and soon you will have the life you've always deserved."

"We," I say, correcting him. "*We* will have the life we both deserve."

Alden smiles softly, even though his eyes hold a hint of sadness, and instead of agreeing with me, he places an achingly sweet kiss on my lips. Whatever that look in his eyes means, I'll make sure he feels truly loved for the first time in his life.

CHAPTER 54

My wolf stirs inside of me, so close to the surface that I can feel her strength, the power she's ready to release. Tomorrow is the day that she will be freed, and Sage will try to control my shifted body. But she will lose.

I finish off the last of my tea, hoping with everything in me that the tea really suppresses Sage for the whole night. I'm claiming my mate tonight, and every nerve in my body is charged with excitement. *And absolute terror.*

"Oh, man, I'm freaking out." I set my cup down and wipe the sheen of sweat from my forehead.

Fay stands from her bed and throws an arm around my shoulder, stopping my pacing across our bedroom floor. "Calm down, Ivy. This is a natural occurrence between two people who love one another. He's your mate."

I groan and throw my head back. "I've barely ever kissed before meeting Alden, so of course I'm nervous about knowing what to do, but it's so much more than that." I look over at Fay, fear in my eyes. "This was a decision planned out and made so that I can fight better. There's so much pressure. Why couldn't we have just fallen in love in the normal way and had a spontaneous night together?"

Fay rubs her hand on my shoulder. "Come on. You told me what he said to you last night. That's not what this is going to be about. Alden loves you, and even though you were forced to do this *tonight*, it's not planned out like some awkward step-by-step manual." She chuckles at that. "Once you step into his room, that's where the planning part ends. It will just be the two of you, and you will do only what makes you comfortable, what feels *right*."

I nod. How is she always right? "Thanks, Fay. I'm glad I have you, you know?"

She grins and bumps my arm with hers. "Of course I know. I'm awesome."

I laugh, my body relaxing slightly from the joy inside of me. I turn to look in the mirror on the wall and double-check my appearance. My hair is loose over my shoulders, the black locks framing my make-up free face. I'm wearing a silky, black top with half sleeves, and a simple pair of jean shorts. *Should I be dressed up?* Do people dress up for a hook-up date? *Oh, gosh, this is practically a booty-call!*

"Stop," Fay says sternly behind me. She is staring at me through the mirror. "I can see the panic in your eyes, and you are overthinking this. Just go to your mate."

I sigh, trying to blow out all of the nervous energy inside of me, and without another thought, I leave my room and make my way downstairs. It takes me only a few minutes to walk to Alden's room beside the library. I wipe my sweaty hands on my shorts and knock on the door. It's now or never.

Alden's door opens and my heart skips a beat at the sight of him. His hair is slightly wet, like he just showered, and he's wearing a simple white t-shirt that hangs over a pair of black sweatpants. He looks like he's ready to climb into bed, and somehow that's way better than if he had dressed up for tonight.

"Hey," he says simply, a small smile on his handsome face. "Come here."

He takes my hand in his and tugs me into his room behind him. My whole body is shaking as I follow him on wobbly legs, but I stop dead in my tracks as I take in his bedroom. Various candles are lit around the room, taking up every flat surface in the space, the flickering light causing a soft, romantic glow. On Alden's coffee table, a bowl of chicken alfredo fettuccine sits steaming, with a side of garlic bread and two plates beside it.

Alden turns toward me, biting his lip with a shrug. "I know it's not much, but I tried my best. Surprisingly, a boarding school is not the ideal place to find a romantic dinner setup." He laughs nervously, looking at me like I might bolt out of here any moment.

The shaking in my body subsides at the nervous look in his eyes. Gosh, he's perfect, and he's *mine*. I take a step toward Alden and place my hand against his chest, feeling his rapid heartbeat against my palm. I stand on my tippy toes and kiss him gently, silently thanking him for being himself.

I pull back to look up into his eyes. "This is incredible, Alden. All of it." I look down at the food and smile. "I wasn't expecting dinner."

He lays a warm hand against my lower back and tilts my chin up with his other hand. "We've never had a real date before. You deserve more than kisses in the woods and dinner in the cafeteria, Ivy."

A huge grin stretches my cheeks as I look deep into his blue eyes. The heat of his hands on me and the look of love in his eyes is my undoing. I close my eyes briefly and search for the rogue soul inside of me that I hate. I sigh happily when I realize Sage is suppressed, leaving Alden and I alone.

I lace my fingers together behind his neck, pressing my body tighter to his. "Do you mind if we skip dinner, Alden?" I lock my gaze with his, willing my nerves to disappear. "I don't want to waste anymore time when I could be mated to you right now."

Alden's eyelashes flutter as he stares down at me, his grip tightening on my back. "Is…is *she* gone right now?"

I nod. "It's just you and me."

Alden's eyes close for just a second before his hands slide down to my thighs and he quickly hoists me off the ground and presses my back to the wall behind me. "Tell me if you need to stop," he whispers in my ear before his mouth takes complete control of mine.

Every nerve in my body reacts to this kiss, and it's like I'm suddenly supercharged. I grip Alden's shoulders and arch my body into his, amazed at the feeling of finally losing control. I open my mouth to him, letting his tongue slip past my lips and taste me, drawing a moan from my throat.

Alden's hands leave my thighs once my legs lock behind his back, securing me to him. He slips his fingers beneath my shirt, letting his thumbs stroke roughly against my ribs and causing me to break our kiss with a sharp breath. I raise my hands above my head and stare into Alden's darkened eyes, silently urging him to make the next move.

His hands grip the insides of my shirt and he quickly tugs the fabric over my head and tosses it to the ground behind him. He doesn't take his eyes off of mine as his lips find mine again. He kisses me like he's starved for the taste of my lips, and it's completely intoxicating.

My hands become eager, searching for the hem of his shirt, but Alden is already there, reaching behind his head and tugging the shirt off in one swift motion. I'm rewarded with the incredible view of thick muscles that cover every inch of him, and I don't hesitate to press my palms to his pecs.

The break from kissing finally allows Alden to look down at my exposed chest, and a low hum leaves his throat as he gazes down at me. His eyes are completely black when he looks back up into my eyes, and he cups my face in his hands, gently stroking his thumb along my swollen lips.

"You're so beautiful, Ivy. I need you to know that. You're everything." His forehead drops to mine and he takes a deep breath in through his nose as if breathing me into him.

I take Alden's hands from my face and slowly guide them down my neck and over my bare body, needing his touch on every part of me. "I'm yours, Alden," I whisper as his hands take over their exploration without my guidance. "Entirely yours."

He groans and his chest presses against mine before he wraps his large arms around me and turns us toward his bed. He drops me on the plush mattress and then stands so that cold air rushes against me where I don't feel him anymore. I want to complain about the distance, until Alden bends forward and pops open the button of my shorts and tugs them off so fast that I shiver from the sudden cold. *No way was that not supernatural speed.*

I've never felt more exposed in my entire life, but somehow I don't mind Alden's hungry eyes roaming over me. I feel...*powerful* under his gaze, and all I want is for him to touch me again.

I sit up in Alden's bed and crawl toward him, a boldness taking over me. He watches my every movement as I kneel on the bed before him and make quick work of removing his pants like he did for me. He kicks the fabric off of his feet and climbs onto the mattress with me, taking me into his arms once again.

Just like that, there are no more barriers between me and him. Alden lowers me onto my back and lays himself over me, his heat pressing down on my body. I wait, suddenly not sure if I should urge him to continue or beg him to take it slow.

I touch his rough cheek with my fingertips. "I'm scared," I say suddenly, not meaning to.

Alden slips a strand of my hair out of my face and his dark eyes bore into mine. "Me too."

My eyes widen at his confession. "Really? *You're* scared?"

His smile calms my racing heart. "Of course I'm scared, Ivy. I love you so damn much, and all I want is to make you happy." His nose rubs against mine. "I'm terrified of hurting you, physically and emotionally."

I rub my hands along his back, reveling in the way his muscles twitch beneath my touch. "I'm not afraid of a little pain, Alden. I'm afraid of not being everything you want me to be." I blush as his eyebrows press together in confusion.

He smiles again and shakes his head back and forth. "What a ridiculous thing to be afraid of. I think it's time you see yourself the way I see you."

I don't have a chance to question him as his lips drop to my neck and he kisses me from my neck to my chest, to my belly and back up to my mouth. His lips take control of mine in a flurry of heat that spreads all the way to my toes, and his hands grab onto my hips as he presses himself into me slowly and methodically.

I gasp and throw my head back, giving him full access to my throat where he peppers me with kisses and nibbles along my skin. I cling onto Alden's shoulders as I match his movements with my own, finding a perfect rhythm. Something spreads from my heart, through the veins in my body, heating every single part of me.

I gasp all over again at the overwhelming feeling of love that fills me, but the feeling is also somehow foreign, like it's not my own emotions that are flooding me. Love is mixed with this heavy feeling of protection and I shiver at the wave of lust that spreads to my toes. The euphoria of being connected in every way with my mate. I close my eyes, and I see myself, like I'm looking through Alden's eyes, watching me beneath him.

"Alden," I whisper, my breathing so heavy that I can barely speak. "What is going on? I feel like I'm in your body, like I can feel what you feel."

His black eyes peer into mine as he pauses against me, his heavy breath fanning my face. "That's the mating bond, Ivy." One of his hands lays against my cheek in a cherishing way. "Now you know how I feel when I look at you."

I blink back a wave of tears that wants to come. "It feels amazing."

He gives me the happiest smile I've ever seen on his perfect lips. "It always feels amazing to love you."

I can't help it. I grip the back of his neck and pull his lips back to mine. He's my fate, everything that I could ever want in this world, and I am going to show him just as much as he has shown me how it feels to be loved.

Alden's movements quicken as his lips tug and taste mine with a new fervor. Every stroke of his tongue, every grip of his fingers and thrust of his hips is matched by my own until the rest of the world disappears. We become completely lost in one another, claiming the other in every possible way.

CHAPTER 55

I raise my hand to knock on Alden's bedroom door, but he's already swinging it open with a wildness in his blue eyes. "What the hell took you so long?" He asks, taking my hand and tugging me across the threshold before kicking the door closed behind me.

I giggle in his arms until his face presses into my hair and his soft lips roam over my neck. Suddenly breathless, I try to speak. "I just took a shower and...and ran over the plan with F–Fay." I gasp as his teeth bite down on my skin before soothing the nip with his tongue. "I was gone for less than an hour."

Alden groans against me, his hands gripping onto my waist as he spins us and starts walking me backwards toward his bed. His dark eyes stare down at me and his rich voice floods my mind. *"Now that you're officially mine, I crave you even more."*

My eyes fly open so wide that they dry out momentarily. "Did you just say that into my mind?"

He nods, his lips rising into a happy grin. *"I did. Does that freak you out?"*

I shake my head. "No, that's seriously so cool."

"Try it," he tells me out loud. "Just think about what you want to say to me and aim your words in my direction."

I press up on my toes and place my lips gently against his. *"I love you, Alden, and I need you to take me to your bed again."*

Alden groans against my mouth and lifts me without another word before tossing me roughly on top of his bed. I laugh as he pounces on top of me, attacking me with kisses all over while he tickles my waist.

"Hey, stop that right now!" I cry out, tears in my eyes from laughing so hard.

"Make me," Alden whispers into my ear.

His fingers are relentless as he continues his torture, but I use all of my strength to shove against his chest. To my utter surprise and horror, Alden flies backwards off the edge of his bed and lands hard on the stone floor.

I gasp and jump out of the bed to kneel in front of my mate. "Oh my gosh, Alden! Are you okay?"

He blinks up at me with awe in his bright blue eyes. "Wow, I guess your extra strength has kicked in."

I touch his cheek. "I'm so sorry. I didn't know I could actually hurt you." I feel miserable.

Alden surprises me with a laugh as he shakes his head back and forth in amusement. He tugs on my hips until I'm straddling his legs, and he kisses me quickly on the lips. "You didn't hurt me, Baby. I'm okay, but I'm also super impressed." His eyes roam my face. "You're incredible, you know that?"

I blush under his gaze. "All because of you." I snake my fingers into his hair and tug him closer to me. Our lips crash together and his hands dip below my shirt, clinging to my skin, but before we can get carried away, my phone buzzes in my back pocket.

I groan and take the device out of my pocket to find Lorelei's name calling me. "Shoot, Lor never calls." I look apologetically back at Alden. "I have to answer. She probably just wants to wish me a happy birthday."

He smiles back at me and places one soft kiss on my nose. "Go for it. I can wait."

I hit the green answer button and place the phone to my ear. "Hey, Lor!"

"Is this Ivy Hart?" The masculine voice on the other end of the line makes my entire body grow cold, especially when Alden stills below me and his eyes turn completely black.

"Yes, this is her," I answer, fear flooding me.

The man's voice is rough when he speaks again. "You don't know me, but my name is Gregor Laurent. I'm going to need you to put my son on the phone."

My wide gaze flashes to Alden. He's shaking beneath me now, his dark eyes staring at the device in my hand. I don't need to ask who this man's son is, since I know my mate. Alden's demon father has my sister's phone, and I have no idea why.

ALDEN

Ivy is in my arms, her heart in my hands, and her perfect body against my unworthy one. I should be the happiest man on the planet, but the moment my father's voice speaks through Ivy's phone, my happy little world comes crashing down.

Ivy's scared eyes bore into mine as she shakily hands over her phone, placing it into my hand. I feel like I'm in a fog as I switch the phone on speaker mode and hold it between us.

"Father," I say, my voice barely audible. This man doesn't deserve the title as my father, but I need him to tell me what he called to say. Where is Lorelei? How did he find her? How does he know who Ivy even is?

That horrible voice speaks back to me. "Alden, it has been too long since I've seen you, son. How have you been?"

I clear my throat, needing to sound strong. "Why do you have Lorelei's phone?"

My father chuckles darkly. "Straight to the point, then. Okay. First, I need you to know that I have been keeping tabs on you, Alden. For as long as you have been at that ridiculous school, I have known your every move."

Anger pours through me. "You don't deserve to know me. You should have been dead a long time ago."

His low growl rings through the speaker, causing Ivy to shiver where she still sits on my lap. I run my fingers along her back, but I know she can feel the tension within me, especially after we completed our mating bond last night.

"Son, I am trying to be cordial here. Just listen to what I have to say." He pauses before speaking again. "I know about Ivy, and about her soul. I knew you had found your mate months ago, but I only just got word that Sage Whitaker has bled her soul into another, namely, your Ivy."

"We're taking care of it," I say through clenched teeth. "Just leave Lorelei alone."

"Running into Ivy's sister wasn't a part of the plan. I was coming to the asylum just this morning when the investigator I hired said Lorelei Hart is in Sacramento and planning to surprise her sister on her eighteenth birthday. I couldn't pass up the opportunity."

Ivy's eyes are full of tears, and it only fuels my rage. "Leave Lorelei out of this. If you want to get to Sage's soul, just come here. We'll show you that we can get rid of her for good."

"Son," he sighs. "Why would I come to that godforsaken place when I have the leverage I need to bring you to me? I have your mate's sister. She's fine, but I will only release her once you meet with me, tonight. I will personally see to it that Sage's soul is expelled for good, on *my own* turf."

"How can I trust you?" I ask, no part of me willing to trust the man who abused me for so long.

"Simple," he says. "You don't have another choice. Now, I am sending you an address. Meet me there before Ivy's shift tonight and we will finally witness that bitch's end. Together."

I open my mouth, but the line goes dead as my father hangs up. I drop the phone and grip my hair in my hands, wanting to pull it out from the roots. Ivy's hands fall over mine and she takes my hands from my head.

She looks into my eyes while hers pour over with tears. "We have to go, Alden. I need to save my sister." I wipe the tears from her cheeks as she sniffles.

"This doesn't have to change the plan. We'll get everyone together and meet where he tells us. When your shift comes tonight at midnight, Sage will make her move, and you will fight her off. You can do this."

She nods. "And then we'll take Lorelei home and never have to worry again."

A sickness fills my belly. I haven't told Ivy about my plans in case Sage is able to do another body jump. I can't bear to say goodbye to this woman that I love so much. I will do whatever it takes to keep her safe, even if it kills me in the process.

CHAPTER 56

IVY

Please be okay, please be okay, please be okay. My legs are bouncing and my palms are sweaty as Alden parks the car in the dirt driveway. The old barn in front of us looks dilapidated, the red paint mostly peeled from the wood and the large door hanging from the hinges. Lorelei has to be in there.

It took less than an hour to drive out to this abandoned property. Alden's father texted us the address after hanging up this morning, and we immediately gathered the gang together. Fay, Sebastian, and Silis were already planning on being beside me for my first shift, so they didn't accept my offer for them to back out now.

I feel wired from head to toe, knowing that the moment the moon reaches its highest in the sky, my wolf will break free of my skin. I've been over the specifics with Alden and Stella enough times to feel ready, except that now I will be watched by Alden's demon father and worried about Lorelei the whole time. This isn't how this night was supposed to go.

Fay leans forward from the back seat and taps my shoulder. "We better get out there. It's twenty minutes to midnight."

I nod, trying to suck in a deep breath and not throw myself into a full blown panic attack. "We need to find Lor before anything else. I need to know she's okay."

The five of us climb out of the car and meet in the shine of the headlights, cautiously approaching the dark barn. Alden takes my hand and tugs me behind him in a protective way as he takes the first step into the rotting building.

"Stay behind me, Ivy. Don't let my father touch you." He speaks calmly into my mind, but I can feel the waves of fear rolling off of him. He's afraid of his father, and that's enough to make me want to kill the demon right here and now.

This new sense of protection for my mate is overwhelming, but I welcome it. I'll do anything for Alden, and I won't let his father hurt him ever again.

I blink a few times, letting my eyes adjust to the dark interior of the barn, but it only takes a moment before I can see it all clearly. No lights were switched on, but my eyes take in everything as if it's dawn, and not nearly midnight.

Alden must read my mind and feel my surprise. *"That's your wolf senses. You're so close to the shift now and it means you can see in the dark like the rest of us."*

I want to take the time to marvel at this new ability, but one more step puts me in a position to see half of Lorelei's body sticking out from behind a bale of hay. I gasp and release Alden to run to my sister's side.

"Lor," I call out, falling to my knees and turning Lorelei's limp body so I can scan her face. She looks unharmed, and I press my fingers to her wrist to feel her steady pulse. She's okay. Still, she's out cold.

"She's fine," a familiar voice calls out behind me, and I whip my head around to see an older version of Alden standing against a back wall with his hands in his pockets as if he's just chilling on a summer night. He has darker hair than his son that is cut long, hanging past his ears, and the stubble on his face makes him look unkempt.

The man tosses me Lorelei's phone, and then looks beside me where Alden now stands. "My boy," he says, not smiling like a normal loving father.

Alden growls and he takes a step forward, only to have Silis put a hand on his chest to hold him back. "Don't start a fight, Alden. We need to be ready to help Ivy."

Alden looks back at Silis with a nod. I can feel his anger through our bond, and the pain he holds inside of him as he looks upon his father. It's unbearable. Sebastian and Fay stand hand-in-hand by the broken barn door, both of them scowling at Gregor as well. There is no love in here for the demon.

"Is it just me, or does it feel a little tense in here?" Gregor says, as if teasing at a time like this.

"What the hell is wrong with you?" Alden shouts the question, his jaw tightening. "Why are you making this happen here? Just because of your hatred for Sage?"

Gregor points a finger at me, his blue eyes so much like Alden's that it's startling. "That woman is the reason your mother is dead! You think I can just allow you to take a mate that killed your own flesh and blood?"

I flinch, but Alden lays a hand on my shoulder. "Ivy did nothing. Sage took up space in her body, and we are going to expel her evil soul tonight. There's no reason for you to be here, to take Ivy's sister as a hostage!"

"Well, you can't blame me for wanting to make sure the deed truly gets done. Your heart is on your sleeve, son. I need to make sure that if your mate can't get the job done, you will have the spine to take care of it."

I blanch at his insinuation. I've always known there was a chance that Sage could win this fight and take over my body, but I didn't let myself think that far ahead. Would Alden have to kill me? Would one of my friends do it?

"She's not going to lose," Alden says. He believes in me completely, and I can read his mind now. He truly means it.

"Son–" Gregor starts, but Alden cuts him off.

"How do you know about any of this, anyways? You said you've kept tabs on me, but how?" Desperation is in Alden's eyes as he waits for Gregor's response.

The demon pushes off of the wall and crosses his arms across his broad chest. "You'd be amazed what your demon side is capable of, son. There are a few lonely females in the school faculty that become simpering puddles when hit with my Incubus charm."

"Ew," Fay mutters from across the room. "You seduce our teachers for information about your son?"

Gregor turns to Fay with a deep frown on his face. "You drink blood like it's chocolate milk, little girl. Don't pretend to be better than me."

Sebastian growls beside Fay, his eyes flashing to black as he glares at Gregor. "Don't speak to her, demon."

"She spoke first, *dragon*." He glares right back.

"Enough!" I shout, getting to my feet, only I'm not the one who speaks the word. Sage's anger boils inside of me, and sweat breaks across my forehead as I attempt to shove her back down.

"Ivy?" Alden leans into me, his eyes searching mine. "Sage?"

A sharp, foreign-sounding laugh leaves my lips before I can stop it. "The shift is coming, and it's going to feel so good to have a body again." That's not me talking.

I try to reach out to Alden in my mind, but Gregor's voice fills the barn before I get the chance. "I knew it! She's too weak. Kill her, now!"

"No!" Alden yells, charging his father and crashing to the floor with him.

I mentally grab Sage and shove her back down while she tries clawing through my mind. I open my mouth to tell Gregor that I'm still here, that Sage hasn't won, but the sound of wood cracking has all heads turning toward the barn entrance.

Behind Fay and Sebastian, two large men and a rabid-looking wolf step into the room. Gregor brought help to kill me.

CHAPTER 57

Sebastian steps away from Fay and shifts into his dragon, his large, black frame nearly reaching the ceiling. The wolf charges him, but he clamps his large jaws around the furry body and leaps through the door, breaking through the wood on his way out into the night.

One of the two men locks eyes with me, and he growls deep as two long horns rise from his dark hair. *What the hell?* Gregor shouts for the man to kill me, and he immediately sprints in my direction.

In the blink of an eye, Silis appears right in front of the horned man, and he slices his long claws across the man's chest. Movement behind them catches my eye, and I find Fay in her own battle with the third guy, the two blurring in and out as they fade around the room, throwing punches. He's a vampire.

I close my eyes, searching inside of me for the strength I know I have. I can help them. I can fight. It's what I've been training for this past month. I can feel Sage stirring inside of me, but I hold her back in a way I never could before. *"You won't win,"* I tell her, feeling her pain from my force.

Alden's pain floods my mind, and I whirl toward him to find his father kneeling on his chest with his hands on his throat. I step toward them, needing to help my mate, but a shooting pain of my own slices up my back and into my head, dropping me to my knees beside my unconscious sister.

"Ivy," Alden calls out to me, struggling against his father. "It's the shift. Let it happen. Don't fight it."

I cry out as another wave of pain courses through me. I don't try to fight the pain, but the feeling is agonizing. My entire body is coated in sweat as wave after wave of pain stabs through me. My ankles crack, followed by my knees and then my back, bringing tears to my eyes.

I can do this. I say to myself as I close my eyes tight and welcome my wolf to come forward. A heat floods my chest like a pool of lava rising inside of me. I drop onto all fours, forcing myself a few feet away from Lor so I don't accidentally hurt her.

Black fur sprouts from my skin and an animal roars in my head so loud that I can't hear anything else around me. I have just a moment to gasp for air as the final wave filters through my limbs and my wolf has completely taken over.

Suddenly, a new, vibrant world shines in front of me and all of my pain disappears. Strength ripples through me in the most incredible way, and pure elation has my wolf howling long and loud into the night. I'm amazed at how much control I still have in this form. I always thought I'd be just a passenger once my wolf took control, but I was wrong. I'm a co-pilot.

I want to run. I want to explore the woods and smell the scents that have always been so insignificant to me until now, but the sound of fighting brings me back to the moment like a light shutting off.

I whip my head around, taking in the scene around me. Alden and his father continue to grapple on the ground, neither of them overpowering the other. The vampire and horned man are both lying still on the ground behind Fay who kneels not far from me. She has her eyes closed, two candles lit in front of her as she mumbles something under her breath.

What is happening? I don't know where Silis or Sebastian are, but I know that I can help Alden. I turn back to my mate where he has his hands wrapped around his father's neck this time, and then I feel Sage.

It's like she suddenly has a tight hold on every bone in my body and she forces the shift to happen again. My wolf whines in pain as our body shrinks back to its human form without any way to stop it.

I drop to my bare knees, my wolf shoved deep into the back of my mind. Sage's taunting voice fills the void inside of me. *"Time to say goodbye, Ivy. I can't say I'll miss you."*

Her dark soul fills me, and it's as if my own soul is pressed to the edges, slowly being forced out through my skin. It's excruciating, and it feels like the end of myself.

This is what I've been training for. This is what my friends have given their time for, and my mate has given his heart for. This is my moment to prove that I am not the weak human I was three months ago. I'm a wolf shifter, and I won't go out without a fight.

I focus on that light inside of me, the part that makes me who I am. I recognize the distinguishing light as my own soul, and I hang onto that light with everything that I have. I know what strength feels like, so I draw on that feeling of my muscles straining as I train, my legs stretching as I run.

I know what love feels like, and I flood my mind with the love I have for my friends. For Lorelei, and my parents. And the love that I feel for Alden. Sage's dark soul doesn't recognize love, and I can feel her shrink against the brightness inside of me. Everytime she tries to force me out, I focus on the things that give me strength, and I slowly shrink her black soul, inch by inch.

My entire body aches as I keep my eyes closed tight and I mentally fight Sage's attempts to edge me out of myself. The lightness inside of me grows more and more, and Sage screams from the pain of me pressing down on her.

"I told you I would win, Sage. You never stood a chance."

Her rage is dark and was once all-consuming, but now I match her rage with my own. Her black soul writhes like a snake being burned from the inside out, but that distant voice still reaches me just as I feel the last bits of her soul leave me.

"I told you to learn the difference, Ivy. I'm not dying tonight."

Like a rubber-band snapping, Sage's soul rips from my body, leaving me gasping on the ground for air. I'm naked and shaking, but the new lightness inside me is proof that she is really, truly gone.

I look up, my breathing heavy and sweat dripping from me, just in time to see Fay quit her mumbling, and one of the two candle flames blow out in front of her. Her eyes snap up and focus on something behind me.

I turn around, nearly falling over from the weakness of my limbs, and Alden is standing above his father who is kneeling on the ground with wide blue eyes, seemingly clawing at nothing on his chest. I'm so confused. I look up at Alden who looks shocked as he bleeds from a cut on his head and stares down at Gregor in fear.

"What is going on?" I ask, a sick feeling in my gut. "I won. She's gone." *So why does that feel like a lie?*

"She's not gone, Ivy," Fay says, drawing my eyes back to her. "She had a backup plan. Her soul was going to jump to another body the moment you cast her out. I just narrowed down her choices."

"Help me!" Gregor cries out, and I watch him grip the sides of his head, screaming in pain. "She's inside of me. Please help me," he cries again.

No freaking way.

CHAPTER 58

"Is Sage's soul inside of him?" I shout the question at my friend as Sebastian walks into the barn with a limping Silis under his arm. I'm relieved to see they're okay, but I ignore them as I look back at Fay. "Fay! What did you do?"

"It was supposed to be me," Alden says behind me, his voice hoarse and low.

I spin around, my eyes meeting my mate's as he stands above his father still crying on the ground. "What was supposed to be you, Alden? Someone tell me the damn truth!"

Alden looks broken and I can feel his sadness as if it were my own. Fay tosses a thin blanket over my shoulders, covering up my nakedness, but I ignore her, keeping my eyes on Alden.

He swallows hard. "The night you told me that Sage hinted at having other bodies lined up, I knew that we couldn't allow her to just hop into someone else. She should have died the night my father killed her. We couldn't just let her continue ruining lives."

I shake my head, still lost. "So, you and Fay planned on putting her into your father? Did you know he was going to take Lorelei? That he'd be here tonight?"

"No," Fay says. She's standing beside me now. "I made the choice to transfer Sage's soul into Gregor on the way here. It wasn't going to be his body, but I knew it was the better option." Her violet eyes flash back to Alden and I follow her gaze.

Alden's words register in my mind. *"It was supposed to be me."*

My eyes widen as I stand and take a step toward Alden. "You? You were going to take Sage's soul?" Betrayal fills my heart as he tries to avoid my eyes. "Why would you do that? What could you have gained from that, Alden? A lifetime of fighting her?"

His jaw clenches tightly and his blue eyes finally focus on me. "No. I wasn't going to risk her coming back. I was prepared to finally kill Sage once and for all."

Tears burn my eyes as his meaning finally kicks in. "By killing *yourself*?" He opens his mouth and closes it again, confirming my fears. "So, you guys just made this plan behind my back, to shove Sage's soul inside of my mate and then take the one thing I love most in this world away from me? And you were all okay with this?"

"I didn't give them a choice," Alden says, defending my friends. "It was either kill her now, once and for all, or let her kill another soul and become the murderer she was all over again."

"Alden," Gregor moans his son's name as he falls back onto the ground. His whole body is shaking, and tears stain his cheeks. "I'm so sorry, son." The room is silent as Alden kneels in front of his father. "I hurt you for years. I hurt you because my heart was broken the day I lost your mother. I am so, so sorry."

Alden looks up at me, tears filling his blue eyes. All of the anger I felt moments ago dissolves and I crawl to his side, knowing he needs my support.

Gregor grabs Alden's hand. "I'm not going to win this fight, son. Sage is going to beat me, and then she will have my power as her own. You can't let that happen."

Alden shakes his head. "No matter how badly you hurt me, I can't kill you. You're still my dad."

Gregor groans in pain again, and I can feel the ache in Alden as he watches his father struggle. "You don't need to kill me. I died the day your mother did. It's finally time that I do something right, don't you think?" He reaches a shaking hand into his boot and pulls out a long pocket knife. "I failed as a father, but you turned out pretty great anyways, didn't you?"

Alden's voice rises as he looks behind me toward Fay. "Do the spell again. I'll take her soul. I know I can beat her." His eyes land on me. "Baby, we can find someone else to transfer her soul into once I beat her. Someone who deserves to die. I won't leave you. I—"

Alden's pleading is cut off by the sickening sound of Gregor stabbing the knife into his own chest. We both look down as the life drains from Gregor, taking Sage along with him, and I throw my arms around Alden's neck.

"I'm so sorry it ended this way, Alden." I hold onto him as he cries against me. As much as he hated his father, he did love him once. I can feel the others circle us, lending their support as Alden and I huddle together on the ground.

Alden shakes his head and looks up at our friends before his gaze lands on me. "I think this is the way it needed to end. I never wanted to break your heart. And now, the man I thought I'd always hate has saved the woman that I'll love for eternity." His forehead drops to mine and his voice speaks into my mind. *"Maybe now we can have that future we both deserve."*

"We will," I tell him. And I know it's the truth.

CHAPTER 59

ONE MONTH LATER

"Happy graduation day!" Lorelei yells, causing a bunch of freshly graduated students to cheer all around us.

I giggle at my very noisy sister and throw my arms around her neck, smothering us both in my blue robe. "Thanks, Big Bear. I'm so glad you came today. I was a nervous wreck."

"Why?" She looks around really quick and lowers her voice. "Were you worried you were going to shift on stage?"

I roll my eyes at her. "It doesn't work like that, Lor. Stop thinking that I'm this out-of-control animal."

She shrugs. "I'm still trying to wrap my head around all of this supernatural stuff. How am I supposed to know you won't get nervous and sprout fur?"

I shake my head. "You'll get used to it."

"Get used to what?" Lorelei's fiancé interrupts our quiet conversation, making us both jump.

I look up at the handsome doctor and smile as if we weren't just discussing a world he has no idea exists. "I was just saying that she'll get used to having a grown-up little sister."

He places his knuckles on my head and gives me a noogie. I swear, it's like the man has been my big brother for a lifetime already. "Once a baby sister, always a baby sister, Ivy."

He turns and captures Lorelei in his arms, dropping a kiss on her head. "Ready to go, sweetie?"

"Yeah," Lorelei says, grinning up at him. She leans forward to give me one more hug. "You will come visit me within the month, okay?"

"Yes, I will. And I'll bring Alden."

"Good! I'm excited to show him all of your embarrassing baby pictures. I can already think of a few winners." She winks at me and runs off before I can argue with her.

I look around at the excited students milling about the asylum lobby, laughing with family members and taking pictures in their graduation robes. A month ago, I feared for my life. I didn't know I would make it to graduation or get to see my sister in love. I never imagined I'd be looking at Wolfe Asylum as my forever home, where I will someday be molding the minds of students just like me, with my fated mate by my side.

Someone crashes into my side, lifting me into a huge hug and dragging me out of planning my future. "Ivy! You graduated!"

I turn toward Silis and return his enthusiastic hug. "Great work stating the obvious, Si."

His green eyes glare at me as he tickles my side. "Gosh, do you have to act like a sibling to me already? I miss the times when we had this romantic tension between us— ow!" Silis grabs his arm where Alden just punched him and takes a step away from me. "Dude, I was kidding!"

Alden takes me into his warm arms, dragging my back against his chest. "Stop trying to steal my mate. Get your own."

"No, I'm not ready for both of my boys to be all grown up yet," Stella butts in. "He's still my baby for another three years." She kisses Silis's cheek and ruffles his hair.

"Come on, Mom! Jeez!" Silis hurries to fix his hair before running off toward a group of girls that are gathered by the stairs.

Alden and I both laugh as Stella's jaw drops. "How do I make him focus on his studies instead of girls?"

I shrug. "I don't think that's possible unless you remove all girls from the school."

She chews on the inside of her mouth as if considering my suggestion, and I laugh again, sinking further into Alden's arms.

Stella throws her long arms around the two of us, creating an Ivy sandwich. "I'm so proud of you two, you know that? I'm so glad I get to watch you two grow together and make this place even better than it was before."

"College first, Aunt Stella. You won't get a break for at least four more years," Alden says behind me, not ready to become headmaster of Wolfe Asylum right away.

She shrugs. "But you two will be just an hour away while you traverse college together. I call that a win, unlike Sebastian and Fay who are already in New York!" She groans. "Too many of my babies are leaving me."

I sigh sadly. I already miss Fay, even though I've been shacking up in Alden's room for the past month. Fay is still my best friend. She and Sebastian left yesterday for New York City. Sebastian's family lives in NYC and Bast has planned on going to college up there for his entire life. Fay was more than happy to join him and chase after her art degree. Where better than the big apple to become an artist?

Alden's silky voice speaks into my mind. *"Come with me, Baby. I want a moment alone with you."*

"Sounds perfect," I say back.

I wave to Stella as Alden drags me away. "We'll catch up with you later, Stella."

She smiles back at us with a little wave before falling easily into conversation with other students and their families.

Alden's fingers lace with mine as he tugs me through the halls toward the library. We pass by one of the empty classrooms and Alden halts mid-step at the sight before us.

"Well, that's not something you wanna see," he says through our bond, humor lacing his voice.

I grimace at Gabe and Xena who are currently locked in a round of tonsil hockey in the dark science class. They are all over one another, and I turn to Alden while pretending to gag with my finger pointing to my mouth.

"I honestly can't say I'm surprised," I say, trying to hold back my laughter.

Alden grins and drags me down the hall, leaving the two kissing bullies behind. High school bullies, can't say I'll miss them even a little bit.

As soon as we reach the library, Alden spins me and presses my back to one of the loaded bookcases. His lips crash down on mine and I sigh against him, feeling at home in his arms.

He pulls back enough to look into my eyes, his blue irises shining back at me. "So, how does it feel to finally be done with high school?"

I slip my hands behind his neck, over the collar of his silky robe. "Technically, I should have graduated human high school months ago." I laugh softly, amazed at how far I've come from my old life. "I'm really excited to start the next chapter in our lives."

His smile is intoxicating as he runs his thumb along my cheek. "You know, that first day of Creative Writing class, you looked at me with those beautiful eyes of yours and asked me what I saw in my future."

I nod, remembering it perfectly. "You told me the future never felt promised for you."

He chuckles. "And you told me that I was depressing." He rubs his nose against mine playfully. "Want to know what I see in my future now?" I nod, holding my breath as I await his answer. "I see *you*, Ivy. I see myself kissing you every morning and every night. I see you teaching kids how to find the joy of writing within these walls. I see the family we could one day have together, and so much damn happiness that it should be illegal."

I giggle and drop a soft kiss against his mouth, my heart so full from his words. "I think I can get on board with that future. When can we start?"

He presses his chest to mine, his arms encircling me in their warmth. "Right now is as good a time as any. What do you think?"

I rise up on my toes and press my lips to his, so ready for the future he dreamed up for us. *"Yeah, now is good."*

THE END

REVIEW THIS BOOK

It means so much to me that you bought my book! Writing is such a passion of mine and I look forward to your feedback.

So, if you liked this book, whether it be the characters, settings, or adventures, I'd like to ask you a small favor. Hop on over to Amazon and leave a review with your thoughts. It'd be so great to read what YOU have to say!

From your friend, Abigail Grant

OTHER BOOKS BY ABIGAIL

Exclusive Freebies:

A Vision in Thessaly: The Intended Series Prequel

Shifter Cure: Hidden Cure Series Prequel

A Trial of Vengeance: The Kingdom Trials Prequel

Ash Born: Destiny Born Series Prequel

Amazon Series Pages:

The Intended Series

The Rescued Series

Hidden Cure Series

The Kingdom Trials Series

Destiny Born Series

The Wolf Hunted Series

Wolfe Asylum Series

ABOUT THE AUTHOR

Bestselling author of many YA fantasy romance series, Abigail Grant has always found herself lost in a good book. Whether it be as a teenager sprawled out in her upstairs bedroom reading all hours of the night, or more recently as a wife and mother of three small children, excited for bedtime when she can tell imaginative bedtime stories of magical realms and fierce creatures. Find Abigail all over social media and always releasing new books like wildfire!

Printed in Great Britain
by Amazon

12780686R00234